Valentine Honeyman was born in the Old Kent Road, a very, very long time ago. He has written for radio, television and film, in London and in Los Angeles.

STALKING
RICHARD & JUDY

Valentine
Honeyman

First published in 2009 by Old Street Publishing Ltd
40 Bowling Green Lane, London EC1R 0BJ
www.oldstreetpublishing.co.uk

ISBN 978-1-905847-55-6

For Jean Snow, who never fails to make me laugh

The Book List

I'd *finally* got Gloomy Prue off the phone when it happened. No, sorry, when IT happened. I'd been enjoying four of my favourite things in the whole wide world, as I do every afternoon from five till six: lying on the sofa with a triple G&T, a packet of Bensons, and Richard and Judy on the telly.

Annoyingly, Prue had called just as the show started, but I'd put her on speaker and the telly on subtitles, so I was actually managing to pay full attention to R&J without Prue getting all arsey because I wasn't paying full attention to *her*. To be honest I've not paid full attention to Prue for years. We're like a funny old married couple, except she's a Doomed Spinster and I'm a Cursed Fairy. She's a good person, really she is, but she just can't stop yakking. That woman could gas for Hitler. And oh, she's a moany cow! When God was handing out jollity, Prue must have knelt down to tie her laces.

R&J (as I like to call them) had just finished *You Say, We Pay*. I love that part of the show – at least, I did, before I found out I'd wasted the price of an off-licenceful of gin trying to get through to a number that could have belonged to an old-folks' home in Halifax, for all the chance I had of getting on

You Say, We Pay. You Say, We Take the Piss would have been more accurate.

Before I hyperventilate myself into a full-on funny turn I'll get back to the story. *You Say, We Pay* had just finished, and R&J went into their final segment. They both looked very excited, as was I. It was time to announce the shortlist for their summer books.

I need to tell you something at this point. I'm a writer. I've had five novels published in the past fifteen years, and every one of them has had very nice reviews, in literary circles. And there's the problem. Literary circles. Literary circles are perfectly lovely, but they might as well be knitting circles, for all the money they put in an author's bank account. Which means that I'm permanently broke. And when you phone British Gas in August because you still haven't paid last November's bill, it cuts absolutely no ice when you tell them that your most recent review in the Times Literary Supplement said *"Jeremy Canty's writing is reminiscent of Edith Wharton. A Wharton for this new century and all its millennial neuroses, viewed through the shattered mirror of a very personal pain"*. That's mostly because people who work at the British Gas call centre don't give a toss who Edith Wharton was. How very sensible of them.

Of course, when I say "people", what I mean is *real* people, not the ones who buy the *Times Literary Supplement*. I mean the general public. The sort who slave away all day on minimum wage-and-a-bit, in British Gas call centres. Naturally, the readers of the *TLS* know who Edith Wharton was, but so sodding what? There can't be more than fifty of them. If they *all* buy my latest masterpiece I end up making enough to pay that gas bill, and then treat myself to something utterly self-indulgent. Socks, for instance. In short, all I have to show for fifteen years' impersonating Edith la-di-da Wharton is a bachelor pad in Greenwich (oh, all right, it's a bed-sit with a bathroom. And it's in Woolwich – but Woolwich is in the *Borough* of Greenwich, OK?); a small scrapbook filled with the sort of book reviews that my mother loves to show her friends at church, and an Olympic-standard skill for kissing my bank manager's arse. And believe me, you wouldn't want to kiss my bank manager's *hand*, never mind his arse.

"Ooh, Prue," I said. "I've got to go."

"Ohoowwww," she went. "But I wanted to tell you about…"

"Cajjalayderloveyouooo," I said, cutting the connection. It was one thing to watch *You Say, We Pay* on subtitles, but the summer book list demanded total attention. I was about to hear the names of the lucky bastards – sorry, *fellow writers* – who'd somehow managed to get their books on R&J's list.

You see, for a highly-praised but dirt-poor novelist (me!) the announcement of those books is a form of torture. Let me explain. Say you're a cleaner. You work all year for five-fifty an hour. It's a piss-take of a wage, but there's not much else you can do, and the kids need trainers – from Nike, mind, not the ones off the market that'll force them to spend every lunch-break hiding in the bogs in shame. Well, that pretty much sums up my job, too. I admit that housemaid's knee isn't a big problem in my life, but the wages are about the same.

Now imagine this. Every so often, two fairies fly round the country. From time to time they pick a cleaner out of the blue, and touch her polyester pinny with their magic wands. And lo! Those cleaners become millionaires. Millionaires! Can you imagine what that would be like? Well, that's exactly what happens to a starving writer when he or she gets on the R&J book list. Richard and Judy *are* those fairies, and when they touch a lucky writer with their magic wands, she casts off her polyester pinny and goes out to buy a new one. At Versace. She stops living in a rented bed-sit in Woolwich and gets a crippling mortgage, just like a proper person. She stops looking at her cat's bowl of *Sheba* and wondering why it smells so much nicer than her own bowl of Tesco Value lasagne. In short, she joins the human bloody race. And now you understand why the R&J book list is so important to me. I *am* that poor cow, always hoping that I'll get fingered by Richard. Or Judy. I'd swing both ways to get on that list. In fact, I'd swing by the nipples over a pool of crocodiles. I'd swing by the hair in my nostrils over an… Oh, you get the idea. I'd kill. Anybody. In broad daylight. On CCTV. On *national* TV.

"Well," said Judy. "It's that time again. Time to announce our 2007 summer book list."

"Yes," said Richard, bouncing around in his seat like a toddler on crack. "And I know we say this every year, but honestly – truly – we've really *surpassed* ourselves this time. Haven't we, love?"

As so often, Judy turned to camera and gave her T.W.L. That's Trademark Weary Look. I love Judy's T.W.L.'s, especially the way they come in different strengths. Actually I love Judy's face, full stop. It looks lived-in. To be honest, it looks more than lived-in, it looks squatted in. By really interesting tenants. And have you ever noticed how blue her eyes are? They're so blue they look like she could paint your bathroom walls, just by staring at them. And I know some people think she always looks pissed, but not me. I think she looks like she's just had really knock-your-knickers-off nooky. All the time. And, most important of all, she looks like us.

Her audience. She looks like she tries her best every single day to keep it all together, but stumbles at the last fence. You can just see her, sat in front of the mirror of a morning, trying to do her hair and make up in the five minutes she has between feeding the kids and going to work, and saying "Oh, fuck it – that'll do." OK, in real life she's a squillionaire, and her kids were grown up so long ago that these days Cracked Nipples are something she gets with a glass of wine, like honey-roast peanuts. But in telly land she's still One Of Us. I am devoted to her in a strange and slightly disturbing way.

Which brings me to Richard. I must admit, I do sometimes wonder if Judy got knocked up at sixteen by some boy behind the bike sheds, and was then forced to have the baby adopted. One day, many years later, that baby came looking for his birth-mother, only when he appeared on her doorstep there was this instant and very *wrong* attraction between them, so they decided to pretend they were perfect strangers, and just crossed their fingers and prayed that the world would never discover their secret. As the true R&J fans among you will know, the first words she spoke to Richard were "I'm your mummy," or something similar. Well, you don't need to be Sigmund bleeding Freud to work *that* one out, do you?

Richard's younger than Judy, but he's no spring chicken, you know; but he still looks like someone in a boy band that's recently got together again, after ten years of chart obscurity. It's just not fair. I'm about the same age as him, but I look like his dad. No, sorry. His *grandad*. For starters, where did he get that *hair*? You're not telling me it's his? Of course it's not! It was last seen alive on a Siberian peasant, who sold it to buy vodka and coal. And his *skin!* It looks like twenty virgins have spent the last ten years massaging his face with their love-juices. Or maybe it's just Judy who's been doing it. I bet her love-juices could strip wallpaper, never mind human skin. That's assuming Richard *is* human. Have you ever noticed he's a bit like a better-looking version of Commander Data off *Star Trek?* Anyway, the point is he has no bloody right to look so good, even if he is an android.

Sorry, I do have a habit of going off on one. It's one of my lovable quirks. And if you don't agree, you'd better put this down now and slink out of WH Smith's like you're not one of those cheapskates who comes in every lunch time and reads two chapters but never buys the book. Oh, yes. I know your sort, lady. I do it all the time.

ANYWAY. They started to announce The List.

"Now," said Richard. "Over the coming weeks we'll be going into way, way more depth with each of our books, but today…"

"Yes, *today*," interrupted Judy, without seeming to interrupt at all (I *love* the way she does that), "we just want to give you a taster. We're going to name each of our books, and tell you a little bit about them…."

"After all," interrupted Richard, also without seeming to interrupt. Honestly, what a team. Slick as two seals in a single wetsuit. "Some of you might be going off on your holidays early, after all."

Judy then gave a level two T.W.L..

"God, honestly," she said.

"What? What?" went Richard, all innocence and fringe.

"Well, you're making it sound like we're recommending *airport* novels."

"No I'm not!"

"You *are*."

"I'm not. Seriously. *Seriously.* I would *never* insult our viewers' intelligence like that. All I meant was that some of them might be going off on an early and very well-earned holiday – and *yes*, OK, people don't get a lot of time to read, and holidays are the one time they can play catch-up. That's all I meant."

Oh, joy! These are the moments that keep me faithful to R&J. There was a pause. She looked at the camera for such a long time it was rude. Then she knocked out a level-*three* T.W.L. and went,

"What-*ever.*"

Genius!

"OK, so first on our list," Richard continued, as though his old lady hadn't just bitch-slapped him, "is *Find The Fortune Cookie*, by Bethany Twyler. It's not an easy read, is it, love?"

"No," chimed Judy, "You're right there. For a change."

Richard took that on the chin, smiled to camera, and went on.

"Bethany's book is about the deepest, darkest, and – let's face it – *nastiest* thing that can ever happen to a child. It's a horrifying fact, but children – and I'm sure many of you have guessed this by now, from the title – are regularly abused – and I mean *sexually* abused – by their own fathers."

"Yes," said Judy, picking up this somewhat icky baton, "and Bethany Twyler's book doesn't shy away from that."

"Now," said Richard. "We know that there have been tons and tons of these books in the past few years…"

"Misery Lit," said Judy, arranging her face into a suitably miserable form. I must admit, she's good at that: she only has to let her cheeks sag and she looks like a deflated clown-balloon. "But the thing about *Find The Fortune Cookie* – the thing that makes it so special – is that Bethany's father was Chinese."

"Yes," Richard added, bouncily. "And the title of the book refers to the way that Bethany's father made her search in his trousers for the sort of fortune cookie that no child should ever have to see…"

OK, I admit it. At that point I fell off the sofa, laughing. Yes, all right, I felt sorry for the poor girl and her nasty (yet, happily, profitable) childhood. But it was such a purely Richard moment. What the hell did it matter that Bethany's dirty old man was Chinese? And why (I couldn't help wondering) was she called Bethany Twyler? It didn't sound very Oriental to me. I was gripped.

Richard looked very perky. "I s'pose we tend to think – don't ask me why – that things like incest and sexual abuse are particularly western problems. But, as *Find The Fortune Cookie* shows only too clearly, it's just as common in Asian families."

I lost control at that point. I had to haul myself up off the floor and get myself another G&T.

Like many writers, I can pour an alcoholic drink faster than I can get a glass of water. Sometimes I wonder about installing a G&T tap on my sink, but honestly, it wouldn't be worth it. It could never beat me.

Ten seconds later I was on the sofa again. And then, to go back to the beginning, was when IT happened.

"So that's our first book," said Richard. "Painful, but so raw and honest that *everyone* should read it. Even – possibly – children themselves."

"Hmm," said Judy, rolling her eyes. "Or possibly not."

"No, but really! You can't wrap kids in cotton wool forever. Seriously."

That got a level-*four* T. W.L. They don't happen very often. I actually clapped.

"No, Richard. You're right. But most kids don't go through that sort of nightmare, and there's no reason why they should read about it either. Is there?"

Richard looked glum. As always, he was just being eager, and now Mummy had slapped his wrist. He then did his own trademark look to camera. He put his chin down, pouted beneath his fringe, and poked his finger around somewhere deep in the recesses of his Russian hair. *"Mums, eh? Huh! What do they know?"*

"Anyway," Judy went on briskly. "Our second book actually *is* suitable for children. It's called *In Tooth And Claw,* and it's a wonderful ṭale about a family who decide they've had enough of the rat race in London, so they sell their house and move to an isolated village in the far north of Scotland."

"Yes," continued Richard "and for a while it looks like their dream of paradise has come true. But then, one day, the children discover Something Nasty in the Woodshed."

"Well," laughed Judy, "not quite the woodshed. Actually, it's a rock-pool. But it leads to the most incredible series of discoveries that threaten the whole idea of what a family means."

"It does indeed," said Richard, starting to look excited again. "It's an absolutely amazing read. It's gripping – a real page-turner – and yet it's so sensitive that I guarantee you'll be crying into your single malt by the end."

"Your single *what*?" laughed Judy, rolling here eyes at the camera.

"It was a Scottish reference," he said, looking hurt. "I love a nice single malt."

"He probably does," she said. "I take no notice of his bad habits any more. *Anyway,* it's a fabulous book, and all the more amazing for the fact that it's by a first-time writer called Andrew Goodman."

Suddenly my world shattered into a million little pieces. Actually, my glass of G&T shattered into a million pieces, because I dropped it on the floor. *Andrew Goodman?? ANDREW FUCKING GOODMAN!!!*

It was the worst moment of my entire life. All I could think of, apart from pouring another G&T, drinking it in one gulp, then pouring another one, was to call my proper best friend.

So that's what I did.

Dolly Sets Me Straight

My proper best friend's name is Robyn, and I love almost everything about her, apart from the fact that she lives in Swindon. She lives in Swindon because she's a professional dominatrix (go on, admit it, *you* want to be her best friend, too). The reason it's a good idea for a professional dominatrix to live in Swindon is simple. Well, maybe not simple, but logical. Swindon is the most popular place in the country for companies to hold conferences. And the sort of men who want to be tied up, whipped, and insulted by a woman such as Robyn tend to want it as a special treat. Usually when they're away from the wife for three nights, pissed out of their minds on the contents of the mini-bar, and stand a fair chance of charging it to expenses. You can't help but admire Robyn's business acumen, but I *do* wish she still lived in London. Then again, I've got to hand it to her: Swindon has proved to be Ground Zero for married masochists, and she's got so much work she's had to take on staff. The problem with her success is that I can *never* get her on the phone. So we have to talk via the webcam.

"Hello darling!" said Robyn when she finally noticed her computer was screeching at her. "I'm a bit busy!"

She certainly was. As always. There she stood, all five feet nothing of her, got up in a black patent corset-bustier-thing, fishnet tights and custom-made cat boots, complete with scary-looking claws.

"Is it important, darling?" she said.

"Yes, it's very important, love. And could you put your tits away? You know they scare me."

She must have seen from my face that I was serious.

"Give me a second, hunny-bunny," she replied.

Robyn had a punter on the go. I meant to look away, but as always, I didn't. It was just too entertaining. Via the webcam I watched her stride across the room in her Catwoman boots. There was a very mild-looking creature, strung up from the ceiling by manacles. He had bulldog clips on his nipples, weights attached to his balls, and he was still wearing his specs.

"You are a piece of SHIT!" screeched Robyn. "What are you??"

"A piece of shit, mistress," said the poor drip, who had probably been at a double-glazing conference only an hour before.

"YES! And you're not making me HAPPY, are you?"

"No, mistress."

"You're WORTHLESS!!"

"Yes, mistress."

Robyn gave him a good kick with her claws.

"Oh, *mistress*," he sighed. God knows why I ever think *I'm* strange.

"And BECAUSE you're not making me happy, I'm going to PUNISH you."

"Oh no, mistress. No!" he whimpered. Happily.

"Shut UP, you pathetic EXCUSE for a human being!"

"Yes, mistress. Sorry, mistress."

Oh, for heaven's sake, I thought. Hurry up, Robyn. I *really* need to talk to you, and this G&T is almost dry. Then she scurried up to the webcam again.

"Two secs, hun. Promise. Love you!"

She pulled something from a drawer and then went back to Pathetic Excuse. It was a leather hood.

"Now you're going to PAY, you maggot!" she snarled at the little masochist. I suddenly realised who he reminded me of: Sid Little. Then, after removing his specs, Robyn pulled the leather hood over his head. He moaned and protested in ecstasy. Then Robyn picked up a black rubber dildo and stuck it in his gob.

"That shut him up," she said, sitting down at the computer, as calm and collected as a woman who'd just sold a jar of jam at a W.I. fete. "What's wrong with my favourite fairy?"

"You still haven't put your boobs away."

"Sorry, hun," she said, expertly scooping her terrifying tits into the bustier thing, like a kinky ice-cream vendor. Mistress Whippy, perhaps. "How's that?"

"Much better."

"Good. So tell me everything."

"Oh, Robyn, I just don't know where to start."

"Well, my darling, try. 'Cos I've got to finish off Stan Laurel over there and then I've got a six-thirty."

"I was thinking more Sid Little."

"Hmm," she said, looking over her shoulder at the scrawny little twit as he dangled limply from his manacles with a dildo in his gob. "I think it's a toss-up."

"Are you sure he can breathe, love?" I asked.

"Oh, yeah," she said casually. "Enough."

I couldn't help but laugh.

"Aha!" said Robyn. "Things aren't so bad that you can't laugh, then? And this crisis is so terrible that you call me at work?"

"Actually, it really is. It's beyond terrible. I'm suicidal."

"With a gin in one hand and a fag in the other?"

I paused. She had a point. I hate webcams.

"It's my last meal," I said.

"I always wondered what a condemned drama queen would have for her last meal. Now I know."

"Andrew Goodman is on the Richard and Judy book list."

"Andrew who, darling?"

"Andrew Goodman. I was at Cambridge with him."

"Darling, you were at Cambridge with everyone. So what?"

"No, Robyn, you don't understand."

"Well, hurry, my sweet," she said, glancing over her shoulder again.

"Oh, don't worry, Robyn. You're busy. I'll deal with it on my own. Sorry I called. Go back to bloody work."

One of the things I adore about Robyn is that she knows the difference between a molehill and a mountain. Suddenly she realised that I was genuinely on the edge, and I had her full attention.

"You really are in a state, aren't you?"

"Yes, I really am."

"Well?"

"Well, Andrew Goodman is a talentless, conniving little twat. He couldn't write a decent sentence if his life depended on it. I know, because when we were at Cambridge he was always trying to weasel his way onto the university magazine but he was just too *crap*."

"And?"

"And? What do you mean: *and?* Somehow or other the little bastard has written a novel. His *first* novel. And it's on the Richard and sodding Judy LIST! Do you *know* what that does to me?"

"Well, darling, nothing. Actually. No more than any other talentless undeserving twat would do, anyway. You didn't get this excited when Wayne Rooney got ten zillion quid for his autobiography, did you?"

"No, of course I didn't! That was different!"

"Why? Because you fancy him?"

"No!" I cried (though I do happen to think Wayne Rooney is just about as gorgeous as it gets. There are so many pins in my Colleen doll she looks like an electrocuted hedgehog). "Wayne hasn't written a *novel*, has he? And he's not a talentless TWUNT, unlike Andrew Goodman!"

"Listen, darling. I really am busy. But I'll call you later, I promise."

"Whatever," I said, pouting.

"Don't pout, darling. You haven't got the chin for it."

"I want to pout."

"OK, you have a good old pout. But listen. You've only got two choices. Let it go, or get even."

"I'm *sick* of letting it go, Robyn. Every time someone I know does well in this world, I let it go. When do I get *my* turn?"

"When you get even."

"Oh! And how do you suggest I do that? Hire a hit man to kill Andrew bastard Goodman? What will I pay him with? Signed copies of my books? "

"I'm sure hit men like to read, too."

"Shut up, Robyn."

"No, of course you don't hire a hit man, you whining queen. You get *your* new book on the Richard and Judy list. Simple!"

"Oh, yeah! Simple!"

"Hang on" she said, looking over her shoulder again. "Stan does look a bit blue."

She went over to Stan/Sid, who was indeed going a funny colour. I was seething. Robyn was clearly too much in her sadistic role to be sympathetic. I didn't need Tough Love, I needed love-love. She pulled the dildo out of Stan's mouth and he flopped around gasping with his eyes bulging out, but I was too miserable to care about what happened next. I cut the connection and went to get another G&T.

As I poured myself a drink strong enough to flatten an entire hen-night, my cat rubbed up against my leg and purred. I'd forgotten to feed her. But I was feeling too sorry for myself to give a toss.

"Oh, piss off, Dolly!" I said, shoving her out of the way. "Go and kill a pigeon if you're hungry!"

Honestly, I'm not one of those silly tarts who think that pets can understand us; but sometimes you just don't know. As I stumbled back to the sofa with a fresh gallon of mother's ruin, Dolly sank her claws into my leg.

"Ooooooooow!" I squealed. "You bitch! You *queen!*"

Dolly just sat there looking justified, which of course she was. Then I realised. Robyn was right about Andrew Goodman. I could either let it go, or get even.

I decided then and there that I would get my latest book on next year's Richard and Judy list if it *killed* me. Literally – I would get on that list or die in the bloody attempt.

"Thank you, Dolly," I said. Then I poured my drink down the sink and opened a sachet of *Sheba*.

I had plans to make.

- 3 -

One of Those Nancies

Needless to say, I didn't manage to make any plans that night. In fact, what happened was that I was so pissed and jangly-wangly that when I tore open Dolly's dinner, the smell of cat food tipped me over the edge and I spent the next hour snogging the lav. I hate throwing up more than anything else on this earth. I know bulimia's supposed to be a bad thing but I salute those brave girls, I really do. I can't believe people do it deliberately, just to stay thin. I would have to be in a situation where I'd accidentally swallowed Jeremy Clarkson's underwear before I deliberately made myself puke.

I don't remember crawling into bed, but I do remember waking up, with my door buzzer going at my brain like a chainsaw. The reason I don't actually remember crawling into bed is simple. I hadn't. I lifted my head off what I thought was the pillow, and screamed. My face was glued to the bathroom floor by dried sick. Classy bitch.

The hateful buzzer just went on and on as I forced myself onto all-fours, wondering if I'd finally had the stroke that a chain smoking piss-artist deserves; but no – all my limbs seemed to be working, even though I felt as though someone had encased me in plaster of Paris for a joke. As I struggled to my feet I got two shocks. First, I saw myself in the mirror. Oh dear, oh dear, oh dear. And to think I had the bloody cheek to laugh at the 'slebs looking a teeny bit rough in Heat. I looked so totally Winehouse I was surprised the poor mirror didn't just walk out of the room and check into rehab. The second shock was that I glanced at the clock. 6.30 a.m. Oh, balls, shit and bugger my mother – it was Paul!!

Ah, Paul. Did I tell you I like rough trade? Well, I do. The rougher the better. The sort with scabs on their knuckles, who sign their names with an "X". Paul is the latest, and possibly the roughest. I met him when he was digging a hole in the road. In fact, I very nearly killed him. I was driving into London to have lunch with my publisher. This is a once a year event for writers like me. We get taken to some second-rate restaurant for a set menu and a bottle of house wine. You know, one of those joints where everything looks like it would much rather be somewhere else. The staff, the "diners"– even the bloody knives and forks look ready to do a runner. When my publisher treats me to lunch, the whole thing feels so calculated to the last penny that I'm surprised he doesn't actually bring the accountant. Quite frankly I'd sooner skip the meal and take the Nectar Points.

Anyway, I was driving into town in my so-called car, the most valuable bit of which is the tax disc, when I had to stop at some road works. As always when I'm stopped at road works, I scanned the workmen for talent. And there he was. Oh, my lord. He was perfect. If Mel Gibson and Mark Wahlberg had a baby, Paul would be the result. He stood there, shirtless and sweaty, pneumatic drill between his beefy thighs, and I was so completely besotted that I didn't notice the lights had changed. Unfortunately I was at the front of the queue and the selfish cow behind me in a Range Rover hadn't even bothered to consider that perhaps I was too in love with the road-digger to notice silly little things like lights. So when they changed, she drove forward – straight up my arse. I panicked, turned the wheel, and finished up in the very hole that Mel and Marks' love-child was digging. Oh, if they gave medals for being a hyperventilating homo, I would have scooped the gold that day.

But, as I always say, every hole in the road has a silver lining. By the time I'd swapped details with Range Rover girl, I was getting along like a house on fire with the road-digger, Paul. Not only was it far too late for me to make lunch with my publisher – I couldn't have cared less. So I phoned and made my excuses, then asked Paul if I could buy him a pint, by way of an apology. To my thrilled surprise he said yes, and six pints later he was spread across my bed like a duvet from Planet Perfect – if Planet Perfect was the name of a homeware store. And it really should be, shouldn't it?

Paul lives on The Island. Doesn't that sound glam? *The Island.* Are you thinking Caribbean, billionaires and yachts? Or a novel by Victoria Hislop? Well, think again. I'm talking about the "Island" of Sheppey. For those of you unfamiliar with this charming corner of Kent, I thoroughly recommend a website called sheppyscum.com. That'll tell you what you need to know.

To be fair to Sheppey, it has potential. It's quite close to London, it has something that looks almost like a beach, and once upon a time it was quite the place to go on holiday. I should know: back in the 60s my one and only rich uncle had a "chalet" down there and I spent many a happy childhood summer in the lively pubs, clubs and amusement arcades of Leysdown. But these days, when you can fly to Spain for less money than it costs to park at Gatwick, the only people who holiday on Sheppey are those who can just about afford the bus fare from Sittingbourne, ten miles up the road. The sort of people who sit at home, seriously wondering whether they could sell their kidneys (or their kids, come to that) to pay for scratch-cards and skunk. But one day in the future, when your carbon miles are more valuable than your house, Sheppey will Rise Again.

So, when I tell you that Gorgeous Paul is from The Island, I hope you get the idea. After that first afternoon of stupendous sex I fully expected him to demand money with menaces, then drive back to his wife and three kids with my mobile phone, my DVD player and my credit cards. But he didn't. We were lying in bed, and Paul was smoking his eighth or ninth salami-sized joint. I, on the other hand, was wondering if he'd like me to pack the DVD player and mobile phone in their original boxes to save time, when he turned to me and said,

"I fink I love you."

And I, dopey romantic quoon that I am, looked into his Melblue eyes and said, "I've been in love with you since the second I saw you."

Oh, brother. Do I ever regret *those* words.

I pressed the button to open the outside door and five seconds later Paul was in my flat. As always, he pushed past me without so much as a hello, never mind a kiss. Then he sat on the sofa, started rolling a joint and grunted, "Any breakfast, bub?"

Honestly, it's a mystery to me why Holloway Prison isn't packed to the rafters with working class birds who've murdered their men with blunt instruments. They go to work; they cook, they clean, they bring up the kids – and meanwhile their blokes do sod all except shag, sulk, and resentfully hand over a few bob at the end of the week. I mean, if Noel Edmonds offered you that would *you* say "Deal"?

"Yes, Paul. I've got sausages, bacon, eggs, mushrooms…"

"Yeah, yeah, wotever – not mushrooms, you *know* mushrooms make me puke," he replied, grabbing the remote and switching to BBC Breakfast. "Fuckinell, that Tasha Blinski," he said, lighting the joint and pawing his groin while he lusted after Natasha Kaplinsky. "I'd sort that slag out. Here bub, gissa blow job."

I know it's nothing to be proud of, but cavemen like Paul turn me into a sex-mong. I really am that person from the old joke – the one who'll give them a BJ while they watch the footy, and then turn into a pizza. Or go and cook a pizza, at least. Don't tell me it's politically incorrect, because I already know. Some girls get off on being treated mean, and there's no point fighting it. It's a long tradition. Go and read *Oliver Twist*. Some Nancies need their Bill – and I'm just One of Those Nancies.

But that morning I really wasn't in the mood. Maybe it was because I felt suicidal and I'd spent the night with my face glued to the bathroom floor by my own sick.

"Piss off," I said. "Have a wank."

"Aw, *bub*," he whined. "Go on. You know I love ya."

Believe it or not, that pathetic line usually works when I'm not in the mood to do his bidding. But not that day.

"I mean it," I said, stomping out of the room. "Rub your cock all over Natasha Kaplinsky – and electrocute yourself while you're about it."

* * *

Stomping out of the room isn't all that impressive in a studio flat. Your options are limited when there are only two doors. It's go out the front, or go and sit on the loo. At least I had the presence of mind to slam the door behind me.

Men like Paul instinctively know how to treat someone like me. If I go off on one, no matter *how* much he's to blame (i.e. always), he will never, ever, *ever* try to make peace. I've read entire novels sitting on that loo, waiting for him to say sorry, and all I've ever had to show for it (apart from having read the novel) is blue ankles from the seat cutting off my circulation.

But that morning, for the first time since I'd known him, he actually tapped on the bathroom door.

"Cummun, bub. Wossamatter?"

I didn't answer. Not because I was trying to milk the situation, but simply because I was speechless at Paul showing the slightest sign of concern for my feelings.

"Can I come in?" he asked. Of course, he then barged in without an answer, but the fact that he'd even *asked*…

He actually knelt down to speak to me. Then he touched my cheek. I wondered if I was still asleep.

"Tell ya what, bub," he said. "Forget about the blow job. I'll do us a bit of grub. You clean yourself up, eh? Look like shit. "

Well, it wasn't much of a breakfast, but in Paul's world, *haute cuisine* is cooking something that doesn't go ping when it's done.

* * *

"See," he said, handing me a slice of singed toast with a Marmite skid mark, and looking immensely pleased with himself. "I can cook when I wannoo."

"You should write to Gordon Ramsay. Ask him for a job."

"Hmm," he said, giving the idea some serious thought. "Nah. I'd end up decking him. Ugly cunt."

I should tell you at this point that Paul uses the C-word about once per sentence. He uses it so much that it doesn't have any meaning at all. It's just a noise he makes. He even uses it where normal people would say "Umm". For instance: say I ask him if he'd like ham or cheese in a sandwich. Instead of replying "Umm… cheese" he'll go "Cuuuuunt….. cheese." I've grown so accustomed to the word that I forget it's really not nice. Last month I was having Sunday lunch with my mother and two of her friends, one of whom plays the organ in church and thought *Calendar Girls* was a bit much. So, this very genteel spinster had just told us her terribly amusing tale of Disaster at the Organ that morning. She'd been halfway through the accompaniment to *Oh God, our Help in Ages Past* when she turned over the page in her music, only to discover it had become mixed up with *The Battle Hymn of the Republic*. Well, you know, it wasn't exactly one of those anecdotes you save up for when you're on Parky, but it was a big deal for an 82-year-old who thinks Brighton is Sodom with bandstands. Not that she's wrong. Anyway, before Paul came into my life I would have joined in the laughter and said "Oh, Esme, you big *silly!*" But no. Oh, no, no, no. I waited for the old dears to dry their eyes, turned to Esme the organist, and said, with a smile, "Oh, Esme. You silly *cunt*."

He's got to go, he really has. But I'm temporarily bewitched.

And, meanwhile, in the faint hope this ever becomes a *Book at Bedtime,* I'll do my best to clean him up.

"*Thass* what my baby needed," he said when I'd eaten the solitary slice of toast. "Bitta looking after."

Honestly, from the self-satisfied look on his face you'd think he'd been sleeping at the foot of my bed for six months while I fought scarlet fever.

"Thanks. Is there any more?"

"Don't take the piss," he replied. "Ain't your *servant.*"

An image of Paul as the world's most unlikely butler suddenly flashed into my mind and I started to laugh.

"S'matter wiv you?"

"Nothing, nothing. I'm just wondering what Bertie Wooster would make of you."

" You're *weird,*" he replied. That's Paul's standard answer, when I say something that goes over his head. *You're weird.*

"Yes," I said, still laughing. "I bloody well am."

He looked grumpy and resentful for a moment, knowing I was laughing at him, but not knowing why. He responded by bringing things back to his level.

"Anyway," he said, reaching into his trackie bottoms, "now you're feeling better…"

"Oh, for fuck's sake."

"Fair's *fair,* bub," he grizzled. "I done yer breakfast ditn't I?"

"You made me one measly slice of toast, Paul."

"Well, then," he smirked. "Have a bit of sausage."

Quick piece of advice: blowjobs and hangovers don't mix. You really can't trust your gag-reflex.

After I'd done his bidding, Paul curled up on the sofa for his usual nap before work, and I set about cleaning the bathroom floor. It's amazing the damage that stomach acid and gin can do to cheap vinyl. It was like that scene in *Alien* where the creature's blood burns right through to the level below. I half expected Sigourney Weaver to wave at me from the downstairs flat.

Then I made him a coffee. Four sugars, all milk, and three Hob Nobs on the side. Before waking him I did what I always do: look at him for a minute. When he's conscious I can never do that. He gets annoyed, even though he's secretly enjoying the attention. But when he's asleep I can drink my fill. I know exactly what some women mean when they say about their rowdy kids "I love them when they're asleep". So I sat there for a bit, just loving him. He's more trouble than a tank full of two-year-olds and madder than a marzipan dildo, but when he's quietly snoozing, and I watch his dreaming eyes dart about beneath his thick black lashes, I just want to cry.

"Nnnnh, ta bub," he said as I gave him his coffee. "S'time?"

"Just gone half-seven."

"Better get moving."

He jumped up and went to do his beauty regime. It's not exactly Beverley Hills. He runs a sink full of cold water, dunks his entire head in it, gargles, then comes up for air. As he looks at his reflection he shouts "Yoo ain't handsome, Paul O'Connor! You're *double* handsome! Mwoah!" And he kisses the mirror. No, really, he does. The maddening thing is, he's right. If anything, he's triple handsome. Sometimes I kiss the mirror after he's gone.

"Fuck mine," he said, drying his hair with my bath mat. "You had a right night last night, ditn't yer? Fuckin' floor's melted."

"I was a little overwrought."

"Over-what?"

26

"Upset."

"Who's upset yer? I'll see to the c…."

"No, it's not like that. I'm upset about work."

He stopped rubbing his hair with the bath mat.

"You don't *go*-a work."

"Paul, how many times have we had this conversation? No, I don't go to an office, and I don't dig holes in the road, but I do *work*."

"Yeah, right," he cackled. Then he stuck his nose in the air and typed camply on an imaginary keyboard.

"Go away, you arsehole. I've really had enough of you today."

"You'll never have enough of me, bub. Never. Not till I say so."

He was right, of course. Suddenly I felt completely useless. My whole life seemed to be in the power of other people. My lip started trembling.

"Don't start all that gay shit," he said, sympathetically.

"I *am* gay, Paul!"

"Yur, well, I don't wanna know about all that. Thass your world."

"Oh, for fuc – look, just go to work. Text me if you're coming round later."

"Nah," he said, sitting down and crossing his arms. "I ain't going a-work till you tell us wossappened."

"Why? You'll just take the piss."

"No I won't. 'Cept if you're being a wanker."

"Well, I'm *not* being a wanker."

"Tell us, then."

"*No.* Look, it's nice that you're concerned but really, you wouldn't understand."

"You saying I'm fick?"

"No…"

"Well then, *tell* us. Might get an idea."

I could see he wasn't going to leave until I'd told him the whole story, so I did. When I was finished he slowly rolled himself another joint, to help him think more clearly. I sat and waited for the benefit of his wisdom.

"Why doncha get someone to give this Andrew Wossname…

"Goodman."

"….Goodman a smack? My mate Terry'll do it for a Rio."

"A Rio?"

"Ferdinand, wanker. A Rio Ferdi-*nand*."

"What? I haven't got a thousand pounds! Anyway, that's not the point. Having Andrew Goodman beaten to a pulp won't get *my* book on the list, will it?"

"Make you feel better, though."

"Yes," I sighed. "But not much."

"Alright, alright," he said, lighting his joint and puffing on it with a Churchillian air. "So you've gotta get your book on this list…"

"Yes, Paul."

"Hmm… What about givin' 'em a bung?"

"*Bribery?*"

"Just *said* that, ditn't I?"

"This isn't football!"

"That cunt Richard – he'd take a bung for definite."

"What on earth makes you think that?"

"Got done for shoplifting, ditn't he?"

"No, he *didn't*. It was all a mistake."

"Yeah, right. Wot-ever."

"God. Look, even if he *would*, what am I supposed to do?

Borrow fifty grand from the bank and then sidle up to Richard Madeley in a car park with a brown paper bag?"

Paul took a toke on his joint and gave me a smug look.

"Works for football."

I'd really had enough.

"For Christ's sake! I don't live in your world, Paul! Not everybody can be bribed, or intimidated, or blackmailed! Some people are decent and honest and, well, straight!"

"S'that right?" he said sarkily. "Well, then. You're fucked."

I have a very heavy bust of Mozart in my room. I looked at it, wondering how well I'd adjust to life in Holloway.

"So, this bird," said Paul. "What about her?"

"Which bird?"

"The one you told us about. Wot picks the books for Richard and Judy."

"Oh. Laura Morris. What about her?"

"She's the one you gotta get at."

"There you go again! What do you mean, 'get at'? She's not Ronnie fucking Kray!"

"Did I say that?"

"No, but…"

"Listen. Just cos you went-a college and all that bollocks don't mean you're clever. I ain't talking about putting the shits up her, or giving her a back-hander or anyfink. I mean *get at*."

"OK, fine. How??"

"Get yer feet under the table."

"*What* bloody table?!"

"Alright, bub! Chill-pill. *Her* fuckin table. Find out about her. Find out where she lives. She got a bloke? Got a window cleaner? Might need a gardener. Anyfink. Just get in there. Make her fink you're her mate. Then you can get her to look at your book."

"Oh, right. So I start out as the gardener, then I tell her I do a bit of writing on the side, and *then* I slip her a copy of my latest novel. Brilliant!"

"No, wanker. You never tell her who you are, do yer? You're just her mate, far as she's concerned. Then you pick yer moment."

Mozart was looking more tempting by the second.

"OK, thanks. You're going to be late for work if you don't get going."

"Don't mug me off, cunt. "

"I'm not mugging you off, really I'm not. But *please*. Let me deal with this my way."

"Wossat, then? Woss your big idea? Go on, tell us."

"There are ways. People. Channels."

"Yur, right," he mocked. "*Pee*-pull. *Char*-nuls."

Then he stood up and made his way to the door, laughing his head off. As he went he turned to me and cackled,

"Here, bub – send us a text if you get lucky wiv any of them *charnuls*, yeah?"

After he'd gone I sat and seethed for ten minutes. Bloody chav moron. What did *he* know?

I grabbed a sheet of paper and sat down to make all the plans I'd meant to make the night before. Not ridiculous Paul-type plans, based on storylines from *EastEnders* or X-Box games, or whatever else fills the imaginations of idiots. Sensible plans, like… um… Well…

Two hours later, the only thing I'd filled was my ashtray. The sheet of paper remained as empty as Paris Hilton's role on earth. Then I realised. Paul had a point.

- 4 -

We The People

They call Laura Morris "the most powerful woman in British publishing", but she's not actually in publishing: she's the person responsible for choosing the books that get on the Richard and Judy list. So, to be accurate, she's the most powerful woman *not* in British Publishing.

Along with every other struggling author I've thought about Laura a lot. I've even dreamed about her. I imagine her life to be a bit like the lives of those judges in Sicily who decide to take a stand against the Mafia. If you think that the World of Publishing is run by sensitive types who spend all day lying in dimly-lit rooms, suffering from migraines brought on by anxiously reading manuscripts written on vellum with quill-pens, hoping to discover a literary genius, think again. Publishing people are just like the *cosa nostra*, only with bad clothes and membership cards for English Heritage.

Poor Laura Morris. In theory her job is pretty simple. She reads books and then decides which ones are just right for R&J to recommend to their viewers. How hard could that be? But think about it. Every morning her phone starts ringing. By lunch-time she's been invited ten times to the best restaurants in London.

She's taken delivery of six baskets of fruit, four bouquets of flowers, two brown envelopes full of cash (returned, of course), and one death-threat against her family. All from those sensitive publishing types.

Everybody wants to get their book in her list. To be honest, I'd feel quite honoured if I just managed to get one of my books in her *bin*. But it simply doesn't happen, not in the real world. Except for Andrew Goodman. Andrew fucking Goodman had managed to get his *first novel* right there – on The List!

I sat and stared at the empty sheet of paper for an hour without a single idea in my head. Paul was absolutely right. I wasn't going to achieve anything through the legitimate channels. I really did need to *get at* Laura Morris. But how, how, *how?*

The only thing in my head was a bloody awful ache. When my phone rang I was actually glad it was Gloomy Prue.

"Oh," she whined, without saying hello. "So you're alive, then?"

"Sort of. Shouldn't I be?"

"Only that you promised you'd call me back yesterday? After Richard and Judy?"

"Oh, bugger. Sorry. I was in a bit of a state. "

"I was *worried.* "

"Yes, well, I said I was sorry."

"It's easy to be sorry, Jeremy. Sorry's just a word."

It certainly is, I thought.

"Anyway," I said, breezily. "Here I am! All in one piece. Is something up?"

"No. Why?"

"Nothing. Just that it's early."

"Oh. So now I can't I phone you at ten in the morning?"

"Prue, you can call me any time. You know that. "

"*Thank* you."

"But, as a rule, you don't. So I wondered if something was wrong?"

There was a long pause. I could tell Prue was desperate to spill her guts about her own problems, but now she felt guilty because she'd been such a twat. So I let her twist in the wind.

"Oh, it doesn't matter," she said. "I only wanted to tell you the rest of the story about that guy."

"The one you met at speed dating?" I guessed.

"*No.*"

Oops, wrong guess.

"The one I met off soulmates.com."

"Right. Sorry. Yes. Him. I'm all ears."

"It's OK," she said, suddenly sounding very business-like. "I'm on my coffee-break. Got to get back to work. Big day today."

"Oh. Um. What's happening today?"

"God! I *told* you. It's the Woman of the Year Awards. Honestly, do you *ever* listen?"

"Yes, yes. You did tell me. Who's going to win?"

"I can't tell you that*!* It's Top Secret! My life wouldn't be worth *living* if it got out!"

"Prue, it's not like I've got the *News of the World* on speed-dial."

"I know my job's a joke to you," she sighed. "But there *are* people who'd sell the information."

"Well, sorry I can't be trusted. I'll wait to read it in the paper tomorrow. Speak to you later, bye."

Gloomy Prue has this weird habit. One among many. She spends five minutes being a miserable cow, and just when I've had enough of it she seems to realise that I'm the only person in the world who puts up with her. So then, as I'm replacing the phone, she changes her tune.

"Ooh, no!" she implored. "Don't be like that! Don't *go!*"

Too late, I thought, the phone halfway to its cradle. That'll teach *you*. And then, *just* as I was cutting the connection, I heard Prue yelling,"It's Laura Morris! LAURA MORRIS is Woman of the Year!"

"What?" I shouted, snatching the phone. "Hello? *Hello?*"

Bugger. I'd cut her off. The one time in living memory that I really didn't want to. Brilliant.

"*We The People,*" said a mean little voice.

"Hi – could I speak to Prue Mandelson, please?"

"S'calling?" asked Mean Girl.

"Jeremy Canty."

"Jeremy *Cun*….?"

"No. *Can. Can*-ty."

"Bear with me."

I don't know about you, but I often wonder where they find the receptionists for advertising and PR companies. When they put the ad in the paper, does it say: "WANTED: LAZY, SARCAS-TIC LITTLE MADAM"? No. Does it say: "PREFERENCE WILL BE GIVEN TO APPLICANTS WITH THE SOCIAL SKILLS OF LIAM GALLAGHER"? No. So why do they *always* hire a lazy, sarcastic little madam with the social skills of Liam Gallagher? It's a Modern Mystery. Or maybe it isn't. Breast size could be involved.

"Hello. *We The People.*"

"Yes, I'm still here."

"And you are?"

"The same person from *one* minute ago whose name you've forgotten. Jeremy Canty. Still holding for Prue Mandelson... "

"Bear with me."

Gloomy Prue works in PR. I know it's hard to believe, but she does. And the company really is called *We The People*. Yes: without the comma. Maybe I'm a bitter old writer, but I don't feel happy when the first three words of the American Constitution are hijacked by a bunch of overpaid gits, any more than I feel happy when their colleagues in advertising use Beethoven's Ninth Symphony to sell lavatory cleaner.

"Sinnameeting."

"Hello? Sorry?"

"She's... IN... A... MEETING."

"Right. Any idea when she'll be free?"

"Prolly not today. It's the Woman…"

"…of the Year lunch."

"Well, if you *knew* that, why did you…"

"Oh, I just wanted to waste your time," I said. "Thanks, anyway."

Great. Bloody *great*. The ONE time in twenty-seven years that I actually *wanted* to speak to Gloomy Prue and she wasn't available! My hangover, like an unwashed squatter, had set up home in my head, and it clearly wasn't going to budge unless I called in the heavy mob. So I went to pour a G&T. Even *I* feel a bit louche with something stiff in my hand before lunch-time.

Dolly was scratching at the window to be let in. I'd been so wrecked the night before that I didn't even remember letting her out. As she nuzzled against my leg I wondered, "What Would Dolly Do?" I don't mean Dolly, my cat. Obviously. I mean Dolly Parton, the woman – no, the *diva* – my cat is named after.

On the subject of divas, gay men fall into two camps. As it were. Either they worship one, or they're too worried about acting butch to admit it. I don't have a lot of time for "straight-acting" homosexuals. For a start, what they really mean by straight-acting is "not acting effeminate". And then they hate all other gay men who are camp or flamboyant. Errr... why? Personally, I admire the Graham Nortons and Julian Clarys of this world. The minute they open their gobs they're telling everybody they're gay. I think that's a lot braver than pretending to be heterosexual, don't you? And finally, just how "straight" *are* these straight-acting queens? The two things that mark out heterosexual men, in my not inconsiderable experience, are (a) a desire to have sex with women and (b) the (slightly bigger) desire to have a fight with other men at the slightest provocation. Well, I've been going to gay clubs for thirty years and the most violent things I've ever witnessed are hair-pulling and heavy sarcasm. Oh, and one last thing: the hetties really *hate* it when queens try to be one of the lads. They *know*, you see? They laugh at you behind your back. Get over yourselves, you butch queens. Let your Inner Julian out for a camper scamper!

Anyway, I myself am proud to admit that I do have a diva, and she's Miss Dolly Parton. I've flirted with Cher, over the years, but in the end, nothing compares to Our Doll. The impoverished childhood, with thirty-six brothers and sisters in a mountain shack made of nothing but cardboard, chicken wire and lurve. The struggle to make her mark in the Nashville of the '60s, where most of the men couldn't see past her bosom. The voice; the look; the intelligence; the wit; the charm; the generous heart. The sheer *talent*.

"Hmm," I said to Dolly, who was having one of her rare affectionate moments and allowing me to stroke her under the chin. "What *would* Miss Parton do?"

She'd take charge, I thought. *She'd* find a way to get at Laura Morris.

Then my phone rang again. I ran to grab it, hoping that Prue was calling back, but it was Robyn.

"This is an honour," I said. "An old-fashioned phone call on an old-fashioned phone."

"Darling, quick! Turn your computer on!"

"It is on."

"Then come and speak to me!"

"I am speaking to you."

"No, I mean look at me! Hurry!"

I went to the computer and clicked on Robyn's icon. The window opened up and there was a gigantic, blue fluffy rabbit.

"Hello?" I said.

"Well? What do you think?" asked the rabbit.

"Robyn? Is that you?"

"No, darling, it's a giant fucking rabbit!"

"Oh. It is you. Why are you wearing a blue rabbit costume?"

"Never mind that. What do you think?"

"Urrrm. What am I meant to think?"

"Do I look nice, darling?"

"Blue rabbits always look nice. To me. But not as nice as pink elephants."

"Thank you. But can you see my tits?"

I looked.

"Yes, Robyn. You look like a lovely blue fluffy rabbit with enormous tits."

"FANTASTIC! OK, I'll speak to you later."

"No – you can't cut me off! Tell me!"

"I'm starting a new line."

"In what? Children's toys?"

"No, darling, perversion. I'm a furry."

"A furry what?"

"Honestly! I can't believe you don't know about furries! Google, darling. Google!"

"Couldn't you just tell me instead?"

She sighed.

"Furries, darling, are people who get their rocks off dressing up as fluffy toys. Isn't it wonderful?"

"Is it?" I asked.

"It's a lot less trouble than whipping them. Only trouble is they all want different animals. I've got one this evening wants a bloody giraffe. And these cozzies cost a *fortune*."

"Hmm. Doesn't sound like good business sense to me, Robby."

Robyn removed her rabbit-head and sighed.

"You're right, darling. It's a shit idea. But I'm just so bored with nipple clamps."

"Oh, isn't *everyone*? My mother was saying the same thing to me only yesterday."

"Then your mother is a very sensible woman, as I've said before."

"I think you should stick to nipple clamps and whipping, hun."

"But I'm bored. Bored, bored, bored! Masochists are so dull!"

Even in my own weird life, it's not often I find myself at ten-thirty in the morning, drinking a large G&T and having a conversation with a giant blue rabbit about the pros and cons of earning a living by torturing strange little men, as opposed to dressing up as a cuddly toy and stroking them.

"Look, Robyn," I said, "if you're bored being Mistress Whippy of Swindon, why don't you come back to London?"

"And do what?"

"Your old job? "

"Ugh! No! I never want to see latex again, unless I'm wearing it!"

Robyn's "real" job is – or was – as a special-effects makeup artist. If you've ever seen an episode of *Casualty* from the early nineties I can pretty much guarantee Robyn was responsible for the bits that made you wish you hadn't had kidneys for tea.

"But love, if you came back to London you could move round the corner and then I'd have someone to go dancing with again."

"Darling, I'd never move to Woolwich! Woolwich is for people who've just spent three days clinging to the underside of a lorry."

"Ta."

"And besides. You've got Prue to go dancing with."

"Excuse me? *Prue?* Prue is to dancing what Jordan is to natural beauty."

"Natural beauty is very over-rated. "

"Yes, I'd expect a giant rabbit to say that. But dancing isn't. And anyway, I've just about had enough of that whingeing cow."

"Do I detect an atmosphere?"

"Yes, you bloody well do."

"Marvellous! Let me – nnnh – just get out of this – hrmph – stupid outfit… I'm fucking boiling ALIVE…"

"Mmm. Blue rabbit stew. My favourite."

"Shut up and help."

"Help? You're in Swindon."

"Yes, but – look," she said, hopping around. "I'm stuck!"

"Ah… You need to undo that zip. No, not that one! The

one that starts behind your right ear and goes down under your boob."

"Oh," she said, twisting her neck. "That one! Agh!"

As she undid the crucial zip, all Robyn's over-ripe charms burst out of the rabbit costume at once, like September figs.

"That's better. Now, tell me *everything*."

"Erm, Robyn? You're naked again."

"Oh, for God's sake! They're just tits."

"No, actually. There's minge, too."

She looked down to check my story – as if the horrified look on my face wasn't proof enough that I'd had an Unscheduled Beaver Encounter.

"Fanny-phobe," she said.

"Couldn't we talk on the phone instead?"

"I'll still be naked."

"Yes, but I won't have to watch Burnham Wood coming to high Dunsinane."

"What? Are you being cultured?"

"Bit of Shakespeare, luv. Give it a Google."

"Well, I would, but as you're *insisting* I abandon the computer…"

Whenever I make a mountain out of a mole hill, Robyn is absolutely brilliant at bashing it back down again. Where Gloomy Prue will always throw petrol on the bonfire of my hysteria, Robby's the one standing by with the asbestos blanket. You know those movies where someone's having the screaming abdabs, and nobody knows what to do to calm them down, until a sensible person steps forward and slaps them? That's Robyn. A natural slapper.

After ten minutes of snot-clogged self-pity, I finally paused.

"Are you done, hun?" asked Robyn briskly.

"Yes," I snivelled.

"I was beginning to wonder if you ever would be. What time is it?"

"Oh, don't worry!" I snapped. "It's not even eleven, yet! Plenty of time to squeeze back into your bunny outfit before the Fabulous Furry Freaks appear!"

"Actually, I wasn't thinking about that. I was thinking about how much time you've got to make yourself look *not* like a drunk who's spent all night sleeping in his own sick, and then get a taxi to the Woman of the Year Lunch."

"What? Are you *mad*? What good will that do?"

"None, for all I know."

"Then what's the p-…?"

"The *point* is that it's got to be better than sitting there getting pissed at eleven in the morning and doing nothing."

"You don't *understand*."

"What don't I understand?"

"I'm not brave like you! You'd go out and grab a rampaging elephant by the balls."

"Life *is* a rampaging elephant, my angel."

"Yes, but… But…"

"But what?"

"Nothing."

"Hmm. Listen, I think I should start getting back into this outfit. "

"Fine. I'll speak to you later."

"OK. But let me leave you with one last thought."

"Which is?"

"I bet Andrew Goodman would get a taxi. Byee!"

Oh, I hated her. I hated, hated, *HATED* her!!! But…

Ten minutes later I was in the back of a cab.

- 5 -

Woman of the Year

I loathe going into central London. The only people who seem happy to be there are the young, the rich and the mad.

The moment I watched my cab drive away I realised I'd made a mistake. I was in Soho, outside the offices of *We The People*, but Prue had almost certainly left for the Woman of the Year lunch. Bugger. Oh, well. I was there, so I thought I might as well go in.

Before I even reached the desk I knew that the girl sitting behind it was the same one I'd spoken to earlier. She looked exactly as I'd imagined. Pretty, poisonous and stacked.

"Hi!" I said, airily.

I know I'm getting on a bit, but I'm still quite cute. I was lying when I said I looked like Richard Madeley's granddad. Women usually react quite well to me. But not this one. She stretched her hand out, without meeting my eye.

"Hello?" I said, wondering why she wanted to shake my hand.

"Want me to sign for that?" she asked – and I realised she'd assumed that the large Jiffy-bag I was carrying meant that I was a courier.

"What? Oh, *this*. No, no."

In fact it contained a ready-mixed bottle of G&T, but I wasn't about to tell *her* that.

"Ohhhh-kaaaay," she replied. "What?"

"I've come to see Prue Mandelson. Prue. I'm a friend."

"Out of the office today. But you already know that, don't you?"

I swear to God, if my bottle of ready-mix had been concrete, not G&T, I would've pulled it out of that Jiffy bag and lamped her.

"Ah, right," I smiled, thinking on my feet. "So she's already gone? To the Woman of the Year lunch?"

"Yes," she replied, looking a tad less confident.

"*Shit*," I said. "I'm such a *moron*."

She didn't exactly smile, but at least she stopped looking at me like a pregnancy test that had turned unexpectedly blue.

"She left about ten minutes ago. She'll be at the venue."

"Durrr," I said, in what I thought was a cute-dopey way, hoping she'd spill the beans about 'the venue'. She didn't. "Bear with me," I smiled, pulling my mobile out, and dialling the first number that came into my head.

"Hi, Prue," I said to thin air. "It's Jeremy! Listen, sorry I was late, but now I'm stuck at your office. Can you call me back when you get this and tell me where to come? Love you!"

I closed my phone and smiled helplessly.

"Oh, well. Just have to wait. She's going to be *so* angry when she finds out I was left standing around here, like a twat."

That tactic didn't work, either. *Christ*, I wanted to scream, it's not Shangri-fucking-La! Of course, if I ever actually listened to Gloomy Prue, I would already have known.

A minute passed. Then my phone rang. Dreadfully, it was Paul. Not surprising, I realised, since it was his number I'd called. But even as my heart sank, my brain bobbed to the surface.

"*Prue, honey!*"

"Allo?" asked Paul, suspiciously. "Who dat?"

"God, I'm *so* sorry, pumpkin. I've come to your office by mistake!"

"Iss *me,* ya cunt," said Paul. "You juss rang. Who's *Pumpkin*?"

"Oh, I know, I *know*. But I've *always* been a dizzy bitch, love! Just tell me where to come and I'll grab a cab."

"I'm tellin ya for real, Jeremy. You better not be seeing no-one else," growled Paul. "OOO is *Pump-fuckin-kin?*"

"Hello? Prue? You're breaking up, love…. Prue…. *Prue*…?"

I cut Paul off and immediately started stabbing at my phone. Out of the corner of my eye I could see Princess Pissy was on the verge of believing me. I dialled 118 118.

"Hello," said a very bored voice. "What name please?"

"Oh, for fuc….." I yelled. And then, knowing I needed to make a really big gesture, I threw my mobile across the floor. "No signal! *Bloody* T-Mobile!"

Miss Hospitality 2007 still looked uncertain. I had nothing to lose.

"*Please*. Where do I have to go?"

There was a long pause. She actually took the time to scratch a tiny star from one of her fake fingernails. I thought about introducing her to Robyn. She was clearly in the wrong profession.

"This is more than my job's worth," she said.

"I know, I know."

"If you're a nutter and I get the sack… my boyfriend will *hurt* you. 'Kay?"

She looked so scarily serious that I giggled. "I might like that."

"You so wouldn't?"

"No, no. Sorry. Joking."

" 'Kay. It's at Saint Bernadette."

"Of course*!"* I said, slapping myself on the forehead. "*How* could I forget that? Thank you! Right, guess I'll need a cab."

"Corner of Soho Square's best," she replied, turning away and answering the phone. "Hello? *We The People?* How can I help you?"

For once in my life there followed a run of tiny miracles. First, my phone was still in one piece. It had collided with some sort of soft sculpture. Or perhaps it was a chair. It's hard to tell what's what in those Soho reception areas. Second, I got a cab the moment I stepped outside the building. And third, there was next to no traffic between Soho and Saint Bernadette.

For those of you tuning in from the provinces, Saint Bernadette is not a convent, it's a fashionable restaurant. Very popular with skinny Soho types. That's strange, because the menu is what might best be called meaty. For years I wondered about this, because I couldn't possibly afford to go there. The starters at Saint Bernadette cost more than some cars in Woolwich. Then, finally, somebody rich took me there for dinner. I looked at the menu. Every single thing was made from those parts of a cow that the rest of us call shoes. Then I looked at the punters, all of whom looked like they could do with a month being force-fed Big Macs. And *then* I worked it out. Saint Bernadette isn't a restaurant for people who eat; it's a restaurant for people who snort. Who cares if there's a twenty-quid cow's rectum on your plate when the only porcelain you'll be eating from is the top of a loo?

My happy mood disappeared the moment I arrived. Yes, I was at the venue, but so what? There was a young PR girl on the door, checking the guest list. The guest list that didn't include me. Admittedly, she looked a lot less trouble than the Rottweiler at *We The People,* but the two dickey-bowed storm troopers either side of her did not. On the other hand, they did look like they'd just stepped out from one of my stickier dreams, but somehow I didn't think that telling them as much would get me under the silk rope.

So, I stood on the pavement, watching the guests arrive for the Woman of the Year lunch. Oh, what fun! When you're feeling like a complete failure, is there *anything* to lift the spirits better than a parade of expensively-dressed, laughing, successful people? No, indeed.

I looked at my watch. It was almost one. No sign whatsoever of Prue. Then it hit me. I'd been so busy pretending to phone her that I hadn't actually tried to phone her.

"Hello?"

"It's me."

"Yes, Jeremy, I know," hissed Prue. "For God's sake! I can't speak to you *now!* I'm hosting the Woman of the Year lunch!"

"And I'm outside."

"Outside where?"

"Saint Bernadette."

"You're *what?*"

"It's an emergency."

"What sort of emergency justifies calling me *now*? Are there tanks coming down the Commercial Road?"

"Look, can you *please* pop out and speak to me for a minute?"

There was a pause while Prue did a lot of air-kissing in the background.

"This'd better be *good*," she said, once she'd finished. "*Where* are you?"

"I told you. Right outside. Literally."

Thirty seconds later, Prue bustled past the bouncers. For the ten-thousandth time I marvelled at her fashion sense. She always dresses straight out of *Vogue*, but the effect is like stone cladding on a Pitsea prefab. The concept is fine, but the context is so, *so* wrong.

"Wow! You look fab!" I said, trying not to look too aghast at the smock-dress, black leggings and flat shoes. On Sienna Miller the combo would've looked great. On Prue…

"What on *earth* is going on?" she barked.

"Not sure," I said, gaily. "Some sort of awards thingy."

"Jeremy, *please*."

"OK, look. I'll be quick…"

Despite her flaws, Prue has an annoying habit of coming up trumps, which always makes me feel shitty for bitching about her. She went back inside, promising she'd do whatever she could to help. The fact that she was sitting at the same table as Laura Morris gave me a shred of hope.

After that, I was at a bit of a loose end. I hung about for a while, after the last of the guests had gone in, hoping to get lucky with one of the bow-tied brutes, but they were both competing for the little PR girl, so I wandered off, wishing I had a fanny. I thought about splurging on my third taxi of the day, but then realised that mingling with the rich and famous had warped my mind when I reached in my pocket and found I had four pounds sixty to my name. So I made my way to the nearest Tube.

I once read that "being a writer" is the third-most fantasised-about career, after "being a footballer" and "being an actor". I think it must have been a long time ago, when most of the population could actually read and write, but all the same. People do dream about it. Well, apologies to those few of you who still have the fantasy, but the reality is shite. Then again, so is being a footballer, or an actor, or a model, or a singer, or every single one of those jobs that people dream about. 99% of professional footballers earn less money than your bog-standard plumber. They work just as hard as the Beckhams and the Rooneys, but they never had the same gifts. Once you start on the models, singers, actors, dancers (and writers).... Five hundred quid a week is a dream! The trouble is, when you've been given a bit of a talent for something, it takes over your life. You just can't stop yourself from doing it, even when you've realised that you're always going to be poor. You keep plugging away, hoping you'll Get Lucky. But as the years go by, you start to see that maybe the reason why you never hit the Big Time is nothing to do with bad luck. Maybe it's just that you're a bit crap.

Oh dear. Sorry. Just wanted to let you know what I was thinking about while I sat on the Tube. Sitting on the Tube always makes me depressed.

Woolwich doesn't have a Tube station of its own, because it's a flood risk. The nearest Tube is East Greenwich, home of The Dome, which is about three miles from my flat. These days The Dome has been reinvented as the O2, but back in 2007 it was just a big, silly hubcap. I still fantasise about getting five minutes in a padded room with a baseball bat and the git who thought that paying forty quid to climb up a giant plastic vagina was a family day out.

By the time I got home it was five to five. Five to five is a special time for everyone from my generation. We can't help shouting CRACKERJACK!! Oh, ask your mum.

But it's still a good time of day, even now. Five to five means you can feed the cat, the kids, or any other annoying mammals in your life. Then you can pour a drink, grab your fags and settle down on the sofa for… yes! Richard and Judy!!

Judy was looking very fresh – as she often does on a Tuesday, I've noticed. My latest obsession was trying to count the flicky-uppy bits at the sides of her hairdo. They seemed to multiply by the day. If her hair was green and her head was pointy, she'd look like a Christmas tree. She'd look lovely with shiny balls. And speaking of shiny balls, Richard was positively shimmering. He looked like he'd just been injected with every monkey gland in London Zoo, and then been given a good going-over with a can of Pledge.

"Hi," said Judy. "On today's show we're discussing a problem that many women over forty suffer in silence. Flatulence."

"Not that you can," smirked Richard.

"Can what?"

"Suffer in silence. With flatulence."

Judy ignored him. Richard looked naughty and made a parp-ing noise out the corner of his mouth.

"Anyway," Judy carried on. "We'll be looking at different methods for getting rid of the problem."

"Yes, and Judy's tried every one of them. Haven't you, love?"

That got a level eight T.W.L. Actually, it was more of a straight-forward pissed-off look. Richard giggled. I was already helpless.

"And also," she continued, with her usual professionalism, "we've got our child-care guru, Minty Lavier. She's got some great advice about what to do with the kids in the school holidays when you get to that point where you want to throttle the little angels."

"But *first*," beamed Shiny Balls, "we've got an announcement to make."

"An *announcement?*" said Judy, dryly. "It's not Waterloo Station."

Oh, I love that woman! The way she waits for her revenge. She's like Lucrezia Borgia in a cardy.

"Well, what would *you* call it?"

"Nothing. Carry on."

Poor Richard. He really should have been born with a tail to put between his legs.

"OK – a *pro*nouncement, then."

Judy rolled her eyes. "Get on with it!"

He laughed. They always laugh after a spat. Yet another patch in the mysterious quilt that is their genius.

"Right – I'll get there in the end. Today saw the awards for the Woman of the Year, here in London. And we're proud – *very* proud – to announce… To *tell* you, that the winner was our very own Laura Morris!"

"Yes," beamed Judy, radiating Proud Mum. "As you know, Laura is the woman…"

"…no, the genius…"

"Yes, he's right. For a change. The *genius*, who came up with the idea for our Book Club…"

I was so excited at feeling a part of the proceedings that I almost didn't notice the phone ringing. Then I did, and the caller display told me it was Prue.

"Hello?"

"Are you watching the show?"

"What do you think?"

"They had a camera crew there. I should be on in a minute. Looking fat, probably."

"Don't be silly. You're not a bit fat."

"Telly adds ten pounds, though," said Prue, miserably.

"No, I bet you'll look gorge, hun. As always."

"God, I *hope* so. You never know who might be watching."

No, I thought. But on the other hand, you can be pretty certain who *won't*. Heterosexual men looking for a girlfriend, and people in positions of power at the top of the public relations industry.

"Anyway," she went on. "I've got news."

That got my attention.

"Oh. Good news?"

"*Very* good news. Potentially."

"Ah. Potentially?"

"Well, no. Really. *Really* good news. Shall I tell you?"

"Oh, go on , then."

"Am I the best friend *ever?*"

"Prue," I said, visualising myself with a rusty knife. "What sort of a daft question is that? You *know* you are."

"OK. Are you ready for this?"

"Ready as I'll ever be."

"Right. Are you sitting down?"

No, I wanted to say, I'm levitating. With anger.

"I am."

"Then I'll begin. Laura Morris is in desperate need."

"Desperate need of what?"

"A good man. "

"Oh. Great. And where do I come in?"

Prue giggled teasingly. And then her mobile went dead.

- 6 -

My Eight o'clock Giraffe

I tried about twenty times to call Prue back but all I got was her voicemail. By then I'd missed most of Richard and Judy. Not that it mattered. I was in such a state that they couldn't have kept my attention, even if they'd suddenly ripped their clothes off and started doing it doggy-style over the coffee table. I'm sure they'll go there, eventually, with Beechy Colclough and Rebecca Loos egging them on. While I'm on the subject, what *is* Beechy Colclough? It sounds like an Oirish beauty spot, till you see it. Then you decide it's the love-child of a mop and a Muppet.

Unless I find myself unexpectedly caught up in an earthquake I always start work at five past six. You probably have me down as a flaky piss artist, but actually I'm not. Well, *OK*, you got one out of two. But I'm not flaky. I've worked more or less every night for the past twenty years. Work is the one thing in my life that's absolutely reliable, apart from Prue, Robyn and Dolly. And even they can only be relied upon when they're not in the grip of excess oestrogen. Sometimes I really do wish I had a few straight men-friends. Then I come to my senses.

So, I'd fed Dolly and settled down at the computer, when my phone rang. It was Prue.

"Hi," she said. "Are you working?"

"Just starting."

"Sorry. My battery died. *Completely*."

"Well, dying should always be done completely," I replied. "No point keeping people guessing."

"Aww… don't be grumpy."

"I'm not!" I lied. "Just fascinated. Laura Morris needs a good man... and?"

"And I think *you're* the man."

"Ohhhhhh-kay. Why? Has she given up on sex?"

"I don't know. Yes, if she's got any sense. But sex won't come into it. I hope."

"Me too. Any chance you could stop talking in riddles?"

"You *are* grumpy."

"Prue, I'm not. I'm just… edgy."

"OK, I'll tell you. Laura doesn't need a man for *her*. Well, actually, she does. You know her marriage broke up?"

"I didn't."

"Well, it did. Her husband just left her."

"Oh. That's a shame. Why?"

"Why? *Why?* Er, he's a *man*? Honestly, relationships! What's the point? If the Woman of the Year can't…"

"Prue."

"Oh, yes. Sorry. Well, you don't have to worry. She's not looking for a *real* man."

"Thanks for that little ego-stroke."

"She wants a *man's* man."

"A man's man? What does that mean?"

"A gentleman's companion. For her dad."

"A gentleman's companion? It's 2007, not 1907! A gentleman's companion is something you buy at Anne Summers."

"Jeremy, shut up and listen…"

The more I listened, the more I realised I was being offered my chance on Opportunity Knocks. For those of you under a hundred, that was a telly talent show. It was the 1960s version of the X-Factor, except you didn't want to throw everybody involved into a bath of acid. Apparently, Laura Morris's mother had died a couple of years back, and her dad, a typical old working-class geezer, wasn't coping without the missus. So, Laura and her hubby had moved him into their place. That was working fine, until the marriage broke up. But now the old boy was getting a bit isolated. So she wanted a sort of au-pair. With a twist.

"Jesus," I said, when Prue had finished. "That *could* be perfect. I always knew there was a reason why I've put up with you since 1979."

For some reason Prue laughed.

"It *is* perfect, isn't it? "

"It honestly is. Have I told you lately that I love you?

"Actually," said Prue, "not since two days before Christmas."

She meant it. Prue's one of those people who genuinely does write in her diary *"December 23rd – Jeremy told me he loves me"*. And then she's surprised she hasn't got a bloke.

"So what happens next?" I asked. "Did you tell Laura you know the perfect man for the job?"

"Jeremy, I work in PR. What do *you* think?"

"Crikey. So what next?"

"OK. I'll call Laura tomorrow. Tell her that you're very interested. Then it's up to you."

"Fucking hell. Am I really going to do this?"

"Well, have you got a *better* scheme for getting on the Richard and Judy book list?"

"I could try writing the right sort of book."

"You do write the right sort of book! You just need a lucky break."

"Is that all it is?"

"Yes. You *know* it is."

"Have I told you lately that I love you?"

"You have. I'll have to put it in my diary."

"OK. Just checking. Can I go away now and have a think?"

"Don't you mean a drink?" she giggled, like she was Oscar bleeding Wilde.

"No. I really *do* mean a think."

You know I said it takes an earthquake to stop me working? Well, this was an earthquake. Twenty-four hours previously, the thought of worming my way into someone's life, just to use them, would have disgusted me. And yet, there I was, seriously wondering how I could best take advantage of a heartbroken, overworked middle-aged woman and her aging father. What sort of evil bastard was I?

An hour later I'd decided exactly what kind of evil bastard I was. A natural. If Laura Morris needed someone to look after her dear old dad, I was going to make damn sure I got the job. I could see it all so clearly: I'd float in on my magic brolly, like Mary Poppins. Then I'd make myself totally indispensable. Her dad would soon see me as a combination of the son he'd never had, the wife he'd tragically lost and the best friend he'd got a leeeetle bit too fond of when he was in the navy. Oh, yes, I thought, if the old boy needs a helping hand under the tartan knee-blanket, I'll be there. I'd do whatever it took to make Laura trust me. And *then*... Oh, it would only be a matter of time before she took me into her confidence... started telling me about the awful pressure of choosing books for the R&J list... and I could casually offer to ease her terrible burden...

I was so excited at the prospect of it all that I put on my favourite disco record of all time, Dolly's *Baby, I'm Burnin'* , and bounced around, shaking my booty like the big ole Harlem girl I am in my heart. I got so carried away that I didn't hear the hammering at my door before it was almost off its hinges.

It was Paul.

"You got someone in there?" he gurned.

"Yes, Paul. Dolly Parton popped round. Do come in and say hi, y'all."

"Urr," he grunted, shouldering his way past me, then turning the stereo off and the telly on. I slammed the door huffily, still feeling a bit Harlem in my heart.

There's an expression "dumb like a fox" – well, that's Paul. For all the good it did him, the school he attended might as well have been the sort with fish. He tried reading one of my novels, once, but only got as far as chapter one. When I say chapter one, I really do mean the words "chapter" and "one". The first word of the actual book was "phenomenal". Paul gave up the struggle at that stage. But the weird thing is, he's a lot smarter than most people I know. Every last brain cell in his gorgeous head is dedicated to the business of jungle survival. He can spot a liar or a scammer in half a second. And when he really *needs* to learn something he'll do it in a heartbeat. For instance: I've spent countless hours trying to teach my university-educated friends how to use their computers. Like a lot of homos, I'm shit-hot with computers. They're the gay version of car engines: technical and butch, but not so butch you have to spend hours afterwards with a nail-brush and a gallon of Swarfega. After all, there are so many better things to do with a gallon of Swarfega (and, probably, a nail-brush). But, unlike my supposedly intelligent friends, when Paul said "Jeremy, learn us the pooter" (so he could watch lesbian porn and Al-Qaeda beheadings, just in case you're thinking he had a sudden urge to use Wikipedia) he sucked it up like an alcoholic Dyson that had just escaped from The Priory.

I'm telling you this because it was Paul who burst my bubble. After I'd told him about my wildly successful day I flopped down in my chair, waiting for him to applaud my brilliance. He didn't.

"Fuckinell," he said. "You sure she don't need someone to do her garden?"

"No, I'm not. But this is *miles* better!"

"Nah it ain't."

I pouted. "*Why?*"

"Well, her dad don't sound like your sorta geezer. Not if he's like, this old docker from Wallwoof. Probly an ex boxer. National Service. Bitches in Bangkok what shot ping pong balls out their twats. All that."

"Oh, please. I can get on with anybody."

"You reckon? There's one or two boozers down my way I woutn't wanna take yer."

"And I wouldn't want to be asked, *thank* you."

"Look, bub. Ain't being funny or nuffink, but you ain't a bloke's bloke. End of."

"So bloody what?"

"So blardy wart?" he repeated, in his version of my accent –

which sounds like Eliza Doolittle and Henry Higgins sharing a frock. "What if he wants to talk footy?"

"Well, I'd um, I'd…"

"Right. Or what if he's a spaz? You know, arfuritus or summink. What if he can't wash his own arse?"

"Well, that's no problem! I don't have to know about football to use a *sponge!*"

"No, yeah. You're right. But he ain't gunna want a poof doing all that shit, is he? *I* woutn't wanna poof touching me arse."

"Oh, for heaven's sake!" I shouted. "You let *this* poof touch your arse! And besides, it's Laura Morris who'll be employing me, not him."

"You reckon? What kind of a daughter's she, then? If she don't give a fuck what her old man wants?"

He was right, of course. I hated him for it, but he was. Again. My shiny pink bubble of joy suddenly popped and ran down my neck. "And another fing," said Paul, looking pleased with himself. "Your face."

"My *face*? What's wrong with my face?"

"Durrrr. Muppet. She might *reckanise* it. You's a writer, innit?"

"Oh, for fu… shit. You're right. She might. *Shit.*"

"Seeeee? S'ain't gunna be easy, Jeremy."

Until then it really hadn't occurred to me that Laura Morris might recognise my face. True, the paparazzi weren't exactly bashing down my door, but in the little world of literature, some people would recognise me – and Laura Morris was sure to be one of them. I've had my share of publicity. Back when my fourth novel came out, and my face didn't need a bit of work on the suspension, I actually got more fan letters from lonely women than I sold copies of the book.

Paul was right. I couldn't take a chance on Laura recognising me. And I couldn't take a chance on her father hating me, either.

So it was that I found myself saying something I never thought I'd say. Not to Paul, anyway.

"OK. What do you suggest?"

He looked very pleased with himself as he stretched out on the sofa and yawned.

"I suggest," he smirked, "that you cook me a bacon sandwich."

I don't know why I bother cooking anything for Paul. He's so fond of tomato ketchup that it would be easier to skip the food and let him drink from the bottle. Anyway, I made the sandwich. After that he needed a nap. And *then*, when I woke him with his tea and biccies, the Bertrand bleeding Russell of Sheppey was finally ready to give me the benefit of his wisdom.

"Right," he said. "Two fings."

"Should I be taking notes?"

"Dunno. Should I be givin you a slap?"

"Carry on."

"First fing. When you meet this old geezer, yeah?"

"Yes. Got that. God, I *should* take notes."

"When you meet this old geezer, suss him out. Talk about fings you're good at, yeah? But don't make out you know about the bloke stuff, cos he'll know you're shittin' him. If you get stuck, give us a bell and I'll tell ya what to say."

"Riiiiiiight."

"And the second fing. That old slag you know. Get her down here."

"What? Who?"

"The one what kicks pervs in the bollocks."

"Oh. Robyn. Why?"

"For the disguise, innit?"

"What? I can't ask Robyn to come with me!"

Paul got to his feet, then came and patted me on the head.

"Doughnut. She ain't always been on the game, has she? You told me she had a pwoppa job doing make-up and stuff innit?"

"Yes, she was….. oh. I see. Yes."

"Say *fank you, Paul*."

"Thank you, Paul."

"S'alright," he replied, looking at his phone. "Out the way, bub, it's *Emmerdale*."

While Paul gave his full attention to *Emmerdale* I went and sat on the loo with my laptop. I couldn't calm Robyn, because she would almost certainly be torturing a punter, and Paul would hear. The last thing I needed was him standing behind me, wanking. So I sent her an email.

Darling! I know you're busy, but I've got an urgent need for rubber! Let me know when you can talk and I'll call you. Xxxx

Two seconds later Paul barged into the loo. Needless to say, Robyn appeared on my screen at precisely the same time. She was what I can only call vacuum-packed, in this red plastic number that made her look like a pornographic saveloy. Actually, when you think about it, all saveloys are a bit saucy, aren't they?

"It's all right, darling, I'm free! My seven o'clock cancelled. Tell me *everything*."

"Oosat?" asked Paul, twisting his body round as he stood at the sink, peeing up my bathroom wall in the process.

"Fucking *hell*, Paul!"

"Oop, sorry bub," he said, re-directing his dick at the plughole and thoughtfully wiping the wall with the Egyptian cotton hand-towel I'd bought in Selfridge's sale. "Oosat then? "

"Who's *that*?" said Robyn.

"Oh, for God's sake! Why don't I leave the two of you alone? Robyn, Paul. Paul, Robyn."

Paul didn't need any encouragement. He'd already snatched the laptop and grinned at the camera.

"Cwor!" he went. "Allo *darlin!*"

"Ooh! Hello *gorgeous*," said Robyn. "Jeremy hasn't done you justice!"

"No," I mumbled in the background. "Unlike the Crown Prosecution Service."

"Hear that, Jeremy?" Paul leered at me. "She finks I'm gorgeous."

"Yes," I snapped, prising the computer from his paws. "That's because she can't see your soul."

"She's gunna," he chortled. "My ar-soul!" Then he pulled his trackies down and mooned at the camera.

"Christ… Robyn, love, can I call you back when I get rid of my pet chav?"

"Oi!" said Paul, cuffing me round the head.

"Of course, darling! I've got to get changed for my eight o'clock giraffe. Byee!"

Paul had gone back to the living room. He looked sullen.

"Ain't a chav," he said, flicking through the telly channels and settling on an early-evening repeat of the Jeremy Kyle Show.

"I was only joking."

"Fuckin' issit."

"Oh, all right. So you're a chav. I'm sorry if you've been under the impression that you're a lost bloody Romanov."

God, I wanted him to piss off. But I could tell he was now

in the mood to hang around all night, just to annoy me. Fortunately, at that moment, his wife called.

"Yur?" he grunted. "Nah… in the pub, bub… What? Fuck mine, Diane… Yeah, yeah, wotever. See ya… 'Pends on the traffic, innit…"

He closed his phone. I felt hopeful.

"Gottamove, bub," he said. "Missus."

"So I gathered."

"Yur, well, gotta go and watch her mate Michelle's kids, innit. Her old man's been nicked."

"Oh."

"Laters," he said, already on his way. Then he stopped, came back, and gave me a kiss that left me vibrating pinkly for the next two minutes, like a Spam tuning-fork. God damn him for the way he could do that to me.

After he'd gone I was going to call Robyn on the phone, but I couldn't resist trying the computer first. I wasn't disappointed.

"Ooh, hang on! I'm having a fucking awful job with this zip!" said a velour giraffe. "Ack! That's better!"

Robyn span round, very red in the face, and smiled at me.

"Very nice," I said.

"Thank you. Oh, wait. There's a hat!"

She popped the final part of the cozzy on her head. It didn't make her look one bit more like a giraffe. It made her look like Deputy Dawg's slutty girlfriend.

"That's smashing, love. Robyn, look. I need you. Desperately."

"How desperately, darling?"

"Very."

"More desperately than the time you were trapped under

that twenty stone man who'd had a heart attack?"

"OK, not *that* desperately. This time I can still breathe. Just about."

"Carry on, my little drama queen. You mentioned rubber?"

"Yes."

"Well, darling, you're welcome. But you do realise I'm a size eight and you're a fourteen?"

"An eight? An *eight?* In what? Shoes?"

"I've lost a lot of weight since you last saw me, sweetie."

"Robyn, I'm looking at you right now."

"Oh, *that*," she said, with a wave of her hand. "You know what webcams are like for making you look fat! They'd make Posh Spice look like she could drop a few pounds – and let's face it, she'd find life pretty roomy in a tin of sardines."

She did have a point. What *is* it with webcams? Why do they make you look like Fat Pinocchio? I sometimes wonder about those people who actually look normal on a webcam. If you met them in real life, would they weigh two stone and have noses that went *in?*

"Well, hun," I replied. "You'll be thrilled to hear that it's not your clothes I'm after. It's your talent."

"My talent? God, darling, DON'T tell me you're turning straight! It's hot inside this giraffe. I might faint."

"No, I'm not turning straight," I said. Then I thought about it. "Actually, love, I am. Sort of. But I can't do it without *you*."

- 7 -

Barbra Streisand's Rabbi

Most of the time my life moves about as fast as the average bowel movement on *You Are What You Eat*. What in God's name persuades those people to invite "Doctor" Gillian McKeith into their lives? She's not exactly the picture of health, is she? She looks like a gerbil in search of a Macmillan nurse. She takes these fat, jolly people and turns them into fat, miserable people who weigh exactly two pounds less than they did before, except after they've been Gillianed, the poor fuckers can't sneeze without shitting themselves. And then she examines the result! It's disgusting! It's repellent! I've never missed a single episode! Quite frankly, I'm waiting for the day when a family of Falkirk fatties decide they've had enough of lettuce, sunflower seeds and Gillian. Suddenly they rebel, and eat the bitch.

Anyway, as I was saying, my life is pretty slow. I can make my mail last until lunch time, which is good going, considering most of it consists of debt orders and offers from Nigerian psychics. But the next couple of days went by in a blur.

Robyn had been her usual practical self. No sooner had I explained my problem than she was cancelling her punters, packing her bags, and driving down to London. Next morning, before she arrived, I spoke to Gloomy Prue. She'd already called Laura Morris. Curse women and their bloody efficiency! I had no choice but to arrange the interview. I had a ton of questions for Prue, but she got called away by someone in desperate need of PR, so I just had to dive in. The one thing I did establish was that she hadn't used my real surname. I was, as far as Laura Morris was concerned, Jeremy Robson, not Jeremy Canty.

It took me a couple of tries, not to mention a couple of G&Ts, but once I got through to the Richard and Judy bunker, the receptionist already knew my name, and I was immediately connected to Laura. Oh, what it is to be wanted.

"Hello!" I said, trying to sound bouncy and sober at the same time. "Is that Laura?"

"*Jeremy*," answered one of those voices that make you want to befriend their owner immediately. "Thanks for calling so soon. You're a life saver."

"Actually," I joked (well, lied, actually), "I *am* fully trained in CPR."

"CPR?"

"Cardio-pulmonary resuscitation."

"Oh. That's, um, reassuring."

Well done, Jeremy, I thought. Great start. Make her feel good by drawing attention to the fact her dad's on his last legs.

"Congratulations, by the way!" I blurted. "Woman of the Year, eh?"

"Thank you," she replied. "I don't think they would've given me the award if they'd known I was neglecting my own father."

"Well, now…" I waffled, looking around for a shovel so that I could dig my own grave faster. "From what Prue's told me, you're not neglecting him at all."

"That's a very sweet thing to say, Jeremy, but I am. I should be there for him, not spending twelve hours a day in this bloody office."

"Well, *someone's* got to pay the bills."

"Yes," she sighed. "*Someone* has. These days."

Marvellous. Now I'd managed to remind her she'd just been dumped by the hubby.

"Anyway. Prue seems to think we'd be good for each other."

"I hope so. When could you start?"

"Start? Wouldn't you like to interview me first?"

"Look, if you're *half* as good as Prue says, I'll be thrilled."

"Oh."

"Would you like to interview *me?*" she said.

"What? God, no! Well, um… I suppose we *should* meet first."

"Saturday at one?" she said immediately, as busy people do.

"Hold on," I said, making a pathetic attempt to sound as though I was busy, too, and needed to consult my hectic diary. While I rustled a copy of *News Shopper,* hoping it sounded like a Rolodex, I heard a flunky tell Laura that TransWorld publishers were waiting on line one. *TransWorld.* Publishers of Andrew Goodman. Sorry: Andrew *fucking* Goodman.

"Jeremy? Sorry to rush you, but is one o'clock tomorrow OK?"

"Yes, yes. Fine. Where?"

"I was thinking my place? Even *I* take Saturday off. Well, sort of."

"Sure…"

"Look – I'll get my PA to call you with the address. Sorry, I *must* go. Bloody publishers! Don't fancy swapping jobs, do you?"

Oooooooh, I thought, staring at the dead phone. If only you knew…

Robyn arrived at noon that day. You've probably guessed that Robyn loves a bit of dressing-up, so the fact she was wearing a business suit told me she was in the mood to sort things out. We didn't even stop for coffee and a catch-up. She lugged her box of tricks up to my flat, and an hour later I had a beard. And sideburns. And…

"No, Robyn, fuck off! I am *not* wearing a false nose!"

"Darling, it'll look perfect."

"Maybe if I was Nicole Kidman and this was *The Hours*."

"Nicole Kidman? You so wish," she said, applying some fishy-smelling glue to the inside of the fake hooter and plonking it on my face before I could turn away.

"See?" she said, holding up a hand mirror. I saw, all right.

"Love," I sighed. "I look like Barbra Streisand's rabbi."

"Ha-bloody-ha."

"I look ridiculous!"

"No, you silly Mary. You just don't look like *you*."

Robyn frowned and folded her arms, thrusting her embonpoint forward. This is always a terrifying sight. It's the Shock and Awe of Tits.

"I'll tell you what the problem is," she said. "You don't look as pretty as you'd like."

I picked up the mirror again. I had to admit the transformation was effective. The only way I could be identified was by my dental records. But Robyn was right. I didn't look pretty.

"Couldn't I look different *and* cute?"

"You do look cute. Man-cute."

"As opposed to?"

"Boy-cute, of course. And let's be honest, love. You've not been boy-cute since you grew out of those skinny white jeans. Was that '97? Oh, sorry, no! It was '87."

"Cow."

"Oh, get a grip, you silly queen! You're forty-six and this is a crisis! I didn't drive all the way from Swindon to pat your slightly balding old ego on its sad little head."

I pouted.

"I need a wee," she said, standing up with all the dignity that a top-heavy midget can muster.

While she was gone I had another look at my new self. The light in my flat is very cruel. If you really must glance in a mirror you always look like you do when you've left a club at 4 a.m., after six pills, and then catch sight of yourself in the mirror at the minicab office. Why *do* minicab offices always have those mirrors, by the way? Have you ever had a driver with nicely-combed hair? No, me neither. Anyway, As I looked at my new nose, new beard and new sideburns, I realised that Robyn was right. The disguise was perfect. And maybe it *was* time to change my look.

I remembered a queen I pulled last year. Or maybe it was the year before. He was short, wide and hairy, with a face not so much sculpted as kneaded, and I don't even mean at a bakery. We're talking day-centre. Anyway, after we'd had it off and were lying there smoking, and making chit-chat as gay men do, before one of them calls a cab and promises to phone, he took a drag on his fag and said, "You know what? I don't think there's anything sadder than a fading pretty-boy."

I was so shocked by his bad manners I laughed.

"I can't believe you just said that."

"What? Oh, no, love. I didn't mean *you*. I meant..."

"Yeah, whatever," I replied, knowing exactly what he meant. "Your cab'll be here soon. Why don't you wait outside? Love."

Needless to say, a romance didn't follow, but it set me thinking. How *do* you know when you stop being something that just needs a quick flash in the oven and a touch of mint sauce, as opposed to twelve hours in a Slo-Cooker and an awful lot of garlic?

"Did you have a little think while I was away?" asked Robyn as she emerged from the loo.

"Yes."

"And you decided I'm right, didn't you?"

"Maybe."

"Don't start again. I'm warning you. I can be back in Swindon for my six o'clock."

"Oh, OK. Yes. You're right."

"Thank you."

"Apart from the nose."

"But that's the key element! I was up half the night, picking your nose!"

"Eeww."

"The nose," she pronounced, tweaking her own button-version "is the foundation of the face."

"Yes, love, but the one you've given me could be the foundation of St Paul's bleeding cathedral. Besides, it's a different colour from the rest of my face."

"Not any more," she said, producing a sponge and wiping it round my fake schnozz.

"Cor," I said, looking in the mirror. "You're good."

"Thank you. See? That's all there is to it. On with the new nose, a quick wipe of foundation and you're all set."

"All right. Yes."

"Yes what?"

"Yes, mistress. I'll wear the bloody nose!"

"Good boy. Now, pour me a large G&G."

"OK. One large G&T coming up."

"No, darling. G and G. This is no time for tonic."

- 8 -

Marcel Proust is Great in Bed

I must say, the disguise was effective. Next morning, as I sat on the Tube, I spent a good five minutes eyeing this sexy bearded number in the window, before I realised I was actually cruising myself. I especially liked his manly nose.

Laura's place turned out to be in one of those Valhalla-like converted wharves next to Tower Bridge. Choosing books was clearly a lot better paid than writing the bloody things. As I stared up in wonder at the huge brass and chrome doors, feeling like a little gay hobbit, a very loud voice made me jump out of my shoes.

"Jeremy! Hi - I'll buzz you in."

"Oh!" I squeaked, noticing for the first time that a security camera was beaking down at me. "Thanks!"

She came to greet me in the vaulted outer lobby, barefoot, hair like startled straw, and wearing a knee-length tee shirt bearing the words "**MARCEL PROUST IS GREAT IN BED**".

She carried a large steaming mug.

"You're a tea person, right?"

"Yes," I said.

"And no sugar?"

"No sugar."

"There you are, then," she smiled, handing me the mug. "That's for you. *And* I've got bacon sarnies on the go."

By the time I'd followed her into the kitchen I was completely in love, and thoroughly miserable. You know how some people have that knack for making you feel like an evil piece of crap? How do they do that? Oh, hang on. I know how. They're really, really nice. And you actually are an evil piece of crap.

The kitchen was about twice as big as my flat. It had an Italian marble island that I could quite happily have holidayed on. In the middle of the island was a gorgeous German six-ring (and I've met a few of *those*, let me tell you). Laura was struggling with a frying pan the size of a temple gong. All that was needed to complete the picture was a greasy bodybuilder and a big sign saying "The Rank Organisation Presents…"

"Oooh! Ahh!" she said, trying to dodge the spitting fat from twenty rashers of bacon.

"Here," I said, taking over. "Let me. I've had a lot of practice with the full English."

Laura stepped aside willingly and let me tame the unruly pork.

"I s'pose you got lots of practise when you were running that home for disadvantaged kids?" she said.

"Eh? *What* home for… Oh! Prue *told* you about that, did she?"

"Mmm. She's told me a lot about you."

"Prue, tcsch! I do wish she wouldn't big me up to people," I said, wondering what the fuck *else* she'd invented. "She carries on like I'm some sort of saint."

"Mmm," said Laura. Although I was concentrating on the

bacon, I could see she was a bit saucer-eyed. "She told me about the way you'd taken care of that old woman, too."

"Oh. Right. Um… you must mean, um, Maisie?"

"Was it Maisie? The one you met in the street – when you scared off those kids who were trying to mug her? Then you looked after her – until she, well…."

"Yes," I jumped in, thanking Prue in my head and wanting to murder her at the same time. "Dear old Maisie. I do miss her. What a character. Anyway – this bacon's ready!"

"Oh, quick! Here - I've already buttered the bread. Dad *hates* his food cold."

"Does he?"

"Mm. I thought if you took him a bacon sarny and a cuppa it might, well, break the ice?"

"Oh!" I said, suddenly remembering there was a genuine reason for me being there, apart from my own schemes. "Brilliant idea! What's his, um… what shall I call him?"

"Lofty," she replied.

"Lofty? Isn't that a bit familiar for a first encounter?"

"Oh, nooo," she said. "He's not like that. We're not *royalty*, you know."

"OK."

"His room's on the mezzanine," she smiled, handing me a tray.

I'd always thought that "mezzanine" was estate-agent talk for "first floor", but that just goes to show I don't know many rich people. Laura's place did have a mezzanine, and it hung out in space, with a widescreen view of the river. Tower Bridge was so close you could almost touch it, and, as it happened, it was in the act of raising. Although I'd seen it dozens of times, I'd always been outside, on the bridge with the peasants, cursing the interruption to my journey. Now, from a millionaire's perspective, I watched it open-mouthed, like someone slow from Idaho. I may even have drooled. Then I realised I wasn't being the best sort of potential gentleman's companion, because the food was getting cold. So I tapped on Lofty's door.

Old people really aren't funny, are they? They make you worry about your future. One day you're upgrading your mobile every time they bring out a shinier one, and illegally downloading the Arctic Monkeys. Then, all of sudden, you lose it. You go out and buy an entire new wardrobe in mushroom-coloured polyester, and you have to phone your grandchildren before you can use the microwave. Why *is* that? And, more importantly, when?

Lofty's lair was beyond fantastic. It was every gay man's fantasy gaff, with its acres of hardwood floor, its giant span of window, and more halogens than Armani headquarters. Except Lofty had turned it into a nasty little council flat from 1958. The fifty-grand crystal windows were hung with nets that must have cost all of eight quid. The room measured at least twenty-five feet by thirty, but crammed together in the very middle was a ciggy-scorched coffee table and a three-piece suite. It was covered in some terrible nubby green material that looked like someone had started out trying to discover nylon but had then given up and discovered penicillin instead. And, instead of a giant plasma from Bang and Olufsen, there was a tiny pregnant-looking telly made of fake wood, with those ugly buttons for changing channel that look like tin-plated fags.

Lofty himself sat slumped in an armchair, smoking a roll-up. The first thing I noticed was that he was anything but lofty. It was a name he'd been given way back when. School? Army? Anyway, he couldn't have been more than four feet six. He was watching the racing, sort of. I didn't exactly get the impression his heart was doing much racing.

"Hello, Lofty," I said. "I'm Jeremy."

"All right, son. Lofty."

"Yes. Um, I brought you a bacon sarny. And a cuppa."

"Bacon sarny, eh? Don't s'pose she cooked it, did she?"

"Who, Laura? Well, actually, she…"

"…cos she can't boil water, that one. Not like her old mum, God rest her."

"Well, no. I cooked it."

"Right, I'll give it a go, then. Take a seat."

I put the tray down on the coffee table and passed Lofty the sandwich.

"Hmm," he said giving it a good gumming. "Not bad. I can't have it too crispy these days, see? Not like years ago. I had jaws like a bear-trap. Jaws of steel, I had. Not any more."

He shook his head sadly. I really didn't know where to take the conversation next. Piles? Prostate trouble? Maybe care of the elderly wasn't my natural calling.

"Who d'ya fancy?" he suddenly asked. Aha! Good start. I'd prepared for this one.

"Fancy?" I answered casually, pulling a thoughtful face. "Um, let me see. Well, OK, I know she's not to everyone's taste, but I still like Cher. I'd *do* Cher."

"What?"

"Cher. The singer?"

Lofty started laughing. Shit, I thought, he's already worked out I'm a homo. The laugh turned into a series of phlegmy coughs.

"No," he cackled, once he got his breath. "I didn't mean *women*, did I? I meant who d'ya fancy in this *race*."

"Ohhh…" I gasped with relief. "The *race*."

"Yeah – the gee-gees," he laughed. Then he was off again. "Cher – that's good, that is! Cher!"

While he was having another coughing fit I was busy thanking my lucky stars. I know it seems unlikely, but the one subject of working-class male conversation that I'm half comfortable with is horse racing. As a child I was very close to my grandfather, and when *he* was a boy he'd trained as a jockey in Ireland. His dream had never come true, but he'd stayed involved in the world of racing by wasting every penny he ever earned in the bookie's. And the result, for me, was that I was now able to turn to Lofty and say, with complete confidence, "Not *Vodafone's Lad*, I know that much."

"No? I fancied him. He's the favourite."

"No chance. Not with the going as soft as it is today."

"But he's done well on soft going. He's got good feet, that horse."

"Ah," I said with authority. "But not at Folkestone. When the going's soft at Folkestone it's got these funny patches. It wrongfoots the horses."

"I'd *heard* that."

"Unless the jockey really knows his business. And who's riding *Vodafone's Lad*?"

"Lemme see," said Lofty, picking up the newspaper excitedly. "Danny O'Shea."

"Useless. Only rides a winner when the winner's riding him. Don't tell me you've had a bet?"

"No, son, I haven't," said Lofty.

"Glad to hear it. How was that sandwich?"

"Yeah, lovely, ta."

"Glad to hear that, too. Could you eat another one?"

"No, no ta. Tell you what, though," he smiled. "I could murder another cuppa."

"Coming up," I said, getting to my feet.

"Here, son?"

"Yes, Lofty?"

"Laura said you might be, well, keeping me company, like?"

"Did she? I don't think that's up to her, is it?"

"No," he chuckled. "No, you're right."

"I'll get you that cuppa," I said, turning away.

"Here, Jeremy?"

"Yes, Lofty?"

"When you starting, then?"

When I went into the kitchen Laura was pretending to be a housewife. I knew she was pretending because she was scrubbing away frantically at the hob with a Brillo pad. It actually made me wince, to see someone ruining two grand's worth of German stainless steel with a lump of wire wool.

"Oh! Hi!" she said, all surprise. "How was that?"

"Very good. I think we got on."

"Well, of course you did. Of course! Ooh!"

"What?"

"I've just realised!"

"What?"

"It's time for his pills!"

She eyed one of those divided plastic boxes that old people use instead of a memory. It was filled with brightly coloured pills, like something by Damien Hirst, but more useful, and a hundred grand cheaper..

"Shall I…?"

"Ooh, no, you've done enough. I'll just pop up and see him. Won't be a minute."

I smiled to myself as she dashed up the stairs. It was so totally obvious she was using the pills as an excuse to ask Lofty what he thought of me, but I loved her for it. My smile didn't last long, however. That hob was *never* coming back.

"Well!" said Laura, skipping into the kitchen. "When can you start?"

"I passed the interview, then?"

"What? No, no, I wasn't… God, am I that obvious?"

"I can start whenever you want," I smiled.

"Would you mind if I kissed you?"

"Hmm. I don't know if Lofty would approve."

"Purely out of relief."

"Oh, all right. No tongues."

We both laughed, and Laura gave me a kiss on the cheek. Except it was a bit more than that. There were no tongues, of course, but there were eyelashes. I may be a stranger to fanny, but I know all about eyelashes.

"Thank you, Jeremy. Thank, thank you. This is great! I just feel so…"

There was an alarming silence, during which Laura picked up the Brillo pad again. I could see that an overworked woman, newly abandoned by her husband, plus a handsome man with a caring heart and a big butch beard was on the verge of becoming a cocktail that needed only a sparkler and a small umbrella before you could call it Sex Under the Bridge. Just as the silence was reaching the point of no return, and I was wondering if I could snatch the Brillo pad from her hand without looking too gay, I was saved by the bell. Literally. Well, OK, not literally. It was the buzzer.

"Shit!" squealed Laura, like she'd been caught with the window cleaner. "Dougy!"

"Dougy?"

"Can't explain, can't explain!" she said, running away. "Look, sorry – could you get the door? I *hate* him seeing me in a mess like this!"

"Sure," I said. "But who…"

It was too late. She'd gone. The door buzzed again. Well, I thought, this Dougy had better be pretty fucking special.

And, dear reader, as I opened the front door, I can tell you. Pretty fucking special he was. Oh, my *days*, as the colored girls go. No wonder Laura had dashed off to hair and makeup. If I'd had a bit of warning I would've dashed off to hair, makeup and a plastic surgeon. Dougy was about six-two. Or three. It didn't feel like the right moment to whip out a tape measure. From top to toe he looked like someone waiting in line for his turn to be carved on Mount Rushmore. Chiselled? Don't give me chiselled. He was hewn from rock by the hand of God.

"Oooh!" I gasped, before remembering I was supposed to be heterosexual. So, I dropped my voice an octave and growled (or so I thought), "Wotcha, mate."

Brilliant. I sounded like Danny LaRue. Dougy didn't reply. He simply stood there and gave off hormones.

"Laura's just… um…" I blathered. "Laura didn't tell me she had the builders in!"

I stood there, trying not to tremble. Apart from worrying I might spoil my new-found heterosexual status, I was frightened my new-found nose might fall off. Dougy narrowed his dangerous green eyes and scowled. I was in heaven.

"Well, *maybe*," he said, in a really irritating Scots accent, "that's because I'm not her fucking *builder*."

"Sorry," I said, as he shoved past me. "My mistake."
It was then I noticed his muscles were a bit too big, his jeans a bit too small, and that he had Maori tattoos.

"So, if you're not the builder, you must be…"

"Dougy," he hissed, spinning on the heel of his (now that I looked) very *clean* work-boot. "And if it's *any* of your business, hen, I'm Laura's life-coach, slash personal assistant."

He didn't actually say the word "slash". He put his finger in the air and made a little diagonal movement.

"And you must be the new housemaid slash arse-wiper," he went on. "Do you have a name? Or can I call you Miss Thing?"

Fuck, I thought, as I trotted off after his annoyingly high-slung queer rump. Fuck, fuck, *fuck*. I *knew* everything had been going too well.

Brief Encounter

I was sprawled on the sofa, with Robyn on my chest, peeling off my fake nose. She'd already removed the beard and side-burns, which was about as much fun as female circumcision, but the nose called for gas and air.

"Oh! Oww! *Robyn!!*"

"Shut up, you wuss! It's only a bit of glue."

"It might be a bit of glue to *you,* but to me it's a bit of *face.* Owwww!"

"There!" she grinned, triumphantly, like a mad abortionist, waving the rubber nose in the air. It wobbled in her hand, hor-ribly pink; alive and dead at the same time.

"There is absolutely no *way* I can stand that every day! Not for all the tea in China." I wailed, stroking my real nose – or what was left of it.

"*All the tea in China?*" she mocked. "Is that the best you can do? Call yourself a writer?"

"Oh, get stuffed. You try thinking of sparkling metaphors when you're having half your face ripped off."

"Well, darling, never mind all the tea in China. How about *all the money you could make from having a best-seller?*"

She sat there, waiting for an answer. I sometimes wonder if we pick our friends because they have the characteristics we lack ourselves. Robyn is a thousand times braver than me. I envy her balls.

"It's not just the stupid disguise, Robby. It's everything. It's deceiving Laura Morris. Deceiving her dad. Trying to get my book in her hands. And even if all that was easy, there's the small problem of that vile queen, Dougy. The whole thing is fucking ridiculous. It can't be done."

"Hmm. I think they said that about splitting the atom, darling. Or flying to the moon. Or…"

"Yes, all right. But I'm not one of life's brave explorers, am I? I'm *me*."

"There's no such thing as 'me', angel. Every day I meet dreary little men who make *porridge* look interesting – and then I find out they want to have sex with a woman dressed like a velvet giraffe. We all have hidden depths. We just need the courage to go there."

"Oh, be quiet," I said. "You're not on bleeding *Oprah*."

She cocked her head to one side. I mirrored her. She pulled her lips up and gave me one of those vicar's smiles.

"Look, Robby, I'm sorry, but this just isn't happening. I'm sorry. Sorry for dragging you all this way. Sorry for wasting your time. I'm just…"

"Sorry?"

"Yes," I said, standing up and heading for the fridge. "I'm a sorry sack of shit. An excuse for a man. Can we get drunk now?"

"Of course, darling. That'll be lovely. But I do wish you'd consider heroin. That's a *proper* loser's drug. And so much easier on the liver."

There was no point arguing. I didn't have an argument. She was right. I was a coward. A loser. As I poured our drinks I had a little think about my life. How awful was it, really? OK, I wasn't rich and famous; but I scraped by, doing a job I liked. How many people can say that? I had a perfectly adequate little flat. Studio. Bed-sit. Whatever. I had enough money for the rent, and food, and booze and fags. I had friends. A car. Elsewhere in this world there was an Indian beggar, or an Afghan herdsman, spending sixteen hours a day on the simple business of not dying. And in the hour he had between that and exhaustion he was writing beautiful poetry that would never find an audience, much less make him a living. No, I thought, as I finished making our drinks – as far as the life of an artist goes, mine was pretty fine.

"There you go, hun," I said, handing her the glass. "Chin chin."

"Chin chin, darling."

I expected her to start nagging me again, but to my surprise she didn't. She knocked back her drink and then asked if she could take a disco nap.

"A disco nap? Why?"

"Why do you think? Now I've driven all this way we might as well go out on the town."

"Oh, no, Robby. Please. I'm not in the mood."

"Tough titty, darling. I am. And look…"

She rummaged in her overnight case and produced a little plastic bag, which she waved at me. It was full of white pills, and a couple of wraps of gak. I must have smiled.

"*Thought* that would change your mind," she smiled back, heading for the bedroom. "Wake me up about ten, would you? There's an angel. I thought XXL would be nice?"

* * *

A few hours later I was monged off my tits on the strongest E I'd had since 1987, standing in the queue for XXL, with Robyn in drag. I just want to make that clear: not *me* in drag. Robyn.

XXL is a huge gay club, near London Bridge. It caters for bears and their admirers. Bears, in case you don't know, are homosexuals of the butch persuasion. Back in the 70s this type of queen was called a clone, and life was simple. All you had to do was grow a moustache and eat nothing but yoghurt. Christ, even dear old Queen Freddy of Mercury (gawd bless 'er and all who sailed in her) got away with it. I'll never forget the look of shock on my dad's face when he discovered Miss Mercury was not as other men. But, these days, looking butch is all so *complicated,* because gay men never know when to stop. The trouble is, we just can't suppress our inner window-dresser. We have to tweak and polish and rearrange our retail frontage until it could stop the traffic in Bond Street. Or Bondage Street, come to that.

So, as I looked up and down the mile-long queue outside XXL I marvelled at the ingenuity of the 21st-century poof. The casual observer – by which I mean the casual hetty observer – really would have wondered why hundreds of builders, plumbers, roofers and scaffolders were standing in line under a railway arch at twelve o'clock on a Saturday night. Was there some sort of trade fair for insomniac workmen? Or a convention for hard-core fans of Super Mario? Perhaps the AGM of the Bob Hoskins fan club? No, just a load of queens under the mistaken impression that a beer belly and a goatee beard is the same thing as a wife, two kids, and a BTEC in gas-fitting.

Still, I wasn't complaining. It's hard to complain when your brain is getting a prostate massage from the Love Drug; you're with your best friend, and there are hundreds of handsome men who look a bit like that sexy bastard called Dwane, or Wladislaw – the one who came round to fix your blocked toilet last week – even though, in truth, if you said "U-bend" to most of them, they would.

"Ooh, darling!" growled Robyn, poking me in the ribs. "Lovely totty!"

"Hmm," I said, rubbing my ribs. That woman has fingers like chisels.

You've probably decided by now that Robyn's not quite right in the head, and you'd probably be right. She's a lovely woman, and you couldn't wish for a better friend. But she's strange. In fact, whenever I wish I could afford a therapist because I'm so screwed up, all I have to do is think about Robyn for a minute or two, and I feel fine again. When I get a minute I'll tell you about the night we first met, when I was expecting Conan the Barbarian to appear in my flat and instead I got Robyn.

I have no idea why she's not quite right in the head. With some friends you talk about the heavy stuff, and with other friends you don't. And haven't we all got a ton of friends who can't shut the fuck *up* about the heavy stuff? If Gloomy Prue paid me by the hour for talking about the heavy stuff I could have retired to Monaco, years ago. So I'm more than happy not to ask Robyn why she likes to make a living from suspending double-glazing salesmen by the nipples; or wearing a blue giraffe outfit; or, more to the point, dressing as a bricky and going to XXL. For reasons best known to her priest, Robyn sometimes likes to dress as a working man and have anonymous sex in dark corners of gay nightclubs. Then again, so do lots of gay men. The only thing I actually mind is that she makes an annoyingly convincing bricky – albeit a very, very short one.

As if to make my point, at that very moment she got winked at by a stunning lump of six-be-four who was ten yards further down the queue. She winked back at him and then poked me in the ribs. Again.

"Oww!" I squeaked. "Would you leave *off* with the poking? We're not on fucking shore-leave!"

"Ooh," she went. "So much for the Love Drug, darling."

"Shut it, Robyn, or I'll whip off that fake beard of yours. *And* that ridiculous Elvis wiglet."

"*He* doesn't think my beard and wiglet are ridiculous," she replied, winking again at six-be-four.

"No, love, but he would - if I was waving them at him."

We scowled at one another and there was one of those horrid moments when you feel the evening curdling. Is there anything worse than going out fishing with your best girlfriend, only to find that she lands all the prime salmon, while all you catch is crabs?

Fortunately, at that moment a bouncer let us under the rope. I couldn't help noticing that Robyn flashed a smile at him, too.

"I don't think so, love," I said. "He's straight."

"Well, darling. If I don't get lucky before they chuck us out, I can always take off the beard, the ridiculous Elvis wiglet, and get *these* out," she smirked, grabbing her boobs, which at that moment were strapped down with some sort of medieval contraption. Beneath her Puffa jacket they really did look like enormous pecs.

"I just hope they're properly secured," I said, poking her chest. "If those airbags go off, I dread to think what'll happen to the poor sod who's standing in front of you."

"Darling, it'd be a pleasure for him. Like crashing in a Mercedes."

"Hmm. Try telling that to Dodi and Di…"

"Have you two finished?" scowled the pudgy queen on the ticket desk. "Only there's a bit of a queue?"

He did have a point, even if he wasn't making it very graciously.

"Sorry, " I said. "How much is it?"

"Separate or together?"

"Oh. Um…"

"Together," Robyn said, reaching in her jeans. I suddenly felt guilty for being arsey. She's so good at being generous without making you feel small – and when you're as broke as me, you feel small most of the time.

"Forty," said ticket blimp, unsmilingly. For the millionth time I remembered one of the many, many reasons why I hate the gay scene: they take your money like they're doing you a sodding favour.

"Forty what?"

"Pounds, love."

"Yes, *love*. I didn't think you meant drachma. Forty pounds… *what?* Overweight, perhaps?"

"Forty pounds or I'll have you chucked off the premises?" smiled the fat queen unsmilingly. He gave the bouncer a warning look.

"There ya go, mate," growled Robyn cheerily, handing over two twenties and dragging me away. As we moved off, I heard the check-in queen say to the next couple in the queue,

"Lucky bitch. *She* should be paying for *him*."

I actually started to smile. Then I realised that the "she"

was me and the "him" was Robyn. God, I was sooooo drug-fucked.

Inside, it was heaving. One of my smaller ambitions is to find out why almost every gay club in London is under a railway arch. I've given it a lot of thought, over the years and I can only think that queens love to hear the sound of trains, so they can fantasise they're in *Brief Encounter.*

Whatever the reason, it's bloody annoying. Railway arches are terrible places for a party. The low ceilings make the music even more deafening than it is in a proper club, and by midnight there's so much sweat pouring off the walls that the mice are wearing Bermuda shorts and surfing down them.

The club was so packed that I calculated there would be just enough time to get to the bar before last orders. It was ridiculous. At least a thousand half-naked men, average weight eighteen stone, stood between me and a drink. It was like an episode of *Life on Earth,* at the end of the dry season, where drought has driven the entire hippo population of Botswana into the last remaining water-hole.

I do love Ecstasy but it does have that annoying effect of making you believe you'll die of thirst if you don't have a bottle of Evian in your hand. Drugs, huh? They know nothing. The only people who actually die from Ecstasy are the ones who drink too *much* water. If I could've pulled that Ecstasy out of my stomach and given it a slap behind the knees, I would've.

"I've *got* to get a bottle of water!" I shouted at Robyn.

"No you haven't" she shouted back. "You've already drunk six! It's all in your head!"

"I *know!* Most of my life *is!*"

"*What??*"

"Nothing! Do you want one?"

"No thanks, darling! I'll sort myself out later!"

As she shouted, she grinned. Over my shoulder. Six-be-Four had just come in and was shoving his way towards us.

"You *slut*!" I yelled.

"See you when I see you!" bawled Robyn happily, heading for the dark room, followed by Six-be-Four. "Be an *angel* and don't do a Leah!"

Great, I thought as she exited, pursued by a bear. Trapped in a musical hippo-pool; off my box, with nobody to talk to. What a perfect Saturday night. I eyed the bar. My chances of getting to it looked about as good as Kate Moss's in a Sumo wrestling contest, but I had no choice. It was a matter of survival.

I ducked down, turned sideways and slithered through the sweating mass of hairy blubber. Yes, I know I'd thought it was a horrible idea; but, actually, by the time I got to the bar I was enjoying myself so much that I almost went round for another turn.

Anyway, I didn't. I surfaced, accidentally catching my nose in the piquant armpit of a friendly queen who smiled approvingly and said, "Ooh! I thought I was being attacked by a ferret!" Then he bit my neck, ferret-style, and told me his name was Rowan. Rowan. That's not a sexy name, is it? No. Nor was he.

I made a lame ferret-joke about getting down his trousers later, and threw myself across the bar, flapping and gasping like the silly old trout I am.

Managing to make your way to the bar of an insanely busy London club on a Saturday night is one thing. Getting served is an entirely different matter. For starters, every barman is from

Brazil, which is very good in some ways and very bad in others. There must be a factory in Sao Paulo that turns out gayboys with identically perfect bodies, teeth and cheekbones. That's the good bit. Then, just as they're sending them off to U.P.S. for despatch to the developed world, they give them all an identical *attitude*. Getting them to serve you for a first time depends entirely upon how cute they think you are. Getting served the second time depends on whether or not you leave them a big tip. Many are the occasions I've wanted to explain to a Brazilian bar-boy the difference between serving drinks and actually being a whore, but I never have. They're always on to the next punter, the whores.

But, as fate would have it, Juan, or Carlos or Jesus – whatever – immediately came over.

"Olá, handsome!" he said, flashing his Osmonds at me. It was nice to be called handsome. I'm only human.

"Three Evians, please."

"Three? Ai, ai ai! What are you *on*, baby?"

"Oh, no, they're not all for me!"

"*I* no care!" he laughed, like it was the best joke he'd ever heard. "Is only *water*, baby – relax!"

As he went to the fridge I couldn't help smiling at the way he did everything in time to the music. Open the fridge – shake the bum; get the water – shimmy the shoulders; shut the fridge – cha-cha-cha. By the time he returned he'd completely earned his tip, and I felt strangely warm towards South Americans.

"Thanks," I said.

"Any time, baby," he smiled, razzling his shoulders, banging his hand on the edge of the little tin tray that carried the change, and catching the coins as they tumbled back to earth. "You come see me later, OK? I look after *you*, meu amor!"

"OK," I gurned, feeling the E come up and hit me again, as it does. "I'll do that. What's your name….?"

But, of course, he was already gone, trapping the next punter in his charm-beam. You silly old queen, I thought to myself. Thinking he actually fancied you. He's Brazilian, for Christ's sake. Whore!

Still, at least I had enough water to see me through the rest of the night. I could find a quiet spot and wait till Robyn resurfaced. Then we could go home, have a Cadbury's Moment, and I could laugh at her mad adventures.

As I turned away from the bar, Rowan was right in my face. He was actually chomping on his top lip, in a terribly wrong attempt to look like a sexy ferret. Then he made it all worse by going, "Nnnnyurrr – what's up, doc?"

"I'm totally off my tits and I've got to get back to my boyfriend!" I lied, feeling very glad that I'd bought three Evians.

"Oh," said Rowan, looking disappointed. "Lucky him."

"I'm always *saying* that," I laughed, before ducking down and wriggling my way through *Life on Earth* once more.

When I surfaced I was thrilled to find myself in a dark corner that hadn't been overrun with bears. Then, to my sad delight, I saw that there was an aluminium beer-barrel for me to sit on. OK, I admit that finding somewhere to be alone and sit down might not be everyone's idea of a night on the town; but believe me: at forty seven, it so *is*.

I plonked myself on the barrel, sipped at Evian number one, and settled down to enjoy my E. I'm not like most people when I take Ecstasy. I don't want to dance, or hug everybody – and I certainly don't want sex. What I love more than anything is to sit and watch. I watch everything, and everybody, and it all streams directly into my brain, like the best film ever (which, of course, is *The Sound of Music*), crossed with The Big One at Alton Towers. And, quite frankly, what could be better than *The Sound of Music* and a Big One? For a straight man that would be like doing your girlfriend doggy-style whilst watching your team win on Match of the Day.

My vantage point let me watch the men as they came into the club. Every one of them – young, old; handsome, ugly; triumph or disaster – every one entered with the same air of terrified bravado. Crossing the threshold of a gay bar is like going on stage at the Glasgow Empire after the pubs have chucked out. It's *harsh*. Straight people, over the centuries, have perfected a way of looking, but not *looking*. Gay men have not. For all the subtlety that's shown when someone new comes through the door of a gay bar, queens might as well hold up score cards. And so I watched, as man after man came in, head held high; pretending not to care as he was marked out of ten by the merciless mob.

Did I say something about not wanting sex when I'm on an E? Sorry. I lied. What I meant was: I don't *usually* want sex. Until I see something perfect. And, wouldn't you know, just as I was chugging my way through Evian number two, something perfect walked in. He was so perfect I actually felt my brass eye close up like the iris on a 1963 Leica. I won't bother describing him, because if you don't know my taste by now you've clearly not been paying attention.

On account of my strange location, under the stairs, I was in danger of losing sight of him. Well, *that* wasn't going to happen, let me tell you. I jumped off that beer barrel like someone had connected it to the National Grid, and shoved my way back through the crowd.

He seemed to know a lot of people, which was a bad sign. As he made his way to the bar, almost everybody patted him on the shoulder, or shook his hand, or whispered in his ear. It was like watching Bill Clinton work a stadium where *everyone* was called Monica.

In my heart I knew he was probably there to meet his boyfriend; and even if he wasn't, there was a ninety percent chance I wouldn't be his type. No, sorry. Ninety-nine percent. But I was under the influence of illegal drugs; and besides: Jesus had told me I was handsome, and I knew I'd never forgive myself if I didn't give it a try.

Speaking of Jesus, no sooner had God reached the bar than my little Brazilian amigo was there for him – and he already had his drink ready.

Hold fast, I thought. Faint heart never won fair lady. Go for it now, Jeremy, or forever live in shame and regret.

So, I barged one last queen out of my way and, amazingly, found a space at the bar, right next to God. As luck would have it, the E chose that moment to come up again, and my confidence exploded in the air like a big smiley rocket. Bursting with my own loveliness, I turned to God, flashed my best smile, and said:

"Ohhhhhhh. Oooooooooooh. Errrrr. Bleuuurgh…."

Then I threw up on his boots.

Bollocks! Bollocks, bollocks, bollocks, *bollocks!* Robyn had been right, as always. Too much water!

As I felt myself fainting, God, to his everlasting credit, caught hold of me.

"Has someone been playing with illegal substances?" he grinned.

I couldn't help noticing the way his arms bulged as he held my weight.

"Fuck," I moaned, looking at his boots. "Sorry, sorry, sorry."

"It's only water," he laughed. "Happens to the best of us. You OK?"

"Yes," I gasped. "Thanks."

"Not a problem."

"Christ," I said, pulling myself together. "I don't mind you being gorgeous, but do you have to be *nice* as well?"

He laughed again. A real laugh. Crinkly eyes, throat exposed – the works. What a dreamboat.

"I'm Adam," he said, squeezing my hand.

"Oh," I sighed. "I wish I could say mine was Eve! But actually, it's J…."

"Hmm," said an unpleasant Scottish voice from behind me. "I don't give a shit *what* your name is, honey. Just get your drug-fucked paws off my boyfriend's neck, there's a love. Then disappear, before I send you the bill for cleaning your puke off his boots. 'Kay?"

I didn't need to turn round to confirm the owner of the voice. In fact, turning round was the very last thing I wanted to do. I gave Adam a quick look, trying to combine both everlasting gratitude and romantic love, but probably only managing to come across as a tragic old queen. And then I was gone.

The moment I felt safe in the crowd, I turned back to look. I know that's never a good idea, but I had no choice. I had to see for certain. And, sure enough, there was gorgeous, sweet, adorable Adam, with his tongue down the throat of gorgeous, bitter, hateful *Dougy*.

It could have been the worst moment of my entire life. For a second, it was. But then I thought: *fuck* this, I'm not having *two* worst moments in my entire life in one sodding week.

Lofty, I decided right then and there, was about to get a gentleman's companion…

- 10 -

Bingo

Once upon a time I knew this straight boy who'd worked out the perfect Saturday night formula. He went to gay clubs and pretended to be queer. He scanned the fag hags, and when he found one he fancied (and, on the very-*very*-off-off-chance that there's a straight man reading this book, here's a tip: there are always tons of hot, straight women in gay clubs) he'd start a conversation with her. That was easy, of course, because she would think he was gay. Then (because, believe me, they always do) she would say what a terrible shame it was that a boy so cute should be gay. And he would say something along the lines of "Well, maybe I'm just *scared* of women." Five minutes later, they'd be hailing a cab back to hers; where she (poor, deluded creature), could spend all night believing she was showing a homo the error of his ways.

The sheer, breathtaking brilliance of his scheme was that he could then leave the next morning, saying "Thank you so, so much. You're amazing. But really, now, I *know* I'm… I'm…. *truly* gay."

Honestly, how many nasty, nasty men shag nice, nice girls on a Saturday night, then dump them on Sunday morning... and leave them feeling *grateful*? What an evil, evil genius that boy was.

And then there's Robyn. A straight woman who goes to gay clubs and pretends to be a man, so that *she* can dump *them* before Sunday morning. Yes, I know she's got more issues than the *Daily Mail*; but I don't try to make sense of that, either.

Robyn and I walked home from XXL. I couldn't face the Taxi Rank of Shame, with all the other queens who hadn't pulled a bloke, each one desperately pretending that going home alone had been the plan all along – not to mention the possibility of seeing Dougy and Adam emerging together, hand in hand. No, walking home was the best idea.

We'd had a vague plan to hail a cab along the way, but it was a warm night, and we were both still high as kites, with very long strings. I wasn't feeling very chatty; but Robyn soon dealt with that. Every time we saw a phone box she insisted on going in and chopping up two lines of gak. I did try to point out that snorting Class A drugs in a brightly-lit glass cubicle, right by the side of the road in the early hours of Sunday morning, in London, wasn't the cleverest of ideas. She ignored me. After the second phone box I'd stopped arguing and started talking.

"I *knew* going to XXL was a good idea!" she beamed, as we emerged from a particularly nasty phone booth. "It was fate!"

"It was *horrible*," I whined.

"Fate's always horrible, darling. Until you take charge. And now you're going to. *Aren't* you?"

"I might."

"You might?" she shouted. "You might?! Christ, I've whipped masochists with more backbone than you."

I knew she was right, but still I needed to talk it through.

"The thing is, Robby, *why* have I changed my mind about going to work for Laura Morris? The original plan was so I could try to get my book on the list – but now all I want is to do something horrible to that disgusting creep, Dougy."

"Jeremy, listen to me. We're having a Big Moment. You've got to make a decision, my adorable little gay friend. I know you like getting buggered by big, hairy men, but that doesn't mean you have to get buggered by big, hairy *Life*, does it? It's up to you. Go and work for Laura Morris and you could get your book on the list *and* do something unspeakable to Dougy. Or don't. I'll still love you, whatever you decide."

"Will you?"

"You know I would. But I've got to be honest. If you wimp out, I can't promise I'll love you… well… quite as much."

We walked along in silence for a few minutes. It was a bright night, and as we turned a bend in the river, moonlight bounced off the Thames Barrier. We were almost home.

"Robby?"

"What?"

"Have you got any more gak? I'm crashing."

"Sorry. All gone."

"Robby?"

"What?"

"I'm scared."

"You know what, darling? Everybody is."

"I can't do this unless you hold my hand."

"Did I say I wouldn't?"

"No."

We were at the entrance to my flats.

"OK," I said. "Bollocks! I've had enough of getting buggered by big, hairy Life. I'm going for it!"

"Mazeltov!" she smiled. "That's my little Jeremy!"

Robyn didn't have any more charlie, but she did have some bloody fantastic Valley of the Dolls-type sleeping pills. I can't remember falling into bed, but I do remember catching sight of myself in the mirror, and not being able to decide if I was Marilyn or Judy. Again.

Next morning I felt great. I even looked great. I think those supermodels really must be telling the truth when they say that the secret of their flawless complexions is water, water, water. My face looked like it had been visited by a team of scaffolders in the night – and it's not often I can say that.

In fact, I felt so perky I'd popped out to Lidl for freshly-squeezed orange juice, croissants and the *Observer*. I do love Lidl. Their OJ is the *best*. In fact, until I discovered Lidl I'd never realised the word *Waitrose* could be so funny.

"I've decided," said Robyn, munching her third croissant. "Your nose is a bad idea. Your fake nose, I mean."

"You said it was the foundation of the face!"

"It is. But I think you could do without the hassle. Putting it on, taking it off. Making sure the join doesn't show."

"It's a bit bloody late to say that! "

"Why?"

"Why? What will I tell Laura when I turn up to work on Monday with half the nose I had on Saturday? Flesh eating bug? Aggressive leprosy?"

"Darling, not everyone is a novelist."

"Lucky, lucky them."

"What I mean is that most people don't *notice* things the way you do."

"And what if she does?"

"She won't."

"But how do you *know*?"

Robyn clamped the half-eaten croissant between her teeth and fumbled in the pocket of the jacket she'd worn to XXL, which was hanging off the back of her chair.

"*That's* how," she said, handing me three bits of paper. Each one bore a different man's name and phone number. "See my point? They're supposed to be gay men – but they don't even notice *these*."

She jiggled her boobzillas.

"OK, you're probably right."

"I'm definitely right, darling. The beard and sideburns are all you need. And if you're still worried, just wear a pair of glasses for the first few days. That'll throw her off."

"I bet it doesn't throw Dougy Dearest off."

"Darling, Dougy Dearest won't notice a thing. You know what queens like that are like. If they don't fancy you, you might as well be invisible."

"Thanks for reminding me."

"Oh, please. You wouldn't want that piece of shit. Think of the *flies* he'd attract."

"Flies like…. Adam?"

Robyn sighed.

"Look. I *know* you've fallen in love with your Knight in Shining Armour, but how shiny can he really be, if he digs, um… Doug?"

"Believe me, most of the men in XXL last night dug Doug. They'd *kill* to put their little dibbers in his smelly old cabbage patch."

"Yes, but it's what's on the *inside* that matters."

"I can't believe you just said that."

"Well, I did. Because I meant it. And it's true."

"Not when you look like Dougy it isn't. It's amazing how men let their standards drop when beauty rears its ugly head."

"Hmm," said Robyn. "Do you want that last croissant?"

"Be my guest."

"I am your guest."

"Then eat the sodding croissant! I'm off my food, anyway, now you've mentioned Adam."

"Darling, you're such an…. Ooh! Who can that be?"

"I don't know," I said, as my door buzzer went again. "I don't get visitors on a Sunday. I hope you didn't give this address to any of your trade last night."

"Now, why would I do something so cruel? Imagine the look of disappointment on their poor little faces when *you* opened the door."

"Thanks, hun" I said, as my unknown and unwanted visitor kept his (or her) annoying finger on the buzzer. "You must remind me to cut you out of my will."

"Ooh, and I was going to buy myself some new socks with that money."

"Cow."

"Answer the bloody door! It's driving me *mad!*"

It was driving me mad, too. Whoever it was had obviously been brought up with very poor bell-etiquette. Ill-mannered oaf.

You got there before me, didn't you? Yes, of course. It was Paul.

"What are *you* doing here?" I asked as I opened the door.

"Fanks, bub," he replied, bouncing up and down on my mat. "Love you an' all. Gunna let me in?"

"No, Paul, I'm serious. Monday to Friday you treat me like a hotel…"

"Do I fuck! What fuckin hotel? Ain't never been to a notel"

"Oh, all right then! Butlins!"

That shut him up.

"Urr."

"Then, on Saturday and Sunday I get my life back."

"Yeah? What life's that, then? Hur-hur."

I heard Robyn let out a throaty laugh behind me. Paul heard it, too.

"You got someone in there!" he growled, shoving me aside as he pounced across the threshold. "You better say your fuckin prayers, Jeremy, cos I'm…. Oh. Allo darlin."

"Hell-o," said Robyn. "Aren't webcams *terrible?*"

"Pends what they're pointed at," Paul grinned.

"What I meant, darling, was that on the webcam you looked gorgeous. "

"Cor. Fanks."

"Whereas *now*. Well – Elvis *is* alive, and he's in the building. With blue eyes!"

Resistance was futile. I went to put the kettle on, and let the love-fest begin. By the time I'd made the tea I was feeling a little left out.

"Excuse my bad manners," I scowled, plonking their mugs down. "I haven't introduced you. Robyn – this is Paul. He's married with children, but three nights a week he sleeps with another man. And when he's asleep he sometimes says he loves me. And Paul – this is Robyn. She's a whore. That's when she's not having anonymous sex with gay men, or dressing as a blue giraffe."

Even as the words left my mouth I realised my divide-and-rule strategy had a poor chance of success.

"Well, darling, don't fret," said Robyn. "People like Paul and me need at least *one* boring friend."

Paul sniggered. I glared at Robyn, trying to look angry and hurt at the same time.

"*You* started it, darling," she said. "So, if that knotted little hanky of a face you're pulling is your way of saying you want an apology, you can go ahead and blow your nose in it."

She was right, of course. I was being a proper little madam. But you know what it's like when you're in one of those moods. You carry on sawing away at your nose, even though you know your face won't thank you.

"Anyway," I continued, turning my anger on Paul. "I'm still waiting for an answer. What *are* you doing here on a Sunday? Did you get so drunk and stoned last night that you flaked out in your lorry – and now you want a cooked breakfast and a blowjob? Or did her indoors accidentally find out you've got a boyfriend? Is that it? She's thrown you out? Have you come to make an honest woman of me?"

I was shaking with anger. Paul wasn't. He just looked at me.

"As it goes, bub, I was gunna take me littl'un to Digger Weld today. But I come here instead. Told the missus I got a bit of over-time. Told me boy his daddy hat to go work so's we can all go Disney Weld Christmas-time. Lied to both of 'em, ditn't I?"

I glanced at Robyn, willing her to make a discrete exit, but she didn't. She sat there fascinated, like a *tricoteuse*.

"I *come* here," Paul continued, "cos I was worried about you. Cunt."

I burst into tears and ran into the bathroom.

* * *

When I emerged, Paul was gone.

"Feeling a bit less girly?" asked Robyn, without looking up from the newspaper.

"I'm sorry," I said.

"Hmm."

"No, really. I am. Forgive me."

Robyn made a sign of the cross. "You're forgiven. I should order you to say three Hail Marys, but you'd only be praying to yourself."

"Dare I ask where Paul is?"

"Digger World, I think he said. Or Weld. Isn't that accent *adorable?*"

"All of him's adorable," I said. "Much as I hate to admit it."

"You know, I think he loves you? In his way."

"Please don't say that, Robby. If I start crying again I'll look like Christopher Lee's sister."

"No change there, then," she continued. "And you love *him.*"

"Of course I love him! I know he drives me round the bend, but he makes me laugh, and he's bloody miraculous in the sack."

"And it doesn't hurt that he looks like Elvis's blue-eyed brother."

"He really does, doesn't he?"

"Mm-hmm. Shame you've driven him away by being such a twat."

"I will start crying again! I swear to God!"

"Try not to, darling. We're going to the park."

"The park? Which park?"

"Greenwich Park," she smiled, with evil innocence. "Paul's outside, warming up his lorry. "

"I hate you."

"Mm. But not as much as you love me."

It was the first time I'd been in Paul's lorry. What a funny little threesome we made as we drove along, just like three proper road-diggers – in a musical. There was a moment when we stopped at some traffic lights and a bullet-headed geezer in a Shogun literally shook his head and rubbed his eyes, not sure if he was hallucinating. I wanted to lean out of the window and tell him I knew exactly how he felt.

Paul was clearly in the mood to amaze me that day. As we sat under a tree in Greenwich Park, licking ice creams, he reached inside his pocket.

"Fought this'd come in andy," he said, producing a sheet of crumpled paper and a one of those useless midget biros you get in Argos. He smoothed the paper on the grass and licked the tip of the pen. No, I don't know why he did that, either.

"Come in handy?" I asked. "For what?"

"Plans," he replied.

"Plans…."

"Yur, bub, fuckin *plans*. Like in the war time."

"I *think*, darling," Robyn intervened, "Paul means that we – you – should have a proper strategy."

"Corrr," said Paul, looking at Robyn like she was Yoda. "Thassa good word. Yur, bub. A strattygee."

"A strategy?" I asked.

"Darling, are you going to repeat *everything* we say?" asked Robyn. "It's no good you just going to Laura Morris's house tomorrow without a *plan*. Is it?"

"Right," said Paul, licking the pen again. "Number one?"

"Dolly," I said. "That's number one. What do I do with Dolly?"

The two of them looked at me pityingly.

"Well, I'm sorry, but I can't leave her in the flat alone all the time, can I?"

"She's hardly going to turn it into a crack-den, darling."

"Hmm. You don't know Dolly. Besides, I was thinking of more practical things, like who's going to feed her? And let her out?"

"OK, we can think of that later," said Robyn. "Paul, just write it down and we can move on."

"Urr," said Paul, scraping at the paper angrily. "Pen dunt work. Piece-a-shit."

"Well, stop *licking* it, then!" I snapped. "You're not Samuel fucking Pepys!"

"Samuel oo?"

"Look, just give me the bloody pen and paper."

"Nah," he replied, clutching them to himself. "I can write, innit?"

Frowning at me, Robyn reached inside her bag and handed Paul a fountain pen.

"Now, *don't* lick that one, darling," she smiled. "Or you'll look like you've been performing cunnilingus on a squid."

An hour later we hadn't got very far. They say the best ideas can be written on the back of a napkin. Well, if that's true, we were screwed, because we'd soon exhausted Paul's ragged scrap of paper, *and* the pile of actual napkins that Robyn had scrounged from the ice-cream man. All we had to show for our genius was a pile of crumpled napkins and stomach ache from eating every disgusting product the ice-cream man had to sell. I was so full of chemical additives I could have died and not needed embalming.

Eventually the sky started threatening a storm, so we went to the pub. Unlike most of London, Greenwich seems to be getting *less* gay as the years pass. There used to be two grand old ladies of gay pubs in Greenwich. The sort that dated back to a time when gay men had two choices in life: pass for straight, or get beaten up by thugs five nights a week. Nowadays, of course, everything is much more fluffy and tolerant. Unless, that is, you happen to be an effeminate gay man.

Anyway, we found ourselves sitting in the *Rose and Crown,* the only remaining gay(ish) pub in Greenwich. I must admit, I swelled with pride to see how much attention Paul attracted as we walked in. I know I've told you how half the queens in the western world try to look like road-diggers; but when they see the real thing, they sit up, retract their pinkies, and *notice.* And, of course, Paul was, as he never tired of saying, double-handsome.

"This is a fuckin poof pub," he scowled, as I returned from the bar with our drinks.

"Yes, love. What's the problem?"

"Ow many times, Jeremy? Ow many *times*? I – ain't – a – poof!"

"OK, calm down. Turn your back on them, if you're uncomfortable being stared at."

"Urr," he grunted, making a big deal of moving to the other side of the table. I almost apologised to the flotilla of disappointed queens who'd sailed across the bar to get the best view of him. Of course, it was a good job that I didn't bother. Five seconds later Paul moved back to his original position. Stage centre.

"Better this way," he said. "Dunt like havin' all them queers lookin at me arse."

"Hmm," I replied. "Do you want me to get up and move that spotlight? It's not *quite* shining on you."

"You what?"

"Children, children!" cried Robyn, clapping her hands together like Mary Poppins, only with gigantic knockers, "Could we *please* try to make some decisions?"

"Has it occurred to you that maybe the problem is that I don't need to *make* any decisions?"

"No, darling, it hasn't. Because you do. If you just turn up to work at Laura's place, with some vague idea about smuggling your new book under the radar, you will go down in flames. If she doesn't suss you in five minutes I can absolutely guarantee that Dougy Dearest *will*."

Paul nodded wisely. They were right, of course. I was just doing what I've done all my life: putting off the hard stuff.

"OK," I said. "But can we do without the bloody napkins? It's not D-day we're planning."

"That would be lovely," said Robyn.

"Right, then. We've already decided that I won't go and live at Laura's. I can stay over from time to time, if she's out for the night and doesn't want Lofty left alone."

"Agreed. What about the Dougy Question?"

"Simple. I'll just act straight all the time."

"Hur-hur-hur," chuckled Paul. "Like to see *that* on the telly."

If it hadn't been for my determination not to give the queens at the bar the satisfaction of witnessing a murder I swear I would have strangled Paul on the spot.

"At least my life isn't one big *lie*," I hissed at him.

"Urr," he replied, not missing a step. "What we talkin about, then, if it ainna lie?"

"Paul, darling," Robyn intervened, reaching into her bag for cash. "Would you be an angel and get me another drinky?"

"Put it away, doll," he replied, scraping his chair across the floor and scowling at me before he went to the bar.

"Could you at least *try* not to snipe at each other the whole time?" Robyn asked when he'd gone. "It's like watching a Special School production of *A Streetcar Named Desire.*"

"Well," I replied. "He does love his Stella."

Paul came back to our table with steam coming out of his nostrils, and no drinks.

"Can't 'andle this no more Jeremy," he snorted.

"Handle what?"

"That geezer over there just squeezed me arse. Eiver we go now or I smack him."

As we chugged along in Paul's stinking lorry I felt about as miserable as I'd ever felt in my entire life. Part of it was simple tiredness and a come-down after the drugs. But that was a very small part. Far more important was the fact that my life was out of control. A week earlier I'd been the master of my very small universe. I'd had a small reputation as a well-thought-of literary novelist. I'd had a small income, which I'd learned to stretch, so that it covered all the necessities. I'd had a small relationship, which gave me just enough emotional sustenance not to die of heartbreak. And suddenly, because of one little incident, I was on the brink of plunging into some kind of Great Gay Train Robbery. A situation over which I could never exercise control. A situation that could result in me losing the few good things I'd gained in the world.

- 11 -

Reader, I Winked

Eight o'clock, Monday morning, and I'd rung the bell to Laura's palace so many times that I'd started to wonder if I'd made some sort of hideous mistake. Then the door buzzed and opened, spookily, on its own.

It was Lofty who came to greet me. His wet old walnut of a face looked so pleased to see me that I suddenly felt happy to be there. And terribly guilty about my vile plan..

"Allo, son!" he grinned. "Come on in!"

"Thank you, Lofty," I replied. "Has Laura gone to work already?"

"No. She's lost an ear-ring."

"Oh."

"You know what the ladies are like when they lose an ear-ring."

"I certainly do, Lofty. I certainly do," I said, surprising myself with how easily I could turn on the butch camaraderie. "And nipple-rings are *ten* times worse!"

"Eh?"

OK, maybe I needed a bit of practice.

"Jeremy!" said Laura, hurrying into the kitchen, fiddling with her left ear. "Sorry I couldn't answer the door!"

"No, your dad explained. Ear-ring crisis."

"Precisely."

"You found it, then?" asked Lofty, gruffly.

"Yes, dad," she replied, still fiddling. "Under my bed. Bloody thing. I've never got on with these ear-rings. Even when I've found them, I just can't get them in my…"

"Here," I said. "Let me."

Before I knew it, I was fondling my new employer's left ear. While her father watched. I couldn't have felt more awkward if I'd been caught pleasuring the cat. I mean, how many straight men *are* there on earth who actually offer to help a woman with her ear-ring? Well done, Jeremy, I thought. Why didn't you just wear tin-foil hot pants and be done with it?

Then it hit me. Straight men help women with their ear-rings all the time. I'd seen Cary Grant and Sean Connery do it many a time (to women, not each other). Ear-ring insertion is a key element in the human mating ritual.

And, indeed, as she lowered her head and held her hair away from the tiny hole, she looked up at me in a way I'd only ever seen in films. My first instinct was to say "Ooh! Hold that angle, you look like Betty Baccall…" But I didn't. I slipped the ear-ring in and said, "There you go. Easy when you know how."

Laura stood up, shaking out her very nice blonde mane (I suspected the work of Nicky Clark himself, but stopped myself asking). And she followed with another little look. Out of the corner of my eye I could see Lofty looking on, approvingly.

"You've done that before," she smiled. Oh yes, I thought. For my mother and quite a few drag queens.

"I have," I replied. "But rarely with so much pleasure."

Yes, yes, I know I sounded like someone in a Brazilian soap, but guess what? It worked. If Laura had purred any more I would have had to change her litter-tray. And then, dear reader, I winked. Yes, I winked. At least I managed not to run my tongue round my lips as well.

The door buzzed and Laura said,

"Ooh, there's Dave! Jeremy, could you be a total love and chat him up?"

"Well," I replied. "Could I at least look at him first?"

Luckily for me, Lofty let out a big dirty laugh.

"He's funny, this one!"

And that gave me enough time to pull my old Freudian slip down over my bare Jung knees.

"Dave's my driver," smiled Laura. "He's an absolute sweetie, but I swear to God he'll leave me if I keep him waiting any more."

"She's always late," sighed Lofty.

"Just go and be nice to him for a minute, would you? Tell him I'm running a bit late."

"You're the boss," I said.

"Yes, I s'pose I am," she answered, with another little sexually-charged look. Christ, I thought, I've only been here ten minutes and already we're into S&M.

Considering Laura lived in a palace I don't know why I was so shocked; but as I went outside all I could think was crikey, she's got a *driver*.

Dave, it turned out, was quite safe from my attentions. He was one of those middle-aged men who'd let himself go a bit. Well, more than a bit, really. He looked like someone had put a pound of grey hair and eighteen stone of suet into a bucket of glue, then tipped it out on the pavement and stuck a fag in its mouth.

"Hi," I said. "You must be Dave."

"I am," he replied, grinding his ciggy under his boot. "And you're?"

"Jeremy," I said. "Nice to meet you."

"Likewise. So, how late is her ladyship gonna be today?"

"Five minutes?" I ventured.

"Five minutes? Gawd, she can do better than that!"

We shared a laugh. Dave may have looked like something Tracey Emin left in a dustbin, but Laura was right. He was a sweetie.

"Nice motor," I said, admiring the midnight blue Merc.

"Belongs to the firm," he replied, glumly.

"Don't we all?"

"You're not wrong there, bro. So who's you, then? Apart from Jeremy?"

"I've just started. I'm looking after Lofty."

"Oh, right. Nice. You a nurse, then?"

"No, no. I'm… well, I'm not sure. Laura wanted someone to keep him company."

"Sweet. She's a good girl. And Lofty – he's a character."

"I'm working that out."

"Yeah, he's a nice old boy. Had a right life, he has. Reminds me of my dear old dad, God rest him."

"Dave, Dave, Dave!" cried Laura as she hurried towards us. "I am *so* sorry! "

"No worries, babes," smiled Dave, looking at his watch theatrically. "This is good, for you. Specially on a Monday."

Laura smiled. "Have you met Jeremy?"

"No," said Dave. "We stood here and ignored each other."

"Cheeky!" she laughed, slapping his arm playfully.

"No, no, don't," he replied. "You know I love it when you hurt me."

Laura returned his laugh. To my surprise, I found myself feeling a bit jealous. There I was, thinking the ear-ring flirtation was something special, and here *she* was, flirting with a man made out of fag-ash and lard.

"Where to, today, sweetheart?" he asked her. "Straight to the office?"

"Actually, Dave, no. R and J are doing a little thing, out at Elstree."

"Oh, right. Traffic shouldn't be too bad now everyone's at work."

"But first," she answered, "we've got to go and collect Dougy."

At the very mention of his name my anus bit my buttocks.

"Oh," said Dave, looking a bit more annoyed than he should have, in the presence of his employer. "Why couldn't he get the bleedin' tube? Earl's Court ain't exactly on the way to Elstree, is it?"

"I did *ask* him," Laura replied. "But the poor love's been ill all weekend. Didn't get out of bed once."

Oh REALLY, I wanted to scream. He looked FINE on Saturday night!!!!

"Poor old Dougy," sighed Dave, opening the door of the Merc for Laura. "Queer again, eh?"

I know it was wrong of me, encouraging a straight man while he made politically incorrect remarks about a homosexual. But then again, the homosexual in question was Dougy Dearest. So I laughed out loud.

"Jeremy, *honestly,*" smiled Laura as Dave closed the door behind her. "I really didn't have you down as another cave man!"

"Sorry," I said.

Dave pulled a mock-serious face at me.

"Nice to meet you, bro," he said, climbing in the Merc.

Laura's window went down.

"Shit!" she said. "Dad's not had his pills!"

"Well, that's why I'm here," I replied. "So you don't have to worry."

"Thank you, Jeremy," she smiled. "I'm very *glad* you're here."

"Let's hope you feel the same way at the end of the week."

"I'll call you when I get a chance," she said. "God knows what time I'll be home tonight."

I waved goodbye, marvelling at the way the Mercedes moved without making a sound. My own car sounds like someone tied four tin cans to the legs of a cart-horse with Parkinson's.

So, I thought, as I went back inside the palace. Clearly I'm not the only one who hates Dougy Dearest. How very pleasing.

Although Robyn, Paul and I had talked about it the night before, I really didn't know how to set about my new job. Yes, I was a sort of baby-sitter; but Lofty wasn't a baby. And yes, I was a sort of nurse; but Lofty wasn't ill. And yes, my reason for being there was to try to sneak my novel onto the Richard and Judy book list; but if I didn't make a success of my pretend job, I wouldn't be there long enough to do the real one.

When I was back in the apartment I saw no sign of Lofty. There was a crisp copy of the *Guardian* on the kitchen table, next to a *Daily Mirror*; and a fresh pot of coffee on the machine, and I was tempted to sit down and ignore my responsibilities. In fact, I was so tempted to ignore my responsibilities that I actually did. Then my phone rang. It was Robyn.

"Well?" she said.

"Well what?"

"How's it *going*, darling?"

"I've only just got here," I whispered.

"Yes, yes – *and?*"

"I'll tell you later!"

"Aww, no. Tell me now. I'm working later!"

"Robyn, I *can't*. I'm working *now*."

"Yes, of course. Sorry, darling. Just tell me one thing – did she notice your nose had disappeared?"

"What? Oh, no – nothing."

"Told you! Bye - send me an email or something."

I went back to the *Guardian*. Then it hit me. I wasn't working at all. I was reading the paper and drinking coffee.

"Lofty?" I called, from the bottom of the stairs. There was no reply. "Lofty?" I called again.

"Yes, son?" said Lofty, in his frail but strangely rugged wheeze. I jumped. He was standing right beside me.

"There you are," I said. "Thought you were upstairs."

"Nah. I was taking a dump."

"Oh."

"Dunno why, but I can only do it in the downstairs toilet."

"Ah."

"Your arsehole's a funny thing, ain't it?" he said, cheerfully.

"Tell me about it," I replied, perhaps with a touch too much enthusiasm. Luckily, he didn't seem to notice.

"Dunno why, but I've got to be feeling just right before I can go. Know what I mean?"

"Yes, Lofty, I do. I spent most of my school days with stomach ache."

"Cos you couldn't take a dump before you was at home?"

"Indeed."

"See? A man needs to feel *safe* before he opens his back passage."

This time, I actually managed to control my inner Alan Carr.

"Anyway," I said. "What shall we do today?"

Lofty looked puzzled.

"Come again?"

"What shall we do today?"

"Yeah, yeah, I heard you," he replied, a bit tetchily. "But I dunno what you mean."

"Um," I said, wondering how much clearer a question could be. "Well, I don't know what you like to do with your days."

Lofty picked up the *Daily Mirror*, tucked it under his arm and walked away.

"I'll have a think and let you know," he said, heading off. This time there was no mistaking his bad mood. And just in case there was, he stomped heavily on each of the inlaid maple stairs, then slammed the door of his quarters very loudly.

I really had no idea what I'd done wrong. I lit a fag, then paced up and down for a minute, racking my brains. That produced no ideas whatsoever. So I phoned Robyn.

"I thought you were working, darling," she sniffed.

"Yes, so did I!"

"Ooh, do I detect mild hysteria?"

"Yes!"

"And it's not even ten o'clock! Maaarvelous! Tell all!"

"That's the bloody problem. I have *no* idea. Laura's just gone to work, and I thought I was getting on fine, then Lofty flounced out on me. Now he's upstairs, sulking!"

"What did you say to him?"

"Nothing! I swear!"

"No, really. Rewind, darling. *What* did you say?"

So I told her.

"Lovely, lovely Jeremy, are you completely stupid?"

"What? What?"

"He doesn't do *anything* with his days, my petal. That's why he's sulking. He thought you were taking the piss."

"Bugger! Of course he did. Now what do I do?"

"I'll tell you what you *mustn't* do."

"What?"

"Apologise. If you apologise he'll say he doesn't know what you're talking about, and that'll make everything ten times worse."

"But I want to apologise!"

"Darling, trust me on this. Think of something else, or you won't have the job by tomorrow. Off you go. Call me later.

As always in difficult situations, my first instinct was to find some alcohol. But, considering I'd already made a bad start, I thought that raiding my new employer's drinks cabinet at nine in the morning might not be wise. So I settled for coffee and cigarettes. After two more of each I was no closer to a solution. By then I could hear the *Jeremy Kyle Show* drifting down the stairs from Lofty's lair. I did wonder, briefly, about knocking on his door and trying to engage the old man in humorous conversation about trashy day-time telly. Then I thought that perhaps he'd take offence at that, too, considering it was the fruits of trashy day-time telly that paid for all this luxury in the first place.

Bloody *old people*, I thought. What gives them the right to behave like toddlers? My own mother, for example, has grown more childishly demanding with every passing year. On the (thankfully rare) occasions when she comes to stay I have to plan the time with as much care as would a Royal Nanny. My flat has to be clean enough to perform open-heart surgery. The sheets on her bed (*my* bed, actually) have to be washed in a certain way, with her preferred type of fabric conditioner. The food I prepare has to look plain enough for a Carmelite nun; but because her taste buds are on the blink, it also has to be so packed with flavour I might as well skip the food altogether and just let her suck an Oxo. I have to come up with entertainments that are exciting, yet safe (I pray for Noel Coward at the National). She likes to meet my friends – but only the ones who indulge her (thank Christ for Gloomy Prue). On and on it goes, with me constantly worrying that she'll throw her toys out of the pram.

And then I realised: old *gay* people don't behave like toddlers. I thought about my friend Michael, a lovely old queen who's exactly the same age as my mother. He would never stamp his foot and scream because I'd given him a steak that needed a bit of chewing, or taken him to a play called *Shopping and Fucking*. And then I realised something else: old straight people behave like toddlers because they want *revenge* on their kids. Perhaps they don't realise it, but all those years of arse-wiping, story-reading and poverty are like money in a psychological misbehaviour-bank. At some point they want it all back. Every last penny. Plus interest.

Suddenly, a marvellous calm descended upon me. Why on earth was I worrying about how to deal with a difficult old person, when my own mother had been training me for years, with the single-minded fanaticism of an East German gymnastics coach?

With all my confidence restored I opened the door of a fridge the size of a barn and located the bacon.

It didn't work straight away. The apartment's aircraft-hangar proportions meant that the smell of frying bacon got lost before it hit the mezzanine. To fill the whole space I would have needed to fry an entire pig. But I knew my plan was a good one. So, taking a sizzling pan-full of free-range rashers, I crept up the stairs and stood outside Lofty's lair, wafting the fumes under the door with a tea-towel. Then I quickly dashed back to the kitchen and waited.

It was a satisfyingly short wait. Less than a minute had passed before I heard Lofty's door open. Still, I said nothing. He closed it. Five seconds later he opened it again and shouted,

"There's brown sauce under the sink!"

I forced myself to count to ten.

"Oi! Jeremy!"

"Hello?"

"I said there's brown sauce under the sink!"

"Why is the brown sauce under the sink?" I asked, five minutes later, as we tucked into our sarnies. "I mean, the red sauce isn't."

Of course, I knew the answer, but Lofty didn't know I knew.

"Oh," he replied. "Brown sauce is *common*, doncha know?"

"And red sauce isn't?"

"Ooooh, no," he said, sarcastically. "Not if it's Heinz's keeee-chup. It's a *brand icon.* "

"Oh, really?" I laughed, as though I didn't know that there

really were people in this world who would allow Heinz ketchup on their breakfast tables, but not brown sauce.

"Well," said Lofty. "Apparently I'd be in the clear if it was H.P. brown sauce. H.P. sauce is a brand icon. But see, I don't like H.P., do I? Too spicy. I like Daddy's."

"Right. So it has to go under the sink?"

"Yep. And I had to plead for *that*."

I must admit, I was surprised. Really, honestly surprised. Laura hadn't given me the slightest whiff of snobbery, or shame about her working class roots. I wanted to let the moment pass, but I simply could not.

"You'd better give me a list," I said.

"List of what?"

"Well… a list of things Laura likes kept under the sink. I thought she was a bit more easy-going than that."

"Oh, don't worry, son. T'ain't Laura, is it? It's *him*."

"Him? But I thought her and her husband had…"

"Nah, nah. Not him. *Him*. He's the one who gives her all these poncey ideas. Dougy."

"Aha. I've only met him for five seconds."

"Five seconds too long, then," hissed Lofty, squeezing an unnecessarily extravagant dollop of Daddy's on the last of the bacon sarnies. "Queer prick."

As a rule, the words "queer prick" wouldn't bring a smile to my face. But, well, you know, like I said…

"Fancy another cuppa?" I smiled.

12 -

That Man from Atlantis

Lofty had insisted we wash and dry the breakfast things at the sink. After getting off on the wrong foot earlier I was terrified of annoying him again, so I did as he wanted, despite the fact that my very soul yearned to have a go with the top-of-the range Miele dishwasher.

"Where do these go?" I asked, indicating the plates I'd just dried.

"Er… that cupboard there," answered Lofty, pointing vaguely.

I found the crockery cupboard on my second attempt.

"And this?" I asked, holding up the frying pan.

"There," he said, with an even vaguer gesture. I guessed that he might mean the drawers under the hob, and I was right. Then I picked up a bundle of cutlery and said,

"And what about…"

"Am I the LADY of the house?" he shouted.

"No, of course not. I was only…"

"Then don't keep asking, right? Find out for yourself."

"O-kay," I replied, quietly, wishing I'd insisted on using the Miele.

While I found places for the rest of the dishes, Lofty sat at the kitchen table and looked at the racing section of the *Daily Mirror*. I pretended I hadn't noticed. He then took an orange highlighter pen from his pocket and began to strike through the names of the horses he fancied. I carried on ignoring him.

"Laura said you've not had your pills," I said.

He struck through the names of another couple of horses.

"Do what?"

"Your pills?"

"What about 'em?"

"You need to take them."

"Oh, right. They're by my bed."

As is the case with many an old, sick person, Lofty's bedside table looked like a Blue Peter model of Manhattan. Pills in tubes; pills in boxes; pills in extravagantly-shaped containers that looked like art museums. Typically, however, The only thing missing was a box in the shape of the Twin Towers, with a plane sticking out of the side.

His pill-dispenser lay there empty. I was a little surprised that Laura hadn't filled them. So I sat on the edge of his bed and tried to make sense of the boxes. It would have been easier to work out the Indian railway timetable in Braille. Two of the red ones, twice a day, on an empty stomach. One of the brown ones, in the morning, with food. Four of the fat green ones, but only on Tuesdays and Thursdays when there's an "R" in the month. Christ, I thought, this must be a laugh when the patient's getting Alzheimer's. No wonder you don't see old people on the streets: they're all stuck indoors, trying to make sense of their medication.

"Right," I said, twenty minutes later, as I staggered into the kitchen, feeling as though I'd accidentally sat a physics A-level.

"Here we go."

Lofty looked disdainfully at the pill box.

"Fuck all that old Fanny Adams," he said.

"Well, the instructions all say different times and different…"

"Here," he said, grabbing the box, tipping all the pills into his palm and knocking them back in one go. "I just take a handful when I remember. Does the trick."

"Does it?" I asked, trying not to look upset at how he'd treated all my hard work.

"I'm still here, ain't I?" he replied, reasonably enough.

"Yes, Lofty, but…"

"Look, son, don't mollycoddle me, all right? "

"I'm not mollycoddling you … I'm supposed to be looking after you. That's my job."

"Tell you what," he said. "If I die 'cos I took too many of them blue ones – or not enough of them brown ones – I promise not to tell Laura. Shake?"

I held out my hand.

"Now," he went on, waving the newspaper at me. "Can you get over here and have a gander at these gee-gees?"

I hate betting shops, I really do. During the forty years since my grandfather first took me to one, they haven't changed a bit. I'm not talking about the way they look – that's definitely changed. These days they all look like tiny branches of Ikea. With their pot plants and their sofas and up lighters, the interiors of modern betting shops look more attractive than the homes of most of their punters. But the men are just the same. Little men, gambling on the big dream; with the same sour smell of those who drink too much and wash too little. Even as a child I felt sad in betting shops, although, back then, I didn't know why. Years later I realised in words what my child's mind had only felt: betting shops feel sad because they're full of men who don't want to go home.

The bookies in Southwark Park Road was no exception, but Lofty's eyes lit up when we entered, and that was all that mattered. I couldn't help wondering what the hunched and downtrodden clientele, surviving on benefits in the mean streets of Bermondsey, would have thought if they knew that the little old man in the corner lived in one of the two-million-pound gaffs just up the road. One of the maddest things about modern London is that it really only has three or four nice areas, all of which are reserved for those who are rich beyond imagining. Nowadays, the merely loaded live in places like Bermondsey or Stoke Newington. Places that once were shit-holes, and still are, no matter what the estate agents pretend.

Lofty and I had sat in the kitchen, picking horses. I'd realised halfway through our conversation that I badly needed to brush up on my knowledge of racing, but a pinch of bullshit and a sprinkle of self-confidence goes a long way. By the time we'd made our decisions he was looking at me as if I were Gandalf of the Gee-Gees – which was appropriate, considering he looked more than a bit Middle-Earth himself.

We lost on the first race, big-time, and Lofty's mood changed.

"Sorry," I said. "It's more of an art than a science."

"No, son – course it is," he said, looking up at the plasma screens. "When's the next race?"

I looked at the screens myself, but out of the corner of my eye I noticed that Lofty was scanning the room with an increasingly glum expression, and then I realised. This was the first time in ages that he'd actually been inside a bookie's. All his bets since God-knows-when had been placed over the phone. And the reason why he'd been so excited by our little trip was not because of the betting: it was because he thought he might see some of his mates. Poor old sod, stuck in his daughter's ivory tower. No wonder he'd made his living-quarters look like a council flat.

At that moment the door opened and a man of Lofty's age tottered into the shop. Suddenly, he looked very excited. He slipped off his stool and made his way towards this other old boy, who had the flat nose and swollen eyelids of an ex-boxer. Ancient as he was, I still quite fancied him.

"Ray!" he cried. "Ray Bohm! Allo, son!"

Ray stopped in his tracks and stared at Lofty.

"Eh?"

"Ray!" said Lofty. "It's me – Lofty. Lofty Morris!"

"Sorry, mate?" asked 'Ray'. Clearly, this man wasn't who Lofty thought he was. Clear to me, at least – but not to Lofty, who ploughed on.

"Yeah, yeah," he grinned. "You must remember me! We used to spar, down the Beckett!"

"And who am I again?" said obviously-not-Ray, starting to sound a bit stroppy.

"Ha-ha!" laughed Lofty, punching him on the shoulder. "You was always a joker, Ray!"

"Mate," the stranger replied, drawing himself up and suddenly looking like the dangerous young man he must once have been. "No offence, but you've got the wrong fella. Name's Jack. Jack Lyon."

It was a truly horrible moment. To make it worse, some of the other punters had sniffed the first sour whiff of trouble, and started to take an interest in the little scene. I watched Lofty draw his arm back, preparing to punch 'Ray' on the shoulder again. I closed my eyes, praying that I wasn't about to witness an undignified punch-up between two septuagenarians, one of whom represented my entire hope for the future. I could just imagine what Laura would say if she came home after my first day at work to discover that her father had been hospitalised after a fist-fight in a betting shop. At the same time, I knew that if I intervened, Lofty would hate me forever.

"You ain't kidding, are ya?" I heard Lofty say to Jack Lyon. Peeping through my half-closed eyes I saw Jack shaking his head.

"No, mate, I ain't. You got me mixed up."

"Fuck mine," said Lofty, casting around desperately for his dignity. "Fuck mine, eh?! Well, I tell ya mate – you got a double!"

"Yeah?" said Jack, moving away. "Poor bastard. Eh? Poor old bastard! Ah-ha-hah-hah!"

"You ain't wrong there mate!" cried Lofty. "We're all poor bastards now, eh? Eh? Ah-ha-hah-hah!"

"Too right, me old mate," said Jack, turning his back on Lofty. "Anyway – be lucky!"

I saw Jack Lyon move towards the counter. On his way he raised his eyebrows at one or two of the other punters. "Nutter" was what his eyebrows said. I prayed that Lofty hadn't noticed, too.

Lofty loped towards me like a trapped fox who'd just chewed his own leg off but didn't want the other foxes to see his pain.

"Who was that?" I asked brightly, desperate not to let him know I'd witnessed every second of his humiliation.

"Oh, just an old mate of mine. Gone a bit senile, I reckon. Poor sod."

"God," I replied. "That's sad."

"Yeah. In't it just? Anyway, look, I don't fancy me chances today. Lady Luck ain't having it."

"OK. Shall we go home?"

"Yeh. Go back, eh?"

Lofty and I didn't exchange a single word on the walk back to Laura's place. There was no way I could make conversation. If I'd tried being bright and breezy he would have known I'd seen everything; and if I'd tried to talk about what really happened he would never have forgiven me.

When we arrived at the flat I asked Lofty if he fancied a spot of lunch. He said no, he fancied a nap. I didn't ask him twice. I watched him climb the stairs with the sort of relief a mother must feel at that point in the day when the little angel finally needs a snooze. Once I was sure he was in his room, I felt magnetically attracted to the giant sofas in the living room, and shuffled towards them, yawning like an autumn dormouse.

Just as I was about to drift off, my phone rang. It was Paul.

"'Sup, cunt?"

"What?" I yawned again. "Oh, not a lot. He's asleep."

"*Result.*"

"Hmnn. It certainly is. I'm pooped."

"Jeremy, you better not be kippin'."

"Why?" I yawned yet again.

"Fuckinell wanker! You ain't there to kip! Get movin'!"

"But what shall I do?"

There was a pause, during which Paul made a selection of snorting noises.

"Are you OK?" I asked. "You sound like you're having an asthma attack."

"More like a fuckin' *art* attack, ya cunt!"

"Why?"

" *'Ooh – what shell I dwoo'*" he mocked. "You ain't there to go bye-byes, ya cock! Fuckin *case* the joint! "

"Case the joint? I'm not burgling her!"

"Aincha?"

"No, I'm…"

"Get movin'!" he said, as a fellow road-digger called to him in the background. "Gotta go. Laters."

He was right, as usual. Suddenly I wished I'd taken things more seriously the day before, when he and Robyn had tried to make plans. Unlike them, I wasn't one of life's natural burglars.

Half an hour and three coffees later, I was getting the idea. I'd discovered Laura's study.

I have to admit, after I first walked into the room, it took me a few moments to catch my breath. Any writer on earth would have felt the same. For a start it was half the size of a football pitch – not that I'd know. Anyway, it was bloody big . There were *three* desks, each craftsman-made, inlaid with the sort of Amazon rainforest hardwoods that looked about as legal as kiddie-porn, and every one had a top-of-the-range Apple Macintosh humming smugly on its surface. I'm never sure why I hate Apple Macs so much. All I know is that, every time I see someone sitting in the front window of Starbucks, and their laptop has that maddening shiny apple on the lid, I wish I had a crossbow.

The walls were decked out with bookshelves – but not the sort of bookshelves that people like me have. Not saggy bits of contiboard propped up on bricks pinched from a skip. Laura's shelves looked like they were from some ancient civilisation, where books were made from stone. I was surprised not to see an attendant sitting there, dressed as Anubis.

And then there was the view. Tower Bridge; the Thames. I felt so inspired it was all I could do not to sit down at one of the computers and start writing.

In fact I did sit down, at one of the desks, to gather my thoughts. I realised I was actually in a very interesting situation. Yes, my mission was to wangle my new book onto the R&J list; but was I missing the bigger picture? The fact was, I'd just started a whole new life. If I played my cards right I could have a very fluffy future. I could stay with Laura and Lofty until he popped his clogs, or had to go into residential care – and by then I'd be sure to know loads of rich, successful, busy people who were desperate for the services of someone like me. Christ, I thought, it was almost a whole new job-category. Nannies for Rich Geriatrics. I could start an agency and sit back. Bollocks to books.

Ah yes, books. Books on every shelf. Books in drunken ziggurats all around the room. Books in manuscript form, heaped everywhere, covered with Post-Its in day-glo yellow, green and magenta. Books by *other* authors; every last one of them jabbing its pointy elbows in all the other books, desperate to shove itself forward and get its cute little face on *Richard and Judy*. It was the bloody books that buggered me.

I picked one at random, sat down with my coffee, and started to read. It was by an author named Imogen d'Arblay-Real (no, honestly, that was her d'Arblay real name) and it was called *The Earth Cries Also*. Well, I don't know about the earth, but by the end of page three I was crying also, from sheer bloody boredom. Despite the weapons-grade coffee I'd been knocking back I felt my eyes getting heavier, so I took a deep breath and skipped gaily through the next few chapters. I gathered something about an environmentalist heroine called Hopi and her perfect boyfriend – except he wasn't perfect, because he was up to his neck in some awful plot by the oil industry to convince the human race that global warming was all a myth. What should poor, sensitive Hopi do? How would she choose between the man she loved and the planet she loved even more?

By then, the only thing that might have kept me reading was if Hopi's beloved planet had opened up and swallowed the sanctimonious cow. When, on page thirty-three, I found a red Post-It with the words "Not really R&J", I felt like buying thirty tickets on EasyJet and throwing a party in Barcelona, just to enlarge my carbon footprint.

Next I chose a book called *What Lies Beneath: A Secret History of Pies*. I thought that may have been a joke title but no, it really was about pies. Once upon a time there was a book called *Longitude*, by Dava Sobel, about a man named John Harrison, who devoted his life to perfecting an accurate ship's chronometer. It was one of those little jewels of a book that shines through the shit, and charms the world. Needless to say, publishers, with their usual comforting absence of imagination, locked on to this new genre. Soon we had books about tulips, and books about the colour purple. They were quite good, too. But now I held in my hands the crumbs from the bottom of the quirky-history biscuit-barrel. *A Secret History of Pies.* Christ. The only good thing was that this piece of rubbish had a red sticker on page twenty eight, and someone had written *Save Us* upon it. No slice of the Richard and Judy pie for *you*, I thought.

I selected another book from the pile. This one was titled *Burka, Schmurka, Mazurka!* From the little I read, it was a bizarre attempt at comedy, about a Jewish woman marrying an Arab, so that she could gain access to a collection of rare mezuzahs (no, I didn't know Arabs collected them, either). This one had a red Post-It on page fourteen – which was eleven pages more than I managed myself.

I reached for another. *Herding Cats in Belgium.* Aha! Red Post-It – page one. I tossed it aside and picked up *Caliban's Daughter.* Post-It. Page five. *The NutraSweet Lemon.* Page eight. *Streetwalking in Wellies.* Seven. *Toblerone is Not a Fruit...* I felt my eyes getting heavy again. The hum of the computers; the comfy chair; the flicker of the sun on the river...

"Well, well, *well*..." said a now-familiar voice through the fog inside my waking head. "Who's been sleeping in MY bed?"

I sat up so fast my hands jerked about spastically and my head wobbled from side to side, like a puppet.

"That was *funny*," said Dougy, somehow managing to purr and hiss at the same time. "Do it again."

"Oh! Hello Dougy!" I stammered, swimming for consciousness with all my strength. "Do what again?"

"That thing with your hands and your head. This time I could sing *The Lonely Goatherd.*"

"Sorry," I stammered. "Must have fallen asleep!"

"Yes, I noticed. In the study."

"Yes, well, um…"

"At my desk."

"God, is it? I'm so sorry. I just…"

"Yes?"

"Is Laura here?"

"Not yet, luckily for you. Carry on. You were saying?"

I swallowed a red-hot hedgehog of fear.

"Well, er, Lofty went for an afternoon nap. And I was a bit bored, so I, um…"

"Thought you'd have a nose around?"

"No! I, I…"

"Hm?"

"Just *wondered*. What was in this room. That was all."

Dougy drummed his fingernails on the desk. They sounded like scuttling rats.

"I see. So. Let me get this, um, straight. You opened that door, saw it was a *private* space, and thought… "

"Nothing! I didn't think anything! I was just *bored*. I wanted something to read!"

"Well, you certainly found the mother-lode, didn't you?"

"Did I?"

"Please. Don't pretend you don't know what's in this room."

"No," I lied, very badly. "What?"

"Honey," he smiled. "Would you do something for me?"

"Of course!"

"Cut. The. Shit. I've seen *All About Eve* more times than you've had hot dinners. No, sorry. Let me think. More times than you've had… Decent haircuts? Now, get out of my chair. Then we can have a little talk. 'Kay?"

I couldn't believe how everything had gone so wrong, so quickly. If I'd *planned* my downfall I couldn't have made a better job of it. Caught red-handed – and not even by Laura. By Dougy*!*

We swapped places. Dougy settled in his chair and made a great fuss about checking the settings on the lumbar support. I really did feel like Goldilocks.

"I didn't touch any…"

"Shut up," he snapped. And even though I knew I hadn't altered anything on his precious bloody chair, he still insisted on adjusting every lever, the twenty-four carat twunt.

"That's better," he went on, spinning around. "Now, where were we? Oh, yes. You were trying to convince me you were just an innocent book-lover, who *happened* to stumble into this room."

Suddenly I felt angry. I wanted to rip off my disguise, kick Dougy Dearest in the balls and walk out. My scheme wasn't worth it. I was in over my head.

Dougy saw the glint in my eye and smiled. He knew I was about to lose it, and I *so* didn't want to satisfy the evil shit. I struggled to control myself but it was too late: my throat was full of bile and I needed to spit it out. At him.

"Dougy, you know what? You can just go and f…"

"Oi! Doug! Dougy!"

We both turned to the corner of the room. Lofty stood in the door.

"Make us a cuppa, Douglas, eh? There's a good lad."

Dougy suddenly looked like a bully without a gang.

"Hello, Lofty," he sort-of-grinned. "How are you, mate?"

"Well, like I said. Spitting feathers."

Lofty's timing was beautiful. He paused for a second; blinked, and then added,

"*Mate*."

"Ah-ha, yes," Dougy replied, attempting a carefree laugh. "I thought that was Jeremy's job."

"Well, Dougy," said Lofty, not missing a beat. "Seeing as you both work for my daughter, I reckon it don't matter. Or I could make it meself…."

"No, no," said Dougy, jumping up from his lovely chair. "I'll make it."

"Good boy," said Lofty, as Dougy slithered past him. "You know the way I like it."

As I stood there, trying to catch my breath, Lofty caught my eye. And winked.

"Thanks," I said, once Dougy had left the room.

"Don't mention it," he replied. "But… what *was* you doing in here?"

"Nothing! Nothing *bad*. You'd gone asleep and I was fed up. That was all."

He gave me a shrewd look. I felt myself blush.

"Listen, son," he said. "I can tell you're a good lad. I like you. But you've gotta watch your back, all right?"

"Yes."

"You know what I'm saying?"

"Yes. Thanks, Lofty."

"Right. That's that. Let's go and have a cuppa. He makes poxy tea, by the way."

- 13 -

Close Encounters

Afternoon tea with Dougy and Lofty was about as appealing a prospect as licking Marmite out of Ann Widdecombe's muff, but I had no choice. I gritted my teeth and made my way to the kitchen.

Luckily, Laura saved the day. She sailed in, bright and gay as a new yacht, weighed down with Tesco bags.

"Thanks, Dougy," she said with breezy sarcasm, dropping her load on the kitchen floor. "I needed the exercise."

Dougy's back was turned to her; but not, however, to me. I saw him clench his over-developed jaw and then compose a happy face.

"Is there any more shopping, Laura?" I asked eagerly.

"Oh, Jeremy. Yes, if you wouldn't mind – in the car."

I slipped past Dougy before he could throw boiling tea at me.

Fat Dave leant against the Mercedes, smoking.

"All right? You come for the rest of this shopping?"

"Yes."

"In the back," he said, pressing a button on his key fob. The boot of the Merc popped open.

"Thanks," I said grimly, as I struggled to pick up the four huge bags, thinking, You lazy fat git.

"Sorry bro, can't do lifting," he said, reading my expression. "Quack's orders. Broke me back, didn't I?"

"Gosh! Really?"

"Falklands," he said, looking tragic. "Ohhh, yesss. Yes, indeed."

I believed that about as much as if he'd said he'd been abducted by aliens, but didn't need to make any more enemies in one day. "Blimey, Dave. I didn't know you were a war hero."

"No, Jeremy, not a lot of people do. Memories, mate. Memories."

"God. Well, I'm honoured. Thank you for telling me."

"It's a small club, mate. Very small."

"You'll have to tell me sometime," I said, wondering how long my shoulder sockets could hold out without catching fire.

"I will, bro. We'll go out one night, yeah? I know some right lairy places. *Proper* lairy."

In case I hadn't understood him, he poked his tongue in his cheek obscenely.

"Great! Look forward to it," I said, as I hobbled off with the bags and tried not to think about Fat Dave with some fifteen-year-old Lithuanian hooker on his lap. As I reached the entrance to the building, he called out to me.

"Oi, Jeremy! Sorry!"

"For what?"

"Well," he laughed. "Sorry you got the short straw with the shopping. As a rule I get to watch fuck-face struggle with it. Brightens me week, ya know..."

"Jeremy, you're an angel and a love," cooed Laura as I staggered into the kitchen like a very old mule with one broken stiletto.

"Pleasure," I replied, noticing that Dougy was zipping round the room, manically emptying bags into cupboards in an attempt to suck up to the boss.

"Dad was saying the two of you were having an afternoon nap?"

Lofty gave me a look.

"Oh, well, yes, we…."

"I'm so sorry," she interrupted. "I really thought today was going to be endless – but then everything went wrong with R 'n' J at Elstree…"

"It did?" I said, before I could get a grip on my natural instinct for gossip. "Sorry. None of my business."

"No – don't worry. I know I can trust you."

Dougy threw a jar of mayonnaise in the fridge with a clang.

"God, Dougy!" Laura squeaked. "Make *more* noise!"

"My hand slipped," he answered.

"Anyway," Laura continued, turning her back on him. "It was no big deal. They were meant to be doing a piece about the new James Bond movie, but it all went tits up."

"Mmmm," said Dougy, licking his lips. "Miss Craig. *She's* all eyes."

"In your dreams," said Laura. "Daniel Craig is as straight as they get."

"As straight as *what* get?" asked Dougy. "Paper clips?"

"Honestly," Laura sighed. "Why do you think every man in the world is a closet queen?"

"Because they *are*," Dougy said, slamming the fridge door with his stallion's arse. "Aren't they, Jeremy?"

Before anyone could see me blush I bent down and picked up a bag of shopping. It wasn't enough to stop Dougy.

"I said aren't they, *Jeremy*?"

"What?" I said, hiding behind a pak choi.

"Men," he pressed on. "They're all closet queens."

"Um…"

"I'M FUCKING NOT!" bellowed Lofty. It was so loud we all turned and looked at him. "I've never done NONE of that lark! NEVER!"

"OK, dad," said Laura softly. "He was joking. Weren't you, Dougy?"

"Yes," gulped Dougy.

"Yeah," scowled Lofty. "Very funny. Ha-fuckin'-ha. I'm off. Ta for everything, son," he said to me, as he headed for the stairs. "See ya tomorrow."

"What is *wrong* with you today?" Laura demanded of Dougy, as soon as her father had disappeared. "You know dad hates all that stuff."

"Sorry, Laura, I…. "

Yes, I thought: you were so desperate to get at *me* you lost sight of the bigger picture.

"Forget it," said Laura tetchily. "It's been one of those days. Look, Dave's outside. Get him to take you home. We'll talk in the morning."

I swear I saw pink steam coming from Dougy's ears. Things were not going to plan. Not his plan, at least. Mine suddenly felt rather lovely.

"Right," he said. "I'll speak to you in the morning."

"Early," replied Laura, crisply. "We've got to make up for today."

"Yes," said Dougy, heading for the door. "Lovely to meet you, Jeremy."

"You, too!" I waved, brightly.

"Phew!" puffed Laura as soon as he'd gone. "He's been a cow today."

"He has?" I blinked innocently, pushing my specs up my nose for good measure.

"Oh, well. I love gay men. I do, honestly. And Dougy's a brilliant PA. But you *know* what they can be like."

I shut my eyes and Googled for an expression. Unfortunately, I didn't find one, so I had to open my eyes again and look blank.

"Or maybe you don't?"

"I don't really know many gay men."

"Really?" she said, with a funny little look.

"No. Should I?"

"Well, you do live in London, and you…. No. No, sorry. Nothing. Tell me about your day. How did you and dad get on?"

"I don't think that's for me to say," I replied, as she went to the fridge and took out a scarily expensive bottle of Chablis.

"No, you're right" she smiled, pulling the cork. " Wine?"

Something told me I should have made an excuse and gone home; but then it had been almost twenty-four hours since I'd last tasted alcohol. My liver was up on its hind legs, clapping its flippers and tooting a trumpet for herring.

"Yes, please," I coughed. At least I managed not to dribble.

Half an hour later we were curled up on separate sofas, and well into bottle number two. Despite the booze, I was managing to be quite the little Poirot; and as Laura got more drunk she started to spill a lot more than her wine.

"Have you ever had anything to do with literary types, Jeremy?" she suddenly asked.

"No," I blinked. "But I wish I did. They must be so exciting."

"Exciting?" she laughed, bitterly "Exciting? Oh, you are a sweet, *sweet* man!"

Ooh, love, I thought – that second bottle of Chablis has really hit the spot.

"Promise me - no, no, *swear* to me you'll never change."

"OK," I said, raising my fingers. "Scout's honour."

She wobbled her head and did that drunk-person-focusing thing.

"That's not Scout's Honour," she cried, with a squeal of laughter. "That's *Guide's* Honour!!"

"Oh!" I laughed, hating my great big, gaping gay soul and hoping I hadn't gone too red. "Well, haha – I was never in either!"

She laughed so hard I half-expected a pelvic floor accident, but then, in a moment, she became deadly serious, as people do when they're pissed. It's funny how films and books are full of tough broads who smoke cheroots and drink entire rugby teams under the table, but you never meet one in real life. In real life all women get pissed on two sniffs of a cork.

"Literary types," she pronounced, raising her chin for a sort of noble effect, "are *cunts*."

"Gosh," I replied, with the sort of innocent expression I'd last worn when I still believed the fat old man in the corner of the shopping centre, with the whisky breath and the WC Fields nose, really was Santa. "Honestly?"

"Cunts!"

"That's amazing!" I said. As if I didn't know.

Laura refilled her bucket of a wine glass for the fifth time. Yes, I was counting. Us piss artists have a dreadful habit of keeping tabs on other people's drinks.

"Oh, anyway, I don't wanna talk about *them*," she slurred. "The thing ish….. I'm jusht no good at being shingle."

You have no idea how much I hated myself at that moment, for not planning things better. There was Laura, blundering into my web like a blind fly who'd lost her guide-dog – and I had no idea what to do next. Should I get myself off the hook by re-inventing Paul as "Paula" and claiming that "she" was my girlfriend? Or should I pretend that I was as free and single as Laura? And if I did *that*, what horrors might follow? Would I find myself facing down the barrel of a fanny for the first time in my life? What the hell would I do with a fanny? Interview it?

"Me neither," I replied, crossing my fingers.

"Really? Sho you don't have anyone speshul?"

Honestly, she really was talking that way.

"No. Well, not for a while."

"Poor poppet," she smiled. "I thought you'd have women battering down your doorsh."

"Only my downstairs neighbour, when I've got the stereo on too loud."

She laughed much too hard at my weak joke, and my anxiety meter shot into the penalty zone. Then she jumped up and came towards me. I felt myself burrow into the sofa in horror, as I foresaw a close encounter of the fourth, fifth, or possibly sixth kind.

"I need a wee-wee," she said. "Don't go away!"

She staggered out of the room, and I sighed with relief; but my feeling of triumph couldn't have had a shorter career if it had just been signed by Simon Cowell. I was in big trouble. Yes, I did want Laura to have a crush on me. But I really hadn't been expecting to *do* anything about it, apart from chat. And yet there I was, while my new employer – my entire *future* – spruced herself up in the bathroom, knowing full well that when she emerged she was expecting one of those special sorts of chat that can be understood in any language.

The last time I could remember being in such a horrible panic I'd woken up at the worst moment. But this wasn't a nightmare, it was a daymare. A real mare. A woman fit to bursting with alcohol, loneliness and oestrogen was about to descend on me, expecting satisfaction. In desperation I shut my eyes and started fantasising about someone from the World Wrestling Foundation. When that didn't work I actually grabbed hold of my cock and started cranking it like the starting handle on an old wreck. Yes, and you can shut up, too.

Despite my desperate exertions I was about as ready to give a performance as Frank Sinatra. Then I heard Laura emerge from the bathroom.

"Please, please, *please*," I begged my cock. "DO something!"

It did something, all right: it went and hid so deep in my bush it would've taken the Beaufort Hunt to find it. Laura emerged from the bathroom; her Laura's heels clattered nearer. I wondered how bad my injuries would be if I jumped out of the window.

Just as I'd feared, she'd used her bathroom visit to freshen up. Her hair was primped; her lippy was scarily wet and red; and she'd gone to town with a certain perfume. A perfume I recognised, because Gloomy Prue has worn it for years.

"Jo Malone" I said, without thinking. "French Lime Blossom,"

Laura stopped in her tracks. I knew I'd already said the wrong thing but did that shut me up? Did it Dorothy Lamour.

"I sometimes go to Jo Malone, just for a sniff," I went on. "I *love* that woman."

"Yes," she said quietly. "I can tell."

There was a long pause. I think I may have looked at the floor. Or the window. I know I didn't look at Laura. And when I did, she seemed a *lot* more sober.

"Jeremy, is there something you're not telling me?"

And there it was. I had two choices. (a) Admit I was actually Prince Prancer from Planet Poof, or (b) leap on Laura and bang her till her teeth fell out. Either way, disaster was bound to ensue. I looked at the floor again, hoping it would suddenly slide to one side and pitch me into a pool of starving sharks. At least that would be quick.

Then something wonderful happened. I burst into tears. Real, proper tears. I was wracked with terrible sobs that came from the bottom of my boots. Though Laura didn't know it, I was every bit as surprised as she. Immediately she swooped down and put her arms round me.

"God, I'm sorry! I'm so sorry! What have I said?"

And then (this was the *really* good bit) I heard myself say, in a voice so genuinely filled with raw pain that it actually scared me,

"Oh, Paula, Paula, *Paulaaaa*...." And then I was off again, a-sobbin' and a-wailin' and a-speakin' in tongues, like Jimmy Swaggart, channelling Liberace.

Laura sat and held me while I cried. After a minute or so I remember thinking *get a grip, you silly queen, there is no Paula!* But then I said,

"You see, Paula was my ex..."

"Yes, yes," said Laura soothingly. "I realise."

"And she... she..."

"Wore Jo Malone French Lime Blossom?"

"Yes," I snivelled. "Always."

"And it reminds you of her?"

I honked like a lovelorn ship in the night. Laura actually jumped.

"Well, of *course* it does," she said hastily, patting me on the back. "Of course. Stupid, stupid me."

I could have left it at that. I *should* have left it at that; but my imagination had ideas of its own.

"Oh, Laura," I wailed. "It's worse than that."

"Yes?" she said, utterly gripped.

"You see," I went on. "Jo Malone French Lime Blossom was what I smelled...."

Laura's eyes bulged in anticipation of a big reveal. I hate to disappoint my readers.

"Yes? What you smelled..."

I gave one last unearthly wail of pain and loss.

"...when they opened.... Paula's.... *casket*..."

I felt poor Laura stiffen with horror. It was hardly surprising – I mean, really, nobody wants to be told they smell like a corpse. Something told me an Oxfam shop somewhere was about to get an unexpected windfall of Jo Malone products.

In a funny way I did fall in love with Laura at that moment. Gay love, anyway. She carried on holding me, despite the fact she probably wanted to run away screaming, then shower in bleach.

Then something happened that I really could have done with, five minutes earlier. Her mobile rang. She answered it so fast I swear I never saw her move.

"Hi Dave!" she said, brightly. "Oh, yes – great idea! Why didn't

I think of that? Yeah, sure – I'll tell him. What would I do without you, eh? What? Cheeky!"

She put the phone back on the table.

"That was Dave."

"Yes," I said, blowing my nose. "Something wrong?"

"Oh, no, no – not at all! He was just saying – I really am stupid..."

"You need to get a different driver, if that's the way he speaks to you," I replied, managing a smile amidst my tears.

"No," she grinned, punching me on the shoulder. "Dave lives in Bexleyheath, or somewhere like that."

"Oh, the Deep South," I said, with a tiny smile. "Where they wear the pointy white hats."

"Oh, don't," she laughed. "Politics is banned in that car. Anyway, he virtually has to drive past your front door on his way home. So he's coming to pick you up."

"That's very kind of him," I said. To my amazement I started blubbing again. Laura sat down and took my hand.

"Jeremy, I'm very sorry I brought all those painful memories to the surface. Will you forgive me?"

"You weren't to know."

"No. But I did get a bit… Well, look. Let's start fresh tomorrow, shall we?"

"Yes," I replied. "If you'd like that."

"God," she said, looking horrified at the prospect of losing me. "Of *course*. I can tell how much dad likes you. I just hope you like him, too."

"He's lovely," I said, with complete sincerity. "We've got a little something going on."

Laura smiled at me. There was no mistaking it: far from putting her off, my tearful outburst had only made her keener;

and now she was standing on the doorstep of Number One, Love Avenue, Lovetown, Loveshire. But I could deal with that another day.

"Yes," she said. "I saw that earlier. He's got good taste, my dad."

"Except in sofas."

"If you can change that," she laughed, "I'll put you in my will."

- 14 -

The Thames Barrier

D arling, I don't know what you're complaining about," said Robyn the blue giraffe. "I think you've made a fabulous start."

"Oh, right," I replied, glumly. "I made Lofty look like a fool; I got caught spying by Dougy Dearest; and then I told Laura she smelled like a dead person. It was practically perfect!"

"No, you didn't," she replied, popping the zips on the giraffe cozzy and filling the screen with flesh. "You gave Lofty a nice afternoon out, then you fell asleep in the study and Dougy found you. So what? He can't prove a thing."

"No, I suppose he c…"

"… And then you made Laura fall in love with you. Without having to shag her brutally on the parquet! Honestly, darling – that *is* practically perfect! Isn't it?"

"Yes," I said. "If you put it like that."

"Well, how else should I put it?" asked Robyn, wrapping herself in a short silk dressing gown that made her look like the sort of housewife who has a different tradesman parked on her front drive for every day of the week. "It couldn't really be much better. Lofty obviously hates Dougy, but he likes *you*. That's money in the bank. And Laura…"

"… *loves* Dougy."

"No she doesn't, she *needs* him. Or so she thinks. But she does love her dad. And now she loves you. It couldn't be better!"

"Hmm. Except I can't give her what she wants."

"Jeremy, angel, you really don't get women at all, do you?"

"Excuse me?" I sniffed. "Every review I've had since 1988 has said that I write women with *uncanny* empathy."

"Ah," said Robyn dryly, lighting a joint. "And show me a book reviewer who last met a real woman."

"What does *that* mean?"

"Oh, I don't know. I just fancied saying it. Can we stick to the bloody point?"

"Which is?"

"Women don't fall in love with men's cocks, darling. They fall in love with men's stories. And now you've told Laura all about poor, dead Paula and her perfumed coffin – well, she won't need shagging till Christmas, 2012. If then."

"OK," I said, after a brief but necessary sulk. "I believe you."

"Good. Now, what are you going to do tomorrow?"

"I don't know."

"Right. In that case, I'll tell you. Do you need to get a pen?"

"Shut up."

"OK – I can guarantee that Dougy won't waste a second before he tells Laura that he found you nosing around."

"Shit. Don't say that!"

"Oh, for Gaaad's sake. I'll bet he's already been on the phone, dripping poison in her ear. But don't worry – you can turn it to your advantage."

"Do tell, mistress."

"The second you're alone with her tomorrow – and you *will* be alone with her tomorrow – you confess."

"Confess?!" I squeaked. "Are you out of your mind?"

"Will you let me finish? I don't mean confess everything. Just tell her all about nosing round in the study because you're so fascinated by her world. Trust me, she'll love you even more than she does now."

"OK. I can see that."

"Good. *Then* you say something simple, along the lines of 'All those books you have to plough through – they look like so much hard work.'"

"Right."

"And then she'll ask if you'd like to read a few and help her out."

"She will?"

"I guarantee it. *And* she'll offer to pay you extra. Which you'll refuse."

Dolly sashayed across the room and nuzzled my leg. I took it as a sign.

"OK, I'll give it a go."

"Good, good, *good* little Jeremy! Now. My turn. Ask me why I was wearing the giraffe outfit."

"I assumed it was for the same reason as the other day? They pay so well."

"Not 'they'. *Him.* Go and get another drink and I'll tell you *everything…*"

'Everything' turned out to be that Mister Blue Giraffe had fallen in love with Mrs Blue Giraffe. No big surprise there – about half of Robyn's punters decide they're in love with her. But Mister Blue Giraffe (whose name, worryingly, was Alan. Never trust an Alan) was different. For a start, he was leaking money like a trans-Siberian pipeline and then (this was the really weird bit) Robyn actually seemed to like him. In fact, she seemed to like him so much she'd decided to give up whoring for a while. In all the years I'd known her, Robyn had never liked *any* man. I had a thousand questions, but by the time she'd told me the basics and smoked her huge joint, she was more horribly stoned than a Saudi adulteress. I couldn't make any sense of her ramblings, so we said goodnight.

I decided to get a bit of work done on my novel. It's only just occurred to me that I haven't once told you anything about it – or about any of my books, come to that. But why would I? This is a story about *me*. It's not meant to win any prizes, or draw attention to its beautiful sentences. It's just me, talking straight at you. Dressed in casuals. Dressed in nothing at all, to be honest. I didn't want to bore the arse off you with the stuff I write to get patted on the back by the *TLS*.

But I think I should say a little, by way of explanation. It seems important at this point in the story. Skip the next paragraph if you disagree. You won't miss much.

The Thames Barrier is the first novel in a trilogy I have planned. Its big theme is lack of communication. There are three families, who represent, roughly, the working, middle and upper classes. The one thing they have in common is the way that London, with its pressures to succeed, make money and do well, prevents all of them from being fully human. If only they could get off the tread-mill they might find the space to do what really matters in this life: connect. Needless to say, some of them do, and some of them don't. I'm quite pleased with it, so far. I'd put it on Richard and Judy's list, even if I hadn't written it myself. No, honestly, I would.

* * *

Right, that's enough of that.

I didn't get any work done, anyway. After being left alone all day, Dolly made it plain that she was in a thoroughly catty mood, and when a cat's in a catty mood, she's a bitch. By the time I'd paid her enough attention to keep her from clawing me to death in the night, and made myself a sarny, I was good for nothing except bed.

"Christ, bro," said Fat Dave as I let him in next morning. " 'Fuck happened to you?"

"Hi, Dave," I replied, still wondering where I was; and when, and who. "What?"

"You look like your face fell off, mate. Good night, was it? Eh, eh? Good night?"

"What? Oh… shit. Shit! It's Tuesday, isn't it?"

"All day, bro!" cackled Dave, as I dived headlong into the bathroom and slammed the door. "All bleeding day!"

In case any of you should ever decide to wear a false beard and sideburns, here's some free advice: don't sleep in them. Or, if you do, get up at least half an hour before your chauffeur arrives.

It took me a couple of minutes in front of the mirror to work out what was face, what was fake, and what was yesterday's latex glue. I looked like a doll that had fallen into a fire.

"Dave," I said, opening the door an inch. "You'll have to give me a minute."

"A minute?" he chuckled. "I'd say ten, bro. Where's your tea-bags?"

"Cupboard above the kettle," I replied. "No sugar for me."

"Me neither. Gotta watch the old weight."

Christ, I thought, as I shut the door. If this is you when you're watching the weight, I'd hate to see the result if you let yourself go. Still, at least I knew he was occupied. I didn't need telling that Dave was one of life's nosey parkers. Five minutes on his own in my living room and he could have written my biography in the style of the *Daily Sport*.

Having dealt with one potential disaster I found myself in the middle of another. I peeled off my beard and sideburns, scrubbed my face clean with a nailbrush (yes, it did hurt, thanks for asking) and then... *where* had I put the glue? It wasn't in the cabinet, and that was that. My bathroom doesn't have any other storage space – though I did once hide some charlie in the toilet cistern. Then I remembered: I'd left the glue in my man bag. And that was in the living room.

I peeped round the edge of the door. Dave was squeezing the teabags and had his back to me. I had no choice: I darted across the room and grabbed my bag. Needless to say, he turned round at that exact moment. Fortunately, I'd forgotten that I was naked.

"Oh, woah, *woah*! " he exclaimed, covering his eyes. "I like you and all that, bro, but only in a manly way!"

"Sorry," I said, scuttling back in the bathroom, thanking God that men like Dave panic at the sight of another man's cock.

Because I'm a lazy, useless waste of space, I hadn't practised putting on my fake facial hair. But it's amazing what sheer terror can do. In less than a minute I'd made a pretty decent job of it, and I was finished in the bathroom before Dave had a chance to read any of the titles on my DVD collection. I really didn't have the energy to explain *GoldyCock and the Three Bears.*

Laura was waiting for us when we arrived at Coriander Wharf. She was literally on the doorstep, and looking bad-tempered.

"Not like her," said Dave, noticing her expression. He sounded a bit worried.

"About bloody time," she said, as he stepped out of the car.

"Laura, I'm so sorry," I said. "It's all my fault. I didn't hear my alarm."

Dave may have been intensely heterosexual, but the look he shot me was quite like love. *There* was a thought I didn't want to dwell on.

"Oh," said Laura, turning her surprisingly scary glare on me. "Well. Try not to do it tomorrow. Some of us *can't* keep people waiting."

With that, she got in the Merc and slammed the door, before Dave had a chance to do it for her. As he went round to his side he blew me a kiss. I hoped that was intensely heterosexual, too.

As I let myself in with the keys she'd given me the night before, I wondered if her bad mood really had been caused by our lateness. Hadn't Dave said to me that *she* was always late? My stomach knotted up as I imagined just how much poison Dougy Dearest might have poured in her ear.

Lofty was in the kitchen. He, at least, looked pleased to see me.

"Morning, son," he smiled, spooning prunes into his mouth. "I bet you just got the rough edge of her tongue, didn't you?"

"Yes, Lofty, I did."

"Take no notice. Got out the wrong side of bed today. She'd already had a barney with him by half-past seven. Then she had a barney with *him*. I reckon she was going for the hat-trick."

"Him?"

"Her old man."

I must have looked a bit dim.

"Her *husband*."

"Ah, I keep forgetting Laura's married."

"Nnh," was his grumpy answer.

"I take it he's not your favourite person?" I asked, trying to curry favour.

"Who, Mick?"

"Is that his name? I don't know."

Lofty's answer took me by surprise.

"Yeah, Mick. Mick Rayner."

Aha. So Morris was her maiden name.

"Nah, Mick's a diamond. Good as gold."

"Oh, I'd just assumed that…"

"…he was an arsehole?"

Lofty very deliberately took his time chewing the last of the prunes, knowing that I would fill the silence.

"Someone told me he'd run off with a twenty-four year old bimbo," I said.

He chuckled.

"Did they? Who?"

"Um, a friend of Laura."

"You sure about that?" he said, slyly. The man was a Deptford David Frost.

Knowing I was being tested, I told the truth.

"Well, no. Not a friend of hers, exactly. A friend of mine."

"Women," said Lofty, sadly. "They love a good gossip, dun't they?"

"You're not wrong there." I said, stroking my fake beard in the hope it would make me look like a man of the world.

"Mick never left her for nobody. He left her 'cos she left *him*."

"Really?" I replied, silently cursing Gloomy Prue and her poor sources.

"Well, not *left* exactly. But she was never here, was she? Working, working, working. Ain't what a bloke wants, is it? Not a bloke with any pride."

"No," I replied, thinking to myself how much I'd like a life of five-star leisure, courtesy of my workaholic wife. "I suppose it's not."

"Her and Mick was teenage sweethearts. Liked him from day one we did, me and the missus. Had a good trade. Never go wrong with plumbing, can you? Well, I'm talking before Poland joined the common bleedin' market. And Laura, well, she was a bit wild in them days. Always running round with a dodgy crowd up town. New Romantics, they called 'em. Loada shit. Drugs… fuck knows. Anyway, she always come back home, 'cos of him. Married at nineteen, they was. My old lady said it was too young, but I said no. I knew he was a good 'un."

I wondered how much he'd overheard the night before, when I'd believed he was shut safely in his suite. If he'd had been wearing a sign on his head saying "DON'T GET ANY IDEAS ABOUT MY DAUGHTER" it couldn't have been more obvious what he was saying to me. To emphasise his feelings, each time he managed to suck a prune to death he made a great show of spitting the pit into his bowl with a clang and a mean expression. I felt as though I'd asked Wyatt Earp for his daughter's hand in marriage. There was only one thing I could say.

"He sounds like a great guy. Can't you get them back together?"

I knew straight away that I'd said the right thing.

"Not on me own I can't," he smiled sadly. "But I might, with a bit of help."

"Well, " I said, trying not to think about how much more complicated my life might just have become. "If you think of any way I can help, let me know."

"I'll do that, son. Right, listen, I need a bath. "

"OK," I gulped, trying to look professional. Please, no, I was actually thinking. Please don't make me soap between the yellowed pub-curtains of your ancient arse. "Um, do you need a hand?"

"Leave off! I can still wash me own bits!"

"Just asking," I said, stifling my relief. "It's my job."

"Yeah, all right. But I'm fine on me own."

"Right."

"On the other hand," he said with a twinkle, "if you hear a scream and an 'orrible, sickening thud, come up."

I laughed.

"Don't lock the door, OK?" I said, as he walked away. "I haven't got the shoulders for busting down solid teak."

I decided to make the most of the time while Lofty was taking his bath by having another poke around in the study. I hadn't exactly been scientific in my approach the day before, and my pep-talk from Robyn had made me realise I needed to get serious.

I could not have turned the door handle any more gently If I'd been disarming a bomb. I actually held my breath and pressed my ear against the wood. "Oh, pull yourself together, Jeremy! " I said out loud. "You're not bloody Raffles!"

As it turned out, it wouldn't have made much difference if I had been Raffles. The door didn't budge. For some reason I then turned the handle in the opposite direction, as though that would make a difference.

"You *bastard*, Dougy," I hissed through teeth clenched so tight I'm amazed they didn't all explode at once and pebble-dash the walls. "You locked the fucking door..."

- 15 -

Don't Tell Dougy

Despite the fact my morals had pretty much packed their trunk and waved goodbye to the circus I was not about to start rifling the flat in search of a key. I would just have to wait until Laura came home before I dealt with the problem.

I made a pot of coffee and thought about my job. Not my real job, obviously: my pretend job. What was I going to do with Lofty? After yesterday's disaster the betting shop didn't seem like a good idea, but what? What do old people *do* all day? Oh, how I wished that he was gay. I know what old *gay* men do all day. They garden, or cook, or go on the Web and look for a bit of jiggy. Pretty much the same as me, in fact – apart from the gardening, which I'd find difficult, without a garden. Uphill gardening, on the other hand…

Yes, old gay men are the same dirty whores as young gay men. I wonder why so many straight men over seventy seem to forget that they ever owned a penis? It's as though they go off one day and leave them behind, like umbrellas on the 8.31 to Waterloo. Somewhere there must be a warehouse, groaning under the weight of ten million mislaid schlongs. On the other hand, I know loads of ancient homos who just carry on Carrying on up the Khyber. In the morning, along with their vitamins and their statins, they pop a Viagra, and they're off. I guess it's all down to what you're used to. Straight men pretend they've had a lot more sex than they really have. They always claim fifty or sixty, but I read somewhere that their lifetime average is actually about nine. Gay men, on the other hand, pretend they've had a lot *less* sex than they really have. At least, they do in polite company. I always lie, and say I've had three or four hundred – and, believe me, that'll raise an eyebrow or two at most dinner parties. The truth is nearer to three or four thousand. Sometimes I can't even get to Thursday without forgetting who I had on Monday. It's the one big plus about being gay. We might not have babies; but, God knows, it's not for want of trying. And let's face it: if straight men could have sex with ten different women a week, without money changing hands, they would. They really, really would.

Lofty did take a worryingly long time in his bathroom. In fact I crept upstairs at one point and loitered outside the door until I heard signs of life. My plans were precarious enough as it was. An unexpected drowning would have made things tricky. But he was fine. In fact, he was singing *Oh, what a Beautiful Mornin'*, in a wispy baritone that sounded like Gordon MacRae, playing the comb-and-paper.

I knew something was in the air when I actually smelled something in the air. A familiar scent wafted down the stairs. It was cheap and nasty, like flowers dipped in diesel; but it was strangely sexy, too. It made me think of my early childhood. In fact, it made me think of my father's friend Alex, who was in the navy, and never got married, and who often stayed with us when he was on leave – apart from when he stayed with his mother. He would let me lie on his chest, while I played with the smoky curls of black hair that crept out from his shirt. Alex always had the same smell that now floated down Laura's stairs. It was the smell of Old Spice.

Ah. Old Spice. I had no idea they still made it. The one perfume it was OK for men to wear, before David Beckham was invented. Then came *Brut,* and that smelled disgusting, too. After that we had *Hai Karate.* Jesus. Were men ever really that insecure about themselves? I'm amazed there wasn't an after-shave in the 70s called *Rape.* I'm almost certain there was one called *Pillage.*

Lofty wafted down the stairs on his cloud of Old Spice. Something was definitely up. If I could wolf-whistle I would have. He was dressed in a suit and tie, and it was hard to decide what shone more brilliantly: his hair, or his shoes.

"How do I look?" he asked, shyly.

"Um. Sharp," I replied, and then sneezed.

"Did I overdo it on the aftershave? I did, didn't I?"

"No," I lied. "It's just right."

"Not poofy?"

"Not at *all,*" I wheezed , with some authority. Christ, I thought. Poofy? I've seen gay men refused entry to clubs for smelling like that. In fact, I once went to a dive in San Francisco where one of the door-staff actually went along the queue, sniffing every armpit – and the men whose body odour most resembled a midsummer hotdog stall got sent straight to the front. God, I stood in that queue for hours. *And* I'd been ultra-careful not to wear any perfume. My crime, I learned later, was coconut conditioner. There's a free tip for you, if you're ever in San Fran, and fancy a night at a leather bar.

"You're probably wondering why I'm all togged up," he asked.

"Umm… I'm guessing it's not for my benefit?"

He pursed his lips, rolled his eyes and put his hand on his hip. I think he was trying to look gay. I played dumb.

"Ooh," I said. "Betty."

He looked disappointed.

"It's like this. I've got a lady friend."

"Aha."

"Well?"

"What?"

"Can I rely on you?"

"Rely on me? That depends what you're asking, Lofty. I'm not into threesomes."

He laughed and laughed and *laughed* at that. He laughed so much his dentures made an obscene little journey out of his mouth. Fortunately, he pulled himself together and sucked them back in, with a farty plop. Mmm, nice.

"You're bloody funny, you are! You should write a book! Be better than the shit they put on Richard and bleedin' Judy, and that's a fact."

"Maybe I will," I said. "Anyway. About this lady friend."

"Yeah, well. Here's the score, right? Thing is, Laura, she thinks I sit here all day, waiting to die. But I don't. I might have dodgy knees, but the bits what matter, well… D'you know what I'm getting at?"

"I think so," I smiled. "You're saying you can still play darts."

That set him off again.

"Darts!" he wheezed. "Yeah, I can still play darts. I can go for the old bull's eye, I can! Darts!"

This time I really thought I'd have to catch his teeth. Honestly, it's not something you can *train* for.

"I never doubted it," I said, wondering where this giggling old goat had come from. The day before, at the bookie's, I'd written him off as a sad shell of a man. Now he was coming over like a cross between the Casanova of Coriander Wharf and Sid James.

"Look, Jeremy, " he said, when he'd finally got his breath back. "What I'm saying is this. Can I rely on you to button it? You scratch my back and I'll scratch yours."

"Of course you can rely on me," I replied. "If that's what you want. But why can't you just tell Laura you don't need a companion? I feel bad, taking her money under false pretences."

"What? Are you round the twist? Tell me own daughter I'm seeing a bird?"

"What's wrong with that?"

"You're having me on! What if I was *your* father? How would you feel about that?"

"Surprised. He's been dead for twelve years."

"Oh. My condonences."

"Thanks," I said, crushing my urge to correct him.

"But anyway, you know what I'm getting at. If your mother wasn't long dead…"

"Now, she *is* alive…"

"Gawdelpus! You know what I mean!"

"Yes, yes, I know what you mean. But I don't think you're right. I think Laura would be pleased to know you're enjoying yourself. In fact, I think she'd be *very* pleased. She'd feel less guilty, apart from anything."

"Well," he said, tugging at his lapels. "You're entitled to your opinion. But *I* don't want her knowing nothing. Got it?"

"Got it," I said. "Whatever you say. I'm here to make your life easier."

"Ta, son. I knew you'd see it my way."

"One thing, though? Please?"

"You name it."

"*Please* try not to die on the job?"

I waved him goodbye, after making him promise he'd give his "lady friend" my mobile number, just in case. He found the whole idea of dying mid-screw hilarious. I didn't bother telling him that I'd read the statistics about old men, vigorous fornication, Viagra and sudden death. Honestly, they'd be better off tying their feet together and hopping across the M25.

That showed *me*, I thought, after he'd gone. So much for my theories about old straight men leaving their cocks on the train. I wondered how often Lofty slipped off to see his bird. We'd have to sort out a diary. Was it a casual thing? Once a week? A month? Or was it serious? Were they going steady? Could people with shaky hands actually *go* steady? Or maybe she didn't have shaky hands. What if she was thirty years his junior? Or fifty, or (Gawdelpus, indeed) sixty? For all I knew she was one of the dozens of teenaged mothers who spent their days promenading their pushchairs and piercings up and down the Southwark Park Road.

Oh, there was no point in wondering. I'd find out soon enough. Meanwhile, I had time to myself. And a brave new world to explore.

Look, I know I said I wasn't about to start rifling through the flat in search of a key. But, well. Oh, just go ahead and hate me. I hated myself.

At least I didn't actually *rifle*. I thought I'd better be more scientific about this.

Since I had no idea how long Lofty would be away on business,

I decided to plan my route, in case I suddenly had to act inno-cent. The locked study was obviously a non-starter, but should I go for the living-room first? No, of course not. I had a perfect right to be in the living room. It wouldn't matter if I got caught poking around in the bloody living room. Laura's bedroom, on the other hand, was a different proposition. My right to be there was about the same as Gary Glitter's to be dispensing Calpol at a Vietnamese pyjama party. So, naturally, that's where I started.

Christ Almighty, I thought, as I opened the door, put me in ringlets and call me Alice. Talk about curiouser and curiouser. Lofty wasn't the only one with a nasty case of Decor Shame. Laura had apparently hired Barbie's interior designer and handed him a blank cheque and a tab of acid. I mean, I'm about as pink as a prawn at a Barbara Cartland convention, but that room was so pink it made Spam look beige.

After I'd recovered from the shock, I tip-toed in. I'm not sure why I tip-toed. Possibly because I was terrified I'd wake the Evil Fairy of Pinkness, who might suddenly appear and turn me into a ruched curtain. And that was the thing: it wasn't just the pinko-mania. It was the Marie Antoinette headboard; the carpet so deep you wanted snow-shoes; the riot of ruche, and, oh, my word... the illuminated display-cabinet full of Beanie Babies.

Straight couples' bedrooms are, as we all know, the ladies' choice. Once a man gets married, or partnered, or whatever, it's goodbye black leather headboards and hello, scatter cushions and tasteful little knick-knacks. And here's a fact: if you *do* know a couple with a black leather headboard, they have a better sex life than you. The same goes for black leather sofas, actually. I once had a fascinating chat with Gloomy Prue's cleaning lady. That woman is the Sherlock Holmes of upholstery. The gunk she found on black leather sofas was enough to make a brothel madam blush. And as for *brown* leather sofas…. Oh, you don't want to know.

The trouble is, some women can't stop at girly. They have to go *little* girly. I couldn't help feeling sorry for Mick Rayner as I gazed at Laura's anti-sexual bedroom.

I started with the bedside cabinet. The top drawer contained a box of tissues, three pairs of laddered tights, and a tube of Canesten. The bottom drawer contained half a dozen Beanie Babies that for some reason weren't up to the demanding standard of the display cabinet. I pulled them out of the drawer, just to see – and there, hidden beneath them, was a vibrator. One of those nasty Germolene-coloured ones that looked like it was made by the National Health Service in 1958, along with hearing aids and artificial limbs. Eeww, Laura, I thought – you really need to go to an Anne Summers party. On the other hand, on closer inspection I saw that there were no stray pubes, and when I switched it on (oh, like you wouldn't) the batteries were as perky as the day they were born. Something told me Laura didn't spend much quality time with her personal personal assistant.

I put the vibrator back and covered it with Beanies, then went to the other bedside cabinet. And then I stopped. What the fuck was I doing, exactly? It was all very well, telling myself that I was on a mission, but I wasn't. I was just being nosey. Poking around in the private life of a very nice person: that's what I was doing.

I sat on the edge of the bed and felt guilty. This wasn't me at all. How would I like it if someone I trusted was poking around in *my* bedside cabinets? Or cabinet, since my bedroom's not big enough for two?

When I stood up I noticed my arse had made a dent, and

as I smoothed it my hand felt something hard beneath the bed-spread. Not a first, I admit. Peeling back the duvet I discovered a little note-pad. It had Beanie Babies on the cover, but we'll ignore that. The contents were *much* more interesting…

On the first page she'd written one word: "LONGLIST". Personally, I'm not sure if longlist is one word or two; but I got the drift. My fingernails tore at that pad like an African tearing the parachute from a bag of mealy-meal.

Page Two: "GENERAL THOUGHTS":

less girly this time?? More edgy???

new direction???

keep bloody publishers guessing!! BASTARDS!!! Maybe SCI-FI ha ha ha????

Sci-fi? *That* made me jump. But not as much as the next sentence:

DON'T TELL DOUGY!!!!

Ooh, I thought, stopping. What did *that* mean?

- 16 -

Digging up the Dad

D on't you feel sorry for teenagers? Everyone seems to hate them, but why? Personally, I think they're lovely, and that's not even because I want to have sex with them. For instance: last year I found myself on a Friday night in a strange town (Norwich, if you must know, and they don't come much stranger) and I needed drugs. Well, what would you do? I'll tell you what *I* did: I drove around until I spotted a gang of hoodies and then I asked them where I could get drugs. Five minutes later I was driving into the Norwich badlands, in a car full of sixteen-year-old boys. We scored some weed, from a man called Dwayne. Then we visited a chippie, and then an off-licence (where I, as the only person of legal age, had to buy the booze). Then we sat in my car, all six of us, eating chips, drinking lager and smoking spliff, while I made them listen to Mozart. Then they made me listen to some hip-hop and we had a good discussion about music. Then they told me their plans for the future, which made me cry – especially the bit where one of them told me he intended to join the army, but he was going to wait a year for his mate to leave school, so they could do it together. I wanted to phone Rolf Harris, because *Two Little Boys* must be ripe for a re-boot.

When we parted company, every one of them hugged me and texted his phone number. It was one of the best nights of my life. Maybe I was lucky in my choice of hoodies, but I don't think so. After all, they weren't *posh* hoodies. They were just council kids, and all they wanted was the same thing kids have always wanted: to be taken seriously. I do wonder sometimes if adults have forgotten how terribly confusing life feels when you're sixteen. You're desperate to be a grown-up, but you're terrified of no longer being a child. It's hardly surprising that they're sometimes a pain in the arse. Weren't you?

Anyway, there's another reason why I feel sorry for teenagers. They take mobile phones for granted. If you tell a bunch of them that the first mobiles looked like breeze-blocks with aerials, and cost a year's wages, they laugh; just as they do if you tell them that it was once possible to buy a house in Islington (a *whole* house) for £15,000!. Poor little things. They wuz robbed.

My generation, on the other hand, remember *Thunderbirds* from 1966. We remember going to school and pretending we could talk to our mates, *and* see them – on our wristwatches! OK, we had to wait forty years before we could live that dream, but crikey, it was worth it. In fact, when Gloomy Prue got a video-phone, I forced her to spend an entire Saturday afternoon calling all her other rich friends with videophones, while we pretended to be Lady Penelope and Parker. What? Oh, of *course* I was Lady P.

Anyway, where was I? Oh, yes. Mobile phones. They have cameras. That made it easy for me to take photos of every page in Laura's secret notebook. Then I crept downstairs and locked myself in the loo.

The pictures on my geriatric mobile are so crap I'd be better off using an Etch-a-Sketch, but with a lot of squinting I managed to get the gist of Laura's secret notebook. It was good that I was on the loo, because what I learned gripped my bowels and squeezed them till they squeaked. You know I'd read the section called "LONGLIST"? Well, there was also a section called "SHORTLIST". And that told me two things I did not want to hear. First, there was only *one place* left on The List. ONE PLACE!!! And second (this was where I actually pooed) Andrew Goodman's SECOND novel was already there. It was called *Digging Up The Dad*. No, really. Seriously. It really, truly was. You hate him too, don't you?

My hand trembled so much I could barely hold the phone; but there was something else on the page I needed to read. It would have been easier if I'd gone back to Laura's bedroom and consulted the original, but I had no idea when Lofty might come home. So I waited until I stopped shaking enough to see the screen, and this is what I read about Andrew Goodman's second work of genius:

"Wasn't sure at first – but D was right – as usual. SO glad he made me read this again. Perfect tragi-comic choice in middle of slightly lightweight shortlist. MUST make sure we balance things with…"

With? WITH? With WHAT? No, I thought. Nooooo! The useless bloody camera on my phone had clipped off the corner of the page!

If I had any sense I would have called Robyn at that moment. She would have told me not to panic, and to wait until another day, when Lofty had just gone off to see his lady-friend. Then I would have known it was safe to go back upstairs and do things I had no right to be doing. But I don't have any sense. And I was in a panic. So, I didn't phone Robyn. Instead, I rushed to Laura's bedroom and pulled the notebook out from its hiding-place.

It didn't take me long to find the right page. For about thirty seconds I was happy. The missing sentence said *"MUST make sure we balance things with something a bit more CHALLENG-ING. Bit more LITERARY…"*

Oh, I thought. Oh, oh, oh! Maybe there's still a chance! Maybe I've got *just* the novel for you! Maybe Jeremy Canty's new book, *The Thames…*

Oh dear, I thought, as the bedroom door opened. Bugger. Well, I did tell you I was only happy for about thirty seconds…

"Hello, Lofty."

"Hello, son," he replied. I wish he'd looked angry but he didn't. It was much worse than that. He looked disappointed. Then I made everything a thousand times worse, with a feeble attempt to slide the notebook under a pillow.

"Bit late for that," he said, quietly. I tried to look at him but suddenly found Beanie Babies terribly interesting.

"I'll be making a cuppa, if you fancy one," he said, leaving.

I wish I'd had a suitcase to pack. Something to give a bit of weight to my departure. But I didn't, so I got my jacket and shuffled sheepishly into the kitchen.

"You off?" asked Lofty, slowly stirring his tea. In my over-heated imagination he was Blofeld stroking his cat.

"I think that's best, don't you?"

"Don't ask me, son. You do what you wanna do."

"Right. Well. Goodbye."

"All right. Be lucky…"

I headed for the door. Then I stopped. There was something I needed to say.

"Lofty? Can I ask you one favour?"

"Try me."

"Please don't tell Laura? Tell her I had to leave because my mother had a stroke or something?"

"Nice."

"Well, OK," I said, realising I'd added yet another turd to the stinking heap I'd already piled up. "Tell her my cat died."

"What for?" he replied, grim-faced.

"Because… Well, because I haven't done anything wrong. Not really wrong, anyway. "

"Nosing round a lady's bedroom? That ain't wrong? It is, where I come from."

"Well… yes. OK, yes. It was wrong. It was. But…"

"Yeah, yeah. Don't worry. Mum's the word."

"Thank you. Sorry. Really. I'm very sorry."

Christ, I thought, as I walked away. What a disaster. I couldn't wait to leave the building and splash some air on my flaming cheeks. Then my phone rang – and I realised it was still in the bloody kitchen.

I couldn't face going back, so I carried on. Then Lofty yelled "Here, Jeremy! Someone on the blower!" So I went back.

It was Paul.

"Yes?" I said, tightly. "What?"

"Oi, cunt. 'Be funny wiv us. Ain't see yer for days. Wossappnin'?"

"I can't talk right now."

"Too busy wiv your new boyfriend?"

"Something like that."

He cackled. "Fought I'd shoot over tonight, bub. What time you home?"

I was about to say "very soon", but something stopped me. "Eight-ish," I said.

"Urr," he replied, sulkily. "Taking the piss, un't they? "

"It's not an *office job*, you moron! "

"Oi! Wanker!"

"Sorry," I said. And I was.

"See ya 'bout eight, then. Ish."

"Yes, OK."

"'ere, Jeremy?"

"*What*? Sorry. What?"

"Love ya."

"I love you, too."

Paul cackled again and ended the call. Then I realised what I'd just said.

"Never told me you had a brother," said Lofty, dryly.

"No," I replied, feeling my cheeks burning, yet again. "It was my…"

"Dad? Oh no, he's passed away."

"No, it was my, um…"

"Bank manager?"

"No…"

"Boyfriend?"

"No," I said, honestly. "He really isn't. He's a friend."

"Don't tell *my* friends I love 'em…"

"Look, Lofty, it hardly matters, does it? I'm going."

"Matters to me, son. Matters a lot. You come here, makin' out you're one thing, then I find out you're a lying, snooping snake in the grass."

"Yes. Yes, I am. But you'll never have to see me again."

"I might do. In court."

"*Court*? What?"

"Attempted burglary. Deception. I could even say you hit me."

"But you said you'd…"

"Yeah, well. Changed me mind. I want an explanation. No. I want the truth."

"But how will you know I'm telling the truth?" I asked, desperate to get away.

"Honest? 'Cos you're a fuckin' *pony* liar. I knew that from day one. But I give you the benefit of the doubt. Old men do that, more fool us. Now I want the real story. I'll know if you're talking bollocks."

"OK," I said, drying my dripping palms on my jacket. "But I'll need a…"

"Plenty in the fridge. I'll get the corkscrew."

So. I told him. I confessed the whole sorry story. To be honest, it was a huge relief to get it off my chest. It almost made me understand Catholics.

When I was finally done he didn't say a word, but he did stand up. Lofty standing up, as you know, isn't all that different from Lofty sitting down. But even little people can be terrifying, if they're angry enough. So I trembled as he walked towards me.

He picked up my man bag and held it out. I felt that he wanted me to stand up, too. So I did.

"Go home," he whispered.

"OK," I replied, taking the bag from him gingerly. I actually walked away backwards, in case he bit me.

"Tomorrow," he said.

"What about tomorrow?"

"We'll talk about this tomorrow. Come your usual time. Now, sling your fucking hook."

- 17 -

One Flew Under
the Cuckoo's Nest

Fuckinell, bub!" grinned Paul, bouncing around on my sofa.
"Talk about a result!"

He was eating pizza with one hand and rolling a joint
with the other. No, I don't know how he does that, either. Honestly, *Cirque du Soleil* don't know what they're missing.

"A result? It was a disaster!"

"Course it fuckin weren't! Old cunt's on your side!"

"Is he?"

"Durrr. Dur-de-durr-dur, yeaaah. Fuck, what you like? Mong."

"Jesus, I think that sentence actually scanned."

"What?"

"Nothing. You were saying?"

"The old geezer. He likes you, innit?"

"Is it? God. I mean, does he?"

"'Does he? Does he fuckin' *double!*"

"Paul, before you spark up that joint, would you mind explaining? In English?"

"Wossa joint gotta do wiv it?"

"I'd just like you to make sense."

"Ur," he said casually, lighting the joint. "What about the four I smoked when I was waitin, then?"

"Carry on" I sighed.

"Look. If Shorty…"

"Lofty."

"Yehwottever. If he wanted to mug you off, he would of. Woultn't say come back tomorrer. Fink about it. S'got plans, innit?"

"Yes, I see your point. But what if I go back tomorrow and the police are there?"

"What?"

"What if *that's* his plan?

"Pleece? What you talkin' about?"

"What do you bloody think I'm talking about?!" I shouted. "The POLICE! Christ, you know who the police are! You're on first name terms with most of them!"

"Mnnh," he replied languidly, lying back and taking a fat hit off his joint. "Only on the Island."

God, why are some people *born* relaxed? Paul could have been on the Titanic and still found time to get a haircut. I, on the other hand, get slightly hysterical if I'm running low on tea bags.

"The police wun't be there, bub. Trust me."

I looked at him with no trust at all, my hands shaking.

"Oi, funny bollocks," he said. "Oi."

"What?"

"Gissakiss…"

People say that heroin is the ultimate drug for making you forget your cares. Personally, I wouldn't know. But even if it is, a five-star shag must take second prize. And that's good enough for me.

We woke up far too late. Paul especially. It was eight o'clock. Typically, I was the one in a panic. Paul simply called his boss and lied about a tragic pile-up on the A2. The third in a month, if I remembered his last two excuses for being late.

After I'd taken a frenzied shower he insisted on driving me to work. Needless to say he didn't feel the need to shower himself. In fact he mocked me about it, all the way from Woolwich to Bermondsey, as though personal hygiene was something reserved for members of bizarre religious cults.

"Listen, bub," he said, as we parked outside Coriander Wharf. "Take it easy. Shorty's on your side."

"I hope so," I replied. "Either that or there'll be half a dozen policeman waiting for me."

"Nah. No fuckin' way. Anyway, if there is, *I'll* be waitin'. You just leg it, and I'll be here wiv me engine running, yeah?"

I know he wasn't exactly a knight in shining armour, and his rusty old lorry was hardly a white charger. But then again, I'm no princess.

"OK," I said. "Wish me luck."

As I walked towards the front entrance I heard a motorbike coming up behind me, and for some reason I felt the urge to hide behind the ugly steel sculpture of a rearing horse that stood in front of Coriander Wharf. My sixth sense was right. One look at the ridiculously tight leathers of the biker and his passenger and I immediately knew who it was: Adam and Heave.

They pulled up right in front of Paul's lorry. He watched them with casual arrogance, as I trembled behind the horse's arse. They removed their helmets. Crushing though it is to admit, they made a gorgeous couple. To my utter despair, I saw that Paul was thinking the same thing. Then they kissed, with the kind of ostentation that gay men can only get away with in London. In Doncaster they would have died under a hail of pies.

Then they walked towards the building. As they passed the lorry, Dougy glanced up at Paul. He grinned. I died a little more.

"Ooh!" said Dougy to Adam. "How gorgeous was *that?*"

"I don't know, baby. I was looking at you."

"Pur-lease," Dougy replied, rolling his eyes. "Look *now* then. Before he drives away."

Adam glanced at Paul.

"See?" said Dougy. "That is a total *ten.*"

"Yes," said Adam. "He is. So what? You're an eleven."

Rather than looking pleased at such devotion, Dougy pulled a sour face.

"Hmm, well. Just you remember that."

"I will," laughed Adam. What a sweetheart, I thought yet again. Personally, I would have battered Dougy to death with his own helmet.

They kissed again and I hung back until Dougy went into the building. Adam Faithful sped off on his bike without a single glance at Paul, then Paul drove his lorry forward a few yards, to where I was hidden. I was about to emerge from behind the horse's arse, but then Dougy reappeared. He looked up the road, to make sure Adam had gone. Then he winked at Paul, who looked at him blankly for a second, before giving him the finger. I forced myself not to laugh as Dougy dashed back inside.

"That was 'im, wunnit?"

I nodded.

"Cock," said Paul. "See what he done? Cheeky cunt. Like I'd be intrested in it."

"Really? But he's so good looking."

"Yur, right. If ya like the Village People."

Oh, how my heart soared.

"Sides, gotchoo, innit?"

"Yes," I smiled. "You've got me."

"Laters," he grinned, tooting his horn as he drove away.

To my huge relief, as I went into the building, Laura and Dougy were hurrying out.

"Ooh!" said Dougy sarcastically. "Nurse Ratchet graces us with her presence!"

"Actually, Dougy," I smiled. "If you're referring to *One Flew Over the Cuckoo's Nest* it was Nurse *Ratched*."

"Whatever. So, what was the problem, honey? Another bad hair day? Or did your Oyster card get rejected?"

"Sorry, Laura," I said, ignoring him. "My neighbour got locked out of her flat. I couldn't really…"

"No problem. Dad's still asleep, anyway. He was up half the night, pacing the floor. God knows why."

"*She's* probably given him the wrong drugs," said Dougy.

"Dougy," I replied. "Would you do me a favour?"

"Of course. Anything to please Sister George!"

"Stop calling me 'she'?"

"Ooooh!" he whinnied. "Get her!"

"Oh, shut up, Dougy!" snapped Laura. "You wouldn't like it if Jeremy started calling you *he*, would you?"

Dougy went bright red and shoved past me.

"I'll call you when I get a chance," said Laura, all apologetic eyebrows.

I almost skipped into the flat. Oh, I thought, if only I could whistle!

However, it took less than half a moment for terror to grip me once again. There could only be one reason why had Lofty been up all night, pacing the floor, and it wasn't indigestion.

I made myself a silent pot of coffee. At least, I tried. Have you ever really noticed how much racket a coffee machine makes? They sound like two teenaged squid, snogging at a bus stop. Every time the bloody thing let out a fresh squelch I glanced nervously up the stairs, expecting Lofty to appear at the top, firing lightning from his fingers.

But he didn't. Around ten-thirty he crept down quietly, looking knackered and ancient.

"Morning, son," he said, quite casually. "Any chance of a cuppa?"

"Coming up," I replied, flying to the kettle.

"Christ. I was up all night."

"Yes," I said, searching through the cupboards, even though I knew perfectly well where the mugs were. "Laura told me."

"Oh, did I keep her awake?"

"Um… I don't know. She just said you were pacing up and down."

"Well, I was. Had a lot on me mind."

We sat in silence for a minute. I dared to steal a glance or two at Lofty, who was staring into space. I'd expected him to look angry, but in fact he looked worried, which was somehow more disturbing. Then he spoke, and what he said was *really* disturbing.

"Jeremy?" he whispered.

"Yes?" I whispered back.

"I wanna ask you summink. But it ain't easy."

My stomach turned the first of several somersaults.

"Ask away," I said. "I'm prepared for anything today."

"Well," he sighed. "You might not be prepared for this. See, I ain't never said this to another bloke, but…"

My eyes widened. What the bloody hell could *that* mean?

"Yes?"

"All right, all right. Best if I just say it."

"I think so," I said, crossing my fingers behind my back. Please, please, *please*, I thought – anything but *that*.

"All right," he said again, swallowing hard. "Can I show you my knob?"

Oh – my – GOD. Ohmygodohmygodohmygod! And I'd thought things couldn't get any worse.

Vile thoughts rolled across my mind like a turd-covered tumbleweed. I tried to reply, but couldn't. My mouth was as dry as a mummy's arsehole. Lofty stared at me, waiting for an answer.

"Gah."

"Eh?"

"Gah…" I said again. Really, it's terribly hard to speak without saliva.

I grabbed my tea and took a swig.

"Lofty, I… I…"

"Fuckinell," he said, looking offended. "It ain't easy for me to ask another bloke to look at me knob, you know. Never mind a poof."

"What?"

"Well. No offence, like, but you know what I mean. Last time a geezer saw me Old John Thomas was when I started me National Service. And now I'm asking you!"

Reality was starting to dawn. Honestly. Me and my imagination.

"Ah. Well, I'm, um, honoured. But… why do you want me to look at it?"

"Ain't cos I want you to give it marks out of bleedin ten, is it? Got a rash."

"A rash."

"Yeah, a rash. "

"Where?"

"Right on me bell-end."

"Ah. OK. Is it sore?"

"Bit."

"Any discharge?"

"Any what?"

"Pus. Green stuff. Leaking."

"Turn it up! Christ!"

"OK. Well, it doesn't sound very serious."

"Easy for you to say."

"Look, why don't we just go the doctor?"

"Do what? I ain't showing me knob to doctor bloody Ooga-Nooga!"

"Why on earth not? You don't mind showing it to a poof!"

"Yeah – a *white* poof!"

"*What?* What difference does that make?"

"Fuck's sake, Jeremy! Don't you know nothing about darkies?"

"What do you think he'd do? Cut it off and eat it for breakfast?"

"No! Laugh at it! "

"*Why?!*"

"Why? Don't ask stupid fuckin questions! Cos they've all got nine fucking inchers, ain't they? *I'd* laugh!"

Oh, if only I could have told him the truth. My experience with black men isn't huge, I admit. But then again, neither were they. Either I've been extremely unlucky, or it's all a myth about the size of their Mandingoes. I've had three black cocks over the years, and if you put them all together, you'd still need a Kit-Kat and a banana to fill Linford Christie's lunch-box.

"I ain't showing it to no coon, and that's that," said Lofty, crossing his arms.

"All right then," I said. "You'd better show it to a poof."

I do envy vaginas. They're so wonderfully private. There they lurk, in their damp triangular privets, looking for all the world just like the next one and the next one and the next one. Oh, I know that the horrid modern fashion for pussy shaving has led to an outbreak of envy among certain women, but they're in a labia-minority, aren't they? And, quite frankly, if my hubby or boyfriend expressed an over-keen desire for me to make my fanny look like that of an eight-year-old girl, I'd think twice before I encouraged him to read to the kids at bedtime. Just a thought.

Penises, on the other hand, have a hard time. And a soft time – more's the pity. Is there anything sillier than a flaccid cock? There it hangs, all forlorn, begging to be blown into, like the teat on a punctured Li-Lo.

Actually, there is something sillier than a flaccid cock. It's a seventy-five year old flaccid cock. Lofty and I had decided that the downstairs bathroom was the best venue for our little game of doctors and nurses, and thus I found myself sitting on the loo, holding his todger, which looked like a sausage, minus the actual sausage. It also looked very sore.

"Get on with it," he said, knees trembling. "I can't keep this up for long."

I couldn't help giving him a look.

"You know what I mean," he replied, staring at the ceiling.

"Well, I said," releasing him. "I think that's your answer."

"What?" he replied, pulling his trousers up so fast he almost fell over.

"You've been keeping it up too long, haven't you? Where do you hide the Viagra?"

"Viagra? Pardon? What you talking abou…"

I coughed.

"Under me bed."

"Mm-hmm. And how old is this lady friend of yours?"

He looked sheepish.

"Promise you won't say a word to Laura?"

"I think our secrets are safe with each other, don't you?"

He nodded. I silently hoped he wasn't about to say sixteen.

"Forty-five."

"You old dog," I grinned, as much from relief as anything.

"Viagra, eh?" he grinned back. "Enough to make you believe in God, ain't it?"

"I wouldn't go that far," I said. "But I can tell you one thing for sure. You haven't caught anything nasty. You've been overdoing it, that's all."

"You sure?"

"Hundred per cent."

"Why?"

"Let's just say I know a lot more about cocks than you, shall we? And leave it at that."

"Yep, yep, yes indeed. Leave it at that. Suits me."

"Good. Do you want Doctor Jeremy to write you a sick note?"

"Nah," he chortled. "I'll tell her meself. Now, do us a bit of breakfast and we can talk about everything else."

- 18 -

Who Knew Prue?

Breakfast wasn't proving easy. Not because of any awkward conversation – we hadn't actually managed to have any conversation. No, it was because Lofty couldn't stop laughing.

"Who'da thought it, eh?" he kept saying. "Friction burns! At my age!"

I put up with it for as long as I could.

"Yes, yes, all right! " I exclaimed tetchily.

"Nurrr," he cackled. "Jealous, are we?"

"No, I'm… well, yes, actually."

That set him off again. Finally, he calmed down.

"Right," he said. "Now, listen. I been thinking. About everything." At bloody last.

"And I'll do you a deal," he continued. "Take it or leave it."

"I'm listening."

"Right. Here's how I see it. You want your book on that list."

"Just a bit."

"Yeah. Well, this is what I'm gonna say to Laura. I'm gonna tell her that I go to bed of an afternoon, and you ain't got nothing to do, right?"

"Right."

"Then I'm gonna tell her all about your posh education and what-not, and suggest you might be just the bloke to look at that pile of old shit she's never got time to read. Get my drift?"

I nodded, unable to believe my luck.

"Thought you'd like it," he went on. "Now, here's your part of the deal."

"OK – but I'm not fondling your cock any more."

Off he went again.

"See? This is it. This is it!"

"What?"

"Why I like you! You're a nice boy, and you make me laugh. You've changed my opinion about poofs, you really have."

"Have I turned you round?" I asked. It was all getting a bit end-of-the pier, so I threw in a saucy wink.

"You have!" he said, wiping tears from his eyes. "You've turned me round!"

I pride myself on keeping a straight face when I've made a joke, but Lofty sounded like a scratchy old 78 recording of *The Laughing Policeman*. It was impossible not to laugh with him.

"Where was I?" he asked, when we'd giggled ourselves dry.

"My part of the deal," I replied.

"Right, right. Here it is. I want you to get Laura and Mick back together."

That wiped the smile off my face.

"What? How am I supposed to do that?"

"Here, hold up. *You're* the one who said you'd do anything to help get 'em back together!"

"Oh. Yes. So I did."

"Right. And that was before I caught you red-handed."

"Mmm."

"Thank you."

"But… what can *I* do?

"How the fuck should I know? You're the bleedin' writer!"

Yes, I wanted to say: but this isn't my genre. And then I saw the way he was looking at me. I've seen it before, on the faces of my small yet dedicated band of groupies. The expectation that I can somehow direct real life in the same way I direct characters in my novels. But this was a different situation. I wasn't sitting in some draughty bookshop in Salisbury, or Grantham, or Hebden Bridge. I couldn't escape by winking at the publicity girl from my publisher, knowing she'd intervene and tell my audience of six spinsters that I really had to catch the train back to London. If I didn't give Lofty the right answer I would blow any chance I had of completing my mission. For days I'd been telling myself I didn't care; that the whole idea was completely ridiculous, and doomed to failure. But suddenly, I did care. A lot. I cared about being so poor that Dolly's food often looked more appetising than my own. I cared about the way a money-grubbing twat like Andrew Goodman had managed to write a best-selling novel on his first attempt, and now looked set to publish another. I cared about Robyn, and Gloomy Prue, and even (God help me) Paul – all of whom had made an effort to shove me through the glass ceiling of my own weakness, and on to success. And, to my surprise, I realised that most of all I cared about Laura: a genuinely good person, so desperately lonely that she would make a drunken move on the first man who seemed the least bit sympathetic – even though he was a complete fraud, from his fake beard through to his fake heterosexuality and his fake dead fiancée.

I felt thoroughly ashamed.

"You're right," I said to Lofty. "I am the bleeding writer. Leave it with me."

"Attaboy," he smiled. "What you gonna do?"

"Crikey," I said. "Give me a minute! I need to think about it."

"Hmm," he replied dubiously. "Yeh, s'pose so. Right, tell you what. I'm gonna give me lady friend a tinkle, then take a poodle round hers. That'll give you plenty of time to come up with something."

"Right," I said, assuming he meant "pootle". With another one of my Max Miller winks I added. "Just so long as *you* don't come up with anything, eh?"

He was still chuckling when he left the apartment.

Despite not having the faintest idea how I could go about fixing Laura's broken marriage, I felt good about myself for the first time since this whole bizarre chapter in my life had begun. Lofty's proposal sounded like a fair deal, and not something shameful in a brown paper bag. Now all I had to do was come up with a plan.

I tried calling Robyn, but her phone was turned off. I called Paul, but all I could hear was the sound of pneumatic drills. In desperation I called Prue – not because I expected her, the least scheming person I know, to solve my problem; but because I needed to talk to *someone*.

As it turned out, Prue was my saviour. Again. Bless her. To make it even better, she'd insisted on rushing across town and taking me to an early lunch at the Butlers Wharf Chop House, a restaurant I couldn't possibly afford, which had the added advantage of being two minutes' walk from Laura's.

Things didn't start promisingly. Prue had a whinge. I love the word 'whinge', don't you? I wonder who thought of combining 'whine' and 'minge' in one innocent little package.

"Honestly," she whinged, while we waited for our first course (she'd resisted, but I was buggered if I was leaving that restaurant without at least three), "why don't you keep me in the *loop?* I'm not completely stupid, you know."

"I know," I replied. "But…"

"What?"

"Well. If you want the truth, you're too nice."

"Too nice?" she said, looking slapped.

"God, Prue! It's not an insult."

"It is!"

"*Why*?"

"Because you always turn to bloody Robyn whenever there's something exciting going on! "

"No I don't," I lied.

"Yes, you *do*. Does it ever occur to you that Robyn's life is exciting enough as it is? That sometimes *I'd* like to be a Bad Girl?"

"No."

"You see, that's the trouble with you," she went on. "Maybe it's because you're a writer."

"What?"

"You think I'm a character in one of your books, don't you? You've got your little picture of me, and it can't change. But that's all about *you*. I'm not that girl in the fucking awful Annie Hall outfit you met at Cambridge. That was thirty years ago."

That raised the hairs on my neck.

"Think about it. Do you honestly think I got to the top in public relations by being *too nice?*"

"Um…"

"The thing is, and don't tell everybody – I'm a bit of a *cow*."

I was mesmerised. It was like watching Shy Di transform into the Princess of Nails, right before my eyes. I needed a moment and, fortunately, a shiny young person brought our starters.

"So," said Prue, spearing a sweetbread, "do you want some free advice from me, *the* person at *We the People?*"

Between my astonishment and my utterly delicious crab ravioli, all I managed was a nod.

"Good," she said, looking more confident than I'd ever seen. (or do I mean *noticed*?) "Here's my idea…"

Her idea, in fact, was great. It was risky and terrifying, but it was also possible. I finished my lunch with an entirely new picture of Prue.

Lofty came home two minutes after me. He looked a bit sickly.

"You OK?" I asked.

He managed a nod, but I wasn't convinced.

"Did she take it all right?"

"Oh, yeah. She took it all right. Three times…"

"*Three times?* But…"

"Took a bluey, didn't I?" he grinned. "On the way."

"But what about your… wasn't it sore?"

"Not really. Rubbed a bit of ointment on it."

"What ointment?"

"Ointment the quack give us for me arfritis. What's it called? Oh, yeah: *I Believe*."

"I Believe?"

"Yeah – I Believe."

Ah, I thought.

"No, not *I Believe*. *I Believe* was a song by Frankie Laine. I believe. You mean *Ibuleve*."

"Yeah, that's the one. Worked a treat, it did."

"Clearly."

"Only *now*," he went on, sitting down very carefully, "Ooh! It's wearing off. Ow! I reckon I've done meself a proper mischief this time."

"Right," I said, briskly. "Let's get this over with, shall we? Drop 'em."

It was rather sweet, the way he obeyed so meekly. The sight of his cock, on the other hand, was far less endearing.

"Jesus, Lofty," I said, as I caught sight of his livid old knob. "What have you been *doing* with it? It looks like a Swan Vesta! "

He paused for a moment, then looked very pleased with himself.

"Same thing anyone does with a Swan Vesta," he smiled. "Setting summink alight!"

"Well. Thank God this isn't Australia. We'd have a full-scale bush-fire on our hands."

"Aha-ha-ha-ha! There he goes again! Oh, he's funny! *Bush*fire! Oh, that's a good 'un! Bushfire!"

Whenever I have a practical tip, I do love to pass it on. My scrambled eggs, for instance, wouldn't be anywhere *near* as nice, if someone hadn't told me to add a teaspoon of cold water to the mix. Anyway, here's another: if you want to have a serious conversation with an old man, try not to do it while he's got his John Thomas in a bag of frozen peas.

Fifteen minutes later, I'd told him 'my' plan for getting Laura and Mick back together.

"S-s-s-sounds like a s-s-s-scheme," said Lofty, through his

chattering false teeth, which sounded like novelty castanets. "W-w-when d'ya want to d-d-do it?"

"I hadn't really thought…"

"R-r-right, then. T-t-t-morrer. Now…. C-c-c-can I t-t-t-take me c-c-c-cock out of these p-p-p-peas?"

I went home by public transport. Christ, it's amazing how quickly you can get a taste for luxury. Two little trips in Fat Dave's Merc and it was all I could do not to pinch my nose in disgust. The Tube wasn't too bad. The Tube at five-thirty is crammed but fairly civilised. The bus, on the other hand… well, the bus is never civilised, is it? In Woolwich you count yourself lucky if you manage to go the whole journey without someone roasting a goat.

At least the slow trip home gave me a chance to think about Prue's plan. It was simple, but it really could work. The idea was that Lofty would stuff an entire roll of loo-paper down the bog in his bathroom. That would cause a mini-flood. He'd then phone Mick Rayner and ask him to come round and fix it. If Mick resisted, Lofty would beg, and say he was scared of upsetting Laura – and besides, she'd be at work all day (as Mick knew only too well), so there would be no danger of them bumping into one another. Then, assuming Mick took the bait, Lofty would phone me. He would then wait in the flat just long enough for Mick to appear, but then he'd make an excuse and leave. I would then turn up at Coriander Wharf and let myself in, casually acting like Laura's new boyfriend. I'd be perfectly friendly to Mick, because I'd have no idea that he was Laura's husband. Mick (and here was the tricky bit) wouldn't beat me to a pulp. I'd chat away to him, bloke-to-bloke, while he was unblocking the loo. And somewhere in our conversation I would casually drop in the fact that I was returning later that evening, to have a night of passion with his wife. Mick would then leave, and with a tiny bit of luck, would burst into the flat later, just as I was about to make love to Laura.

It was risky. But it was perfect. It was perfectly risky.

- 19 -

Crap a Diadem

Bloody hell, Robyn! Why are you being so arsey? It's not a competition!"

"I'm not being arsey, darling. I just don't want you to fuck up."

"No, sorry, you *are* being arsey. I wish I hadn't told you, now."

"Well, really. Fancy taking advice from Gloomy bloody Prue. What does *she* know about how to handle people?"

"Um, she is one of London's top PRs. She handles people all day long."

"Oh, all right. But not *real* people. You should've done what I told you to do."

"But I couldn't, could I? Things changed. And I *tried* to call. You weren't available."

"Hmm. You could have waited, darling. I'd only popped out for lunch."

"Yes, that's just what I did, too!"

It was weird, arguing via the webcam. There's always that slight slo-mo thing. It was like having a punch-up in the space shuttle.

"Look," I went on. "It's done now. It'll either work, or it won't."

"And it won't, darling. There are too many what-ifs. What if Lofty can't get wotsisname to come and fix the boiler?"

"The loo."

"Whatever. And what if he does come, but couldn't give a shit that you're supposedly schtupping his wife? What if he's met someone else and is deliriously happy?"

"Lofty says he's pretty certain that isn't the case."

"Regular little bloodhound, isn't he? OK – so what if Mr Laura –"

"Mick, Robyn, it's Mick. I've told you twice."

"God, stop being so touchy! His name's hardly important, is it? Say he *is* missing her? What if he goes into a violent rage and beats you up? Black and blue are *not* your colours, darling."

"Oh, piss off, you bossy cow. You're worse than my bloody mother!"

I cut the connection and sat there shaking, surprised at how angry I felt. We'd only had a silly tiff. Then I realised it was myself I was angry with. Robyn is the exact opposite of my sexually repressed Evangelical Christian mother in every way except one: she likes to control me. But letting myself be controlled – that was *my* problem.

I noticed that Paul had left an unlit spliff on my coffee table. Perfect. Blessed oblivion. And Coronation Street was about to start. I turned the telly on and sparked Paul's Hindenburg of a joint (honestly, that boy could skin up for Fidel Castro). Then, just as I smiled in anticipation of some low-rent R&R, I saw something in the corner of my eye.

"Oh, *Dolly!* For fuck's s… Bad cat! Drop it! Dolly, drop it!"

But, of course, she wouldn't. Instead she pranced around the room on tip-toes, looking awfully pleased with herself, in that way only a cat can, when she's fresh from murder. Except it wasn't murder. Not quite. The poor sparrow, or magpie, or pigeon (sorry, but they all look the same to me) was still flapping around in a circle. Dolly had its left wing in her mouth and was clearly enjoying herself. I was about to throw a cushion at her, but that raised the hideous prospect of the bleeding bird whirring round my room, making macabre Rorschach patterns on my walls, before flopping down dead. So I simply watched in horror as Dolly did what she so clearly had to do.

Mercifully, it didn't take long. Lovely, elegant Dolly tossed the doomed creature in the air, caught it by the neck, and then, with a horrible crunch, it was all over. For the bird, at least, if not for me, as Dolly proceeded to pick up the corpse in her mouth and lovingly drop it at my feet.

"Thank you, Dolly," I said, deliberately not looking at the horrible thing, in case it had a final flap in its wings. "Would you like that in a pie, or a stew?"

"Meow," she replied, rubbing herself against my leg.

I picked her up, cuddled her, put down my joint, and went to bed. The corpse would have to wait till the next day.

One of the odd things about being an alky is that you only get hangovers when you don't drink. Next morning I felt like someone had stolen my innards in the night, and replaced them with a piss-stained mattress they'd found in an alley. To make things worse, Lofty had insisted on taking me out to a Greasy Spoon for breakfast.

"I love this place," he said, gazing round mistily at the rancid clientele, the brutal fluorescent lights and the sticky plastic tables. Or do I mean the sticky clientele, the rancid fluorescent lights and the brutal tables? Or – oh, whatever. It was a dump.

"Best breakfast in Bermondsey" he went on, proudly.

"Can't wait," I said, trying my hardest to repel the contents of my stomach, as they crawled up my windpipe like the Viet Cong.

Breakfast appeared. Let's just say that it didn't shatter any illusions. God knows what the *worst* breakfast in Bermondsey is like.

"I've done all the work," he said. "Now it's up to you."

"Right," I replied, looking at my food and wondering how much of it I could hide beneath the two old carpet tiles that had gaily billed themselves as 'fryed bred'. "Tell me more."

"Well," he said, tucking in, "had a right good talk to Laura last night, didn't I?"

There was a pause. I could see he was waiting for me to eat, so I put a bit of ugly sausage in my mouth and pretended I was enjoying myself. And let's be honest, we've all done that.

"Yeusss," I mumbled. "And?"

"So, I tell her I think you're a diamond geezer. And then I tell her I reckon you're a bit soft for her, and *she* says…"

"..no, don't tell me."

"No, you're alright. She never said that."

"What?"

"That she thought you was a shirt-lifter."

"Oh. Good. Carry on."

"No, she says she really likes you, right? But the problem is, well, you're a bit *soft*. So I'm thinking to meself, I know my daughter. She don't want a *drip*, do she – no offence – she wants a bloke. But I'm on it. So I say yeah, he is the gentle sort, but maybe it's time you forgot Mick and found a bloke who's more suitable? I reckon Jeremy's *right* up your street, I go. Like, more on your wavelength."

"And *she* said?"

"*She* said," he replied, cackling. "Well, then, dad – don't let him get away!"

"And here we are!" I grinned.

"Yeah, here we are!" he replied, and had one of his laughing fits. I grabbed my chance and chucked half my breakfast under the table.

"Right," I said, when he'd recovered. "Phase One completed, captain."

"No it ain't," he replied.

"Oh. But…"

"Phase *Two* is completed! Phoned Mick first thing, didn't I? He's on a job over in Leytonstone but I gave him a load of old toffee about how I blocked up the bog and anyway, long story short, he's shooting over the river in his dinner break."

"What, *today?*" I squeaked.

"Course. You got time to waste, then?"

"No, but…"

"Crap a diadem, son. Crap a diadem."

"Excuse me?"

"My school motto," he said. "And there's me thinking you'd know your Latin."

"I only did it to O-level."

"Ah. Maybe that's it. *Seize the Day.* That's what it means. Seize the Day. You eating that other sausage?"

For the second time in three days I found myself hiding behind the horse's arse. Still, the weather was lovely, and being outside the building meant I could chain-smoke. Plus, as I discovered, there was a handy space between the horse's arsehole and the horse's tail that made a lovely ashtray.

Mick appeared at 1.07. I made a deliberate note of it, in case of any subsequent court case.

He was neither what I'd expected nor, secretly, hoped. He was lean and tight-knit, with floppy hair and – good grief – glasses. British workmen never wear glasses. Italian workmen wear glasses. He looked like an actor who'd turned up on the set of a Merchant Ivory, only to find he was playing the plumber, and then decided to piss them all off by refusing to ditch the specs.

Anyway, he let himself in. Then I started counting down from ten minutes, as agreed with Lieutenant Lofty. By the time ten minutes was up the arse-tray was overflowing. In so, so, so many senses.

In theory, my part of the deal wasn't difficult. All I had to do was let myself in to the flat, 'accidentally' discover Mick, then let him know that I was Laura's boyfriend. The problem was that I had to do this without him telling me that he was her estranged husband. *That* was the difficult part.

I paced around outside, smoking one last fag, rehearsing the lines I might use. I thought about bursting into the flat, calling "Darling" Darling!!" but that didn't have the ring of success. I thought about confronting him in an aggressive way – "Whooda fucker yoo?". Oh, please. Do me a big gay favour.

Then, as I entered the lobby, I found the solution. There was an obscenely expensive bouquet sitting there. It was meant for Laura's next-door-neighbour, but I figured that 'petty theft' would be pretty low down on my charge-sheet when this witch's brew blew up in my face; so I grabbed the flowers and threw away the card. Then I took a pen from my pocket, wrote a new note on the sheet of the paper I always carry around in case inspiration strikes (not that it ever has), and pressed onward.

I have the shakes at the best of lunch-times, but that day I had to use both hands to get the key in the door. I started tip-toeing across the hall before I remembered that wasn't quite the point. So I threw my shoulders back and strode masterfully into the kitchen, carrying the stolen flowers like the big love-token they were meant to be. I didn't know whether to call Lofty's name or make a lot of noise and let Mick come to me.

As it happened, there was no need to do either. I heard Lofty's loo flush and, five seconds later, Mick appeared. Suddenly he didn't look so mild-mannered and Italian.

"Whooda fucker you?" he growled. I couldn't believe a man in glasses could be so terrifying, and I very nearly said "The florist – the big gay florist!".

Then I pulled myself together.

"I was about to ask you the same question," I said, trying my best to look as though I could cut up rough, when the truth is that I've never cut up anything rougher than doilies.

"I'm Laura's…."

I noticed him noticing the bouquet for the first time. Well, not 'noticing', exactly. Taking in.

"…plumber," he said, swallowing the last syllable like a bitter pill.

"Oh," I smiled. "The plumber. How lovely! I'm Jeremy."

I reached out to shake his hand.

"I wouldn't," he said, threateningly. "Just had 'em down the bog."

"Oh!" I tittered, quickly covering with a manly cough. "What's the problem?"

"Ain't a problem. Not no more."

"Ah. Good. What *was* the problem, then?"

I read his mind, and he was thinking: *this bloke can't be all that close to Laura if he didn't know about the bog.* So I quickly added,

"Laura never said anything when I left this morning."

He clenched his jaw. Considering what was unfolding before him I thought he showed great restraint.

"No, well, now you mention it, Lofty don't want Laura to know."

"Oh, dear. What did he do *this* time?"

"Got a bit carried away with the toilet roll. No problem. All sorted."

"Marvellous, um…?"

"Tony," said Mick. "Tony… Purvis."

"So, I won't tell Laura that you've been, then?"

"Best not."

"What about money?"

"Not a problem. I'll get it off Lofty when I see him."

"If that suits you. Seems like you know them pretty well."

"Yeah," he said, with a dry laugh. "They're like family to me, them two."

"Well, if that's it," I said.

"Just gotta clean up. Five, ten minutes."

"OK, Tony. Must dash. I only came to leave these."

"Nice," he said, admiring the bouquet. "Must be doing all right for yourself."

"Hm, not bad" I said, trying to sound like the kind of smug arse who spends a hundred quid on flowers. "But she's worth it."

"Yeah," he replied. "Nice girl, Laura."

"She certainly is," I beamed, proudly.

Before I left I made sure the note I'd attached to the flowers was plainly visible.

"Darling Melons. If you think they're a bit OTT, blame yourself. You see, it takes a whole garden of flowers to show how much I love you. Think of every bloom as a kiss, and that's how many kisses I'll give you later. Will be home about 8. Stay hungry. Jerrums xxxxxxxxx".

Quite frankly I wanted to give myself a good kicking for writing such slop, even though I knew Laura would never read it. God knows how it made Mick feel.

"Angry," I hoped, as I left the flat. But, I prayed, as I closed the door. Not *too* angry…

- 20 -

Release the Balls

I didn't go back and hide behind the horse's arse, I went to a pub called the Queen's Arms. Actually, I think there should be a pub called the Queen's Arse. I know many a queen who's arse *is* a pub, give or take a few bar-stools and a widescreen telly.

I can't remember if I told you this, but Laura had insisted on paying me daily. One hundred and forty quid, in cash, thank you very kindly. I've never had a hundred and forty quid in my pocket. Ever. Not in cash. There was a time, three or four years ago, where I'd collected so many money-off coupons that I had to carry them round in a shopping bag. I think they added up to eighty quid or so. But, as I was swiftly learning, cash and me are like Paul and Heather, or leather trousers and the average pair of buttocks. We really, truly, honestly think we're made for each other, but one trip out in public and we realise it's all so *wrong*. Two hours in the pub, with a hundred and forty quid, a slot machine, a few new best friends, and I was broke again. Still, at least I felt cheerful (i.e. : pissed) as I let myself back in the flat.

Lofty looked quite cheerful, too.

"Cor!" he cackled. "You won't believe this! Shut your eyes, shut your eyes!

"What?" I said, doing as I was told.

"Right. Open 'em again!"

"Oh, my... Lofty! Please!"

"Look at that, eh? What d'ya reckon?"

"Um," I said, peeping through my fingers. "It looks... Better."

"Better?" he said, putting his todger away. "It looks *blindin'!* It was a *scab*, Jeremy! Nothin 'cept a scab!"

"Congratulations!"

"And it fell off, didn't it? Minute we started..."

"Yes, yes. I get the picture."

He looked a bit disappointed at my lack of pride in his achievement. I felt like a bad parent at a nativity play.

"You old *stud*," I added, with a wink. That seemed to do the trick.

"Right," he said. "How did it go with Mick?"

"Very well, I think. Did you see the flowers?"

"Yurss," he said, seriously. "Can't believe he never killed you on the spot."

"Hmm," I replied. "The night is young."

Lofty did his cackle and reached in his pocket.

"Here," he said, handing me a piece of silver paper. "Just in case it all goes a bit too far."

He winked at me lewdly and I opened the scrunch of foil. Inside was a Viagra. I swallowed it without hesitation or water.

A couple of years ago I decided it really was time I threw a birthday party for myself. I took a bit of a risk, because I invited thirty people to a restaurant, then spent the entire evening praying that they weren't assuming I was going to pay the bill. Luckily, they didn't. I learned a few things that night. I have nice friends, for instance. I also learned this: I'm the only gay man I know who has never had *any* kind of physical intimacy with a woman. I was amazed. Even my friend Dizzy Dave, who's so effeminate he makes chiffon look rugged, had doinked a girlie. I was alone. A beacon of bentness. I can still remember the looks of disbelief on the faces of all those gigantic poofs when I said that I hadn't so much as *kissed* a woman. Ever. Not even when I was six, at a party, and off my tiny tits on fizzy drinks, ice cream and Jelly Tots.

Well. Tonight was proving to be the night. I'd had a bit of luck (or not, depending how you look at it) when Laura phoned and said she'd be home later than planned. I told her straight away that I was already cooking a bit of tea for her dad – and then I played a blinder by saying that I'd also cook dinner for her and me. Even though she was on the mobile in what sounded like a hurricane, there was no mistaking the excitement in her voice as she took me up on the offer.

I learned later that she *was* in a hurricane. Ish. They'd gone back to Elstree to re-do the aborted interview with Daniel Craig, and there were wind machines going bonkers in the background.

I'd gathered this information from Dougy, who'd insisted on traipsing into the flat with Laura, even though her face was making it very plain he wasn't welcome.

"Ooh," he said, "it takes a *lot* to impress me, but it was fanfucking-tabulous on that set today! *You* would have loved it, Jeremy!"

"Really?" I said, adding another spoonful of hot stock to the mushroom risotto I'd decided to prepare for my seduction supper.

"Yes," he went on, clearly angry that I hadn't asked why I would have loved it at Elstree. "It was wall-to-wall testosterone!"

"Oh."

"Anyway," said Dougy, knowing he was losing this one. "How was *your* thrilling day? "

"Great, thanks. Lofty and me had a brilliant time. Went out to a restaurant…"

"A *restaurant?* You mean a greasy spoon. "

"Well," I lied,. "I can't say there was anything particularly greasy. And they gave us proper knives and forks. Just like a real restaurant!"

Laura's timing was impeccable. She handed me a glass of wine, then sipped at her own. I saw the greedy radar of Dougy's eyes do a quick sweep. Realising he hadn't been asked to the party he prepared himself for the inevitable by adopting one of his awful fake grins.

"Oh well," he said. "That's nice. I should be getting along."

"Thanks for today," said Laura. "You've been a brick."

"That's my job," he replied, tensing his silly body in its spray-on shirt. I think he actually was trying to *look* like a brick. Hmm. Only one letter wrong.

"Now, promise me," Laura went on, kissing him on the cheek, "you won't argue with Dave on the way home? He is doing you a favour, after all."

"I *can* get a cab," said Dougy. "God knows I'd hate to make the chauffeur do his fucking job."

"Ooh, no. He's waiting."

"So? Let him go home. Fat fascist."

"Oh, now, behave. He's fine."

"Yes, but…"

"…and besides – if you wait here for a cab our lovely risotto'd get ruined. And I'm starving."

Dougy looked so frustrated I almost felt sorry for him. Almost.

Then the intercom buzzed. "I *can* get another job," said Dave, only half joking

"He's just coming," said Laura. "Aren't you, Dougy?"

"Yes – sssssss," was Dougy's answer. Laura smiled sweetly, as though she really had no idea about the atmosphere.

"Love you, Davey-Wavey," she smiled at Dave, whose glazed ham of a face entirely filled the intercom's tiny screen.

"Yeah," he grunted cheerfully. "I'll remind you of that when the missus leaves me."

"Quick, quick!" said Laura to Dougy, shooing him away.

"Shit," she said to me, just as he slammed the door. "Dougy's forgotten his laptop. Would you…"

"Watch that risotto," I replied, grabbing the bag.

Dougy had already realised his mistake and met me at the door. "Ah," I said. "You'd realised."

"Yes," he replied, snatching his bag. "I'd *realised.*"

I smiled.

"Don't get too sure of yourself," he seethed. "I've got *your* number, ducky."

"Er, OK," I smiled, as he stomped off to the car. Fat Dave, bless 'im, gave me a thumbs-up as he closed Dougy Dearest's door.

So. We'd eaten the mushroom risotto (a triumph). We'd eaten my melting chocolate puddings (another triumph. Thank you, Gary

Rhodes). We'd said goodbye to bottle of wine number one, and were on the last inch of number two.

And we were back where we were a few nights earlier. On the sofas. Except, this time, there was no reason for Laura to hesitate – so we weren't actually on the sofas, we were on *one* sofa.

"You know what?" she said, twining her left foot around my right ankle.

"What?" I replied, trying to look like I was enjoying the situation.

"I bet men are just like women."

"Oh," I laughed nervously. "I hope not."

"No, no – me too. What I *mean* is that I bet you blokes share all your secrets when you're on your own together, just like us girls do. You do, don't you?"

"How can I answer that?" I lied. "I've got no idea what you lot talk about when you're in a group."

As *if*, I thought to myself. I know *exactly* what girls talk about together. It's a gay privilege.

"Well," she went on. "I'm not about to betray the sisterhood."

"I should hope not," I said. "And I'm not about to betray the brotherhood."

"Mm," she chuckled throatily. "Mm-hmm-hmmm."

And then, unbelievably, she managed to wrap her foot even more securely around mine. It was like being raped by ivy.

I did my very best to look excited by her advances, but she must have picked up on my terror.

"God," she said, kittenishly. "Am I being terribly unprofessional?"

No, love, I thought. I'd say you were being the exact opposite.

"You're bad," I grinned, hoping I looked ready for bed, in the knicker-ripping, tongue-thrashing, sheet-ruining sense, and not the Horlicks-drinking, book-reading, bed-socks-wearing sense that I truly felt. Not that I was really feeling anything at all, except arse-opening fear.

Suddenly she released my foot, which was good because DVT was about to set in. I didn't get much chance to massage some life back into it before she slid herself next to me in a sort of spoon-position. I writhed around desperately, which made us more of a Uri Geller-type spoon. Not to be defeated, she twisted her neck round and looked at me hopefully. Somehow I realised that she expected me to do something significant with my right arm. Christ, it was like playing Twister. Forcing myself to focus on the mess of tangled limbs I spotted an opening and slipped my hand in. It came to rest on her trembling boob. At least, I thought it was her trembling boob, before I realised it was her phone vibrating. To my dismay she ignored it.

"Yes," she sighed.

"No," I thought, praying with every breath in my body for the jealous husband to make an unexpected appearance.

He didn't. But I'll tell you what did: my erection. I'd never taken a Viagra before that night, but I bloody will in future. They say you need sexual stimulation for it to work, so I wasn't expecting much. Well, "sexual stimulation" is obviously a pretty broad term, if it includes "lying on a sofa in a horribly painful position, with someone of the wrong gender, whilst terrified of the prospect of imminent physical violence." The stuff is dynamite! No wonder Lofty had blisters on his cock.

"Ooh," giggled Laura, accidentally brushing her hand across

my crotch, just like Hitler accidentally invaded Poland. "Does Mister Stiffy want to play with Miss Horny?"

"That depends," I squeaked.

"Oh, don't spoil the moment," she replied, petulantly. "I've got plenty of *those*."

"Plenty of what? Oh! No, I didn't mean *condoms*. I always carry condoms."

"Stud…" she giggled. Christ, I thought, is that really how you hetties carry on?

"I mean," I went on. "It depends on, well… your *dad*."

Laura suddenly sat up straight and pulled an imaginary cardy over her breasts.

"Thank you very much! You really know how to ruin a moment!"

"Yes, well, I'm sorry – but he *is* upstairs. "

"So? This is *my* place, not his. We're not teenagers."

"Um… We are, in a sense."

"What sort of man says 'in a sense' when he's about to get *laid?*" she said. "Jesus!"

Fortunately, at that moment, the sort of man who would never say 'in a sense' when he was about to get laid, burst into the room. I'd never been so overjoyed at the prospect of physical violence.

The first thing Laura did, upon seeing her husband, was scream. Then it was my turn.

"What the hell are you doing here?" she yelled.

"What the fuck is *he* doing here?" he replied, jabbing his finger in my direction. Just a brief aside: Viagra isn't a miracle drug. It stops working when you're actually in fear for your life.

"That is *none* of your fucking business!" Laura shouted.

"What do you do fer her, eh?" Mick snarled at me. "What do you do that I don't? Read poems?"

"Ooh, no," I said, trying to run away but being forced to hop, because my bloody leg had gone back to sleep. "No, look – you've got this all wrong!"

"All wrong? Do I look like a wanker? "

"No, of course not!" I said, thinking no, actually you look really hot when you're angry.

To his credit, it was just the one punch, but it did throw me right across the room. All I remember after that was scrabbling my way to the door, while Laura was on Mick's back, hissing like a snake on a hotplate. Then I remember...

Lying on my sofa at home, with Paul. He had his back to me, rolling a joint. I was either dead or dreaming.

"Nnnnh," I moaned, tentatively.

"You better tell me woss goin' on, Jeremy. "

"Shit," I said. "I thought I'd imagined you."

"Yurr, you wish. "

"Paul, just let me get a drink," I said, staggering to my feet. " I'm gasping."

"Piss head," he said, glugging on his Stella and lighting the joint.

I'd completely forgotten that Paul didn't know about Gloomy Prue's seduction scheme. Ooh, that sounds like an experimental band from the 60s, doesn't it? Gloomy Prue's Seduction Scheme.

Anyway, he didn't. And now we come to Laura's trembling boob. Blimey, that's another one. Laura's Trembling Boob. Famous, I seem to recall, for having a girl drummer.

Anyway. It hadn't been Laura's trembling boob at all. It was her trembling mobile phone. Except it wasn't. It was *my* mobile. And it had been Paul, calling me. So, when I thought she'd ignored her phone, the reality was that I'd accidentally answered *mine* (are you keeping up?) – and Paul had heard everything. So, when I'd stumbled out of Coriander Wharf with a bloody nose and no idea what century I was in, Paul was pulling up in his lorry, preparing to burst in and play the part of the jealous husband. Well, jealous repressed homosexual lover, actually; but that doesn't have the same ring about it. The thought that the dreadful scene at Laura's could actually have been *worse* filled me with a wonderful floaty feeling.

"Listen, bub," he said, rolling over. "Summink to ask ya."

"What?"

"Alright if I stay here coupla nights?"

"Yes, of course," I replied. "Why?"

"Smee and her. Ain't gettin on, ''" he replied, trying to sound casual.

"She knows, then?"

"No. Well. Not 'xactly."

"Meaning?"

"Finks you're a bird, innit?"

I wanted to be angry but he flashed his baby blues and leant forward to kiss me. Sod it, I thought, and gave in. Then my phone rang. I ignored it but the ansafone clicked on. It was Laura.

"Jeremy?" she whispered. "Are you there?"

I went to answer it. Paul stopped me.

"*Please* pick the phone up, if you are," she went on. "Mick's worried out of his mind."

"Ooh!" I said to Paul. "M…"

"Sshh! Listen!"

"Anyway, look. I won't be going to work in the morning until I've heard from you I am so, *so* sorry about what happened tonight. If there's anything, I can do to make it up to you, just say. OK? Hope you're all right. God bless. And Jeremy? I really do mean it. *Anything*. ' Night."

"Fuckinell," said Paul, planting the kiss on my lips. "I'm shacked up wiv a lottery winner!"

-21-

The Loose Change of Life

When Laura had said how sorry she was about what had happened the previous night, she was being quite specific. Obviously she was sorry about what happened *before* her estranged husband had knocked me across the room; but judging by the look of tousled bliss on her face the next morning, she wasn't very sorry about what happened *after*. Talk about the cat that got the cream. This one had quite clearly licked her paws afterwards.

"Honestly, Laura," I said, sipping at the horrid camomile tea she'd insisted on making me. "Don't worry about it."

"But I *am* worried about it. Very worried. It's…"

"Look. We were both lonely, and pissed. To be honest, I'm glad Mick appeared when he did."

"Oh," she said, looking a bit hurt. Honestly, you girls really *do* want it both ways, don't you? And not in the way men fantasise about.

"No, not because I didn't want something to happen between us," I went on. "Of *course* I did! But, well, it wouldn't have been a good idea, would it? Be honest."

"Because you're still in love with Paula?" she said, her eyes welling up.

"Exactly," I replied, forcing myself not to sneeze.

"But that just makes me feel *worse*," she went on, handing me a tissue (how *do* women always manage to find a tissue from nowhere? Do you keep them in your fannies, or what?).

"Laura," I said, blowing my nose,. "I'm a big boy. I can see how much you still love Mick. I hope it works out. Honestly."

"God, Jeremy. You are the nicest man. Isn't there *anything* I can do to make it up to you?"

Now, I'd rehearsed this bit with Paul, earlier on, with him taking the part of Laura. He wasn't much help, especially as he'd insisted on wearing my fake beard between his legs to help him get into character. It didn't. He just looked like a road-digger with a false beard on his cock.

"Well," I said, nervously. "What I'd really like…"

"I meant what I said, Jeremy. Anything."

"OK. What I'd really like is to help you out a bit. With your work."

"My work? In what way? I mean, I know I said *anything*, but, well, I can't really sack Dougy."

"Oh! No, I didn't mean to suggest… no, God! How could anyone replace Dougy? Besides, I like the job I've got."

"Oh, right," she smiled. "What, then?"

"Well, your dad does like to sleep. A lot."

"Mmm. He always did like his bed. Even when he was younger."

Hmm, I thought, not as much as he likes other people's, the randy old sod.

"And I have *tried* to get him to do things during the day," I said. "But, well, I don't think it's my place to force him."

"No, of course. You're so sensitive, Jeremy."

"I think it's his right to do exactly what he wants at his time of life."

"It is, it is. And he really seems to adore you. I feel quite jealous."

I was so genuinely touched I actually blushed an actual blush.

"Anyway," I went on. "Thing is, I get a bit bored while he's upstairs napping. And Lofty said that you were absolutely snowed under with stuff. Work."

She sighed heavily.

"Tell me about it…"

It was an awkward moment. I knew that she insisted on doing the household washing and ironing herself, probably because it was the one thing she could do to show her dad that she cared. Now I was terrified she might grasp the wrong end of the stick, and ask *me* to take over the job, because Lofty had adopted me as his surrogate son, and I was almost family. I hadn't dragged myself naked across a mile of broken glass to be offered the job of washerwoman. At the same time I didn't want to be too pushy, in case she smelled a rat. And, God knows, I could smell a whole sewer-full of them.

Luckily, she went straight where I'd pointed.

"You mean the Book List?"

"Yes," I said, as innocently as I could, which was probably not very, considering my innocence was lying in a bin somewhere, right next to Rose West's. "I know you've got a ton of reading to do, and, well, I think I'd know what you were looking for."

She bit her lip. Honestly, she literally bit her lip.

"I don't know, Jeremy," she said, looking like a heart surgeon at the end of a five-day shift, wondering if he could get away with letting his swabs-nurse do the quadruple bypass. "It's pretty serious stuff, my job."

You're telling me, I thought.

"If a book gets on the list," she went on. "It's life-changing stuff. I mean, what with all the scandals about phone-ins and how the public can't trust the programme-makers. I really feel… Well, it's *my* responsibility to choose the books."

It was now or never. I had to take the chance.

"And Dougy's," I said.

"Dougy's?"

"Well. You let *him* choose the books. Don't you?"

Half an hour later Laura had gone to work, and I was holding the key to the study. She'd asked me to write reports on the last few books on The List. My hand trembled so much it took me five attempts to get the key into the lock. Pull yourself together, Jeremy, I thought. It's not the tomb of Tutankhamun. Then again, it was. Much as I wanted the treasure within, I was terrified I might be bringing down a curse upon myself.

I counted the heap of unjudged novels. There were thirty-eight. Then, as if by magic, there were thirty-nine. I actually held my breath as I slipped a copy of *The Thames Barrier* into the pile. It might not sound much to you, but I felt like Tom Cruise in *Mission Impossible*. The inside of my pants couldn't have been more endangered if I'd been hanging upside down from a wire, over a booby-trapped floor.

There was no way I could let myself think about the many, many ways it could all go wrong. For a start, I was assuming that dear Dougy didn't have a list of the books. Then there was the not inconsiderable matter of my photo inside the dust-jacket of *The Thames Barrier*. My fake glasses and beard were a pretty good disguise, but were they good enough? Dougy, let's not forget, was a queen – and one of the things about queens is that we tend to *notice things* . A straight man can wear a beard for twenty years, then shave it off. His straight mates will take about a month before they say "Is there something different about you?" and another six months before they actually work it out. A queen, on the other hand, can gain two pounds, and *his* mates will immediately say, "Ooh, *you're* looking podgy, girl!" Women, ask yourself this: if you get a new hairdo, who spots it first? Your boyfriend (as *if*)? Your girlfriends? Or your gay friend? Thank you. I rest my case.

But I just couldn't worry about any of that. I had to press on. I felt like I'd arrived on the beach at Dunkirk and it was far too late to mince back to the safety of my amphibious landing-craft. Or something.

Thirty-nine books. I wondered how many I could get away with pretending to read each day. If Laura was expecting me to read every one from cover to cover, I was screwed. Then I realised: a precedent had already been set. All the books on the reject pile had Post-Its before page thirty. I could get away with a series of quick reports, and if Laura questioned my incredible speed, I could say I was only doing what others had done before me. She couldn't really argue.

With that thought in mind I got going.

Around lunchtime, something incredibly sweet happened. Lofty came into the study with a pile of sarnies and two mugs of tea.

"How's it goin', son?" he said, plonking down a plateful of paving-slabs.

"Pretty good. Very good, actually."

"Thought you might fancy a bite," he said, shyly shoving the sarnies towards me. "Done a bit of a selection."

"Thanks, Lofty," I said, noticing that his idea of a selection meant cheese with pickle, cheese with tomato or cheese with cheese. "I'm really hungry, actually."

"Good," he smiled. "Man oughta have an appetite."

"Yes," I said, digging into a sandwich. "I'm starting to realise that."

Lofty making lunch for us was weird enough; but, around six o'clock, things got weirder. I'd been hammering away on Laura's Apple Mac (ooh, I suppose they are quite nice, actually), and I'd managed to write ten reports. Considering I hadn't read anything more than a paragraph of each book, plus the notes inside the dust-jackets, it was some of the most creative writing I'd done for ages. Much as I'd wanted to, I'd resisted the temptation to write a glowing report on *The Thames Barrier*. I knew that had to wait until tomorrow, at the very least.

Then I heard someone enter the flat. Assuming it was Laura I put my head down and looked lost in thought. But it wasn't Laura. It was Mick.

He poked his head round the door and I almost levitated with fear.

"Ullo," he said.

"Hi Mick," I replied, suddenly aware that my fingernails had cut through the leather on Laura's two-grand office chair. "I'm just finishing up, here..."

Without warning he came towards me, very fast. I shoved my chair away from the desk and tried to jump up at the same time. The result was that I went twat over beehive and hit my head on the other desk. Dougy's sodding desk.

"You all right?" said Mick, kneeling down beside me and

rubbing my head. "What was that all about?"

"Umm," I replied, realising that I'd completely over-reacted. "I think it was about you catching me with your wife last night."

"Yeah – and I was coming in here to apologise!"

We both started laughing at that. Mick reached out to help me up, and as I stood I suddenly felt faint. My legs buckled. Mick caught me in time and then gently lay me on the floor. I really thought I was about to lose consciousness, when I was jolted awake by the verbal equivalent of a bucket of icy water in the face.

"AHAHAHAHAHAHA!!!!!" screeched an unearthly hag's voice. "I Knew it, I KNEW IT! You saucy little fucking *queen*! Just WAIT till Laura hears about… Oh! OH! Hello, Mick!"

Poor Dougy. If he hadn't been such a gangrenous wound of a human being I would have felt sorry for him. He'd let himself in to the apartment, probably already seething because Laura had told him that she'd asked me to read some books; then he'd marched to the study, hoping to catch me in some minor crime that he could make a song and dance about. And then all his dreams had come true. He'd found me, eyelids fluttering, in the arms of another man. Unfortunately for Dougy, Mick had his back to him, thereby allowing his poisonous pink imagination full rein. Oops-a-daisy, ducky.

- 22 -

Clothes Maketh the Man

I know it's been said before (by Robyn, mostly) but for someone who makes his living from writing about human beings I really don't have much of a grip on the funny little creatures. When I got home the flat was clean, tidy, hoovered; and Paul was standing at the hob. You might want to hear that again. Paul. Was. Standing. At. The. Hob. And he wasn't standing there just to light his joint off the gas. He was *cooking*.

Truly, I thought the knock on the head had affected me.

"What are you doing?" I asked, dumbfounded.

"Avvin' a shit," he replied.

Really, it was all too much. I went and collapsed on the sofa. Then he brought me a drink. Paul. Brought. Me. A – oh, I'm sorry, but.

"Thank you," I said, trying not to faint again when I saw that he'd put a slice of lemon in it. "Paul?"

"Thass me, bub. All day."

"I really hit my head earlier. I got sort of knocked out. Am I, um, dreaming?"

He paused. Stood up. As he headed back to the cooker he grunted one word.

"Cunt."

Ah. I *was* awake.

While we ate Paul's surprisingly nice spaghetti bolognaise (or "me signachure dish" as he'd insisted on calling it, before I found the jar in the bin and pointed out that he wasn't actually called Dolmio), I told him about the day's developments. He jumped around like a kid who'd asked Santa for Scalextric and got a real racing car instead. I do wish I could feel the same excitement at the prospect of danger.

"Fuc-kin' *result!*" he said. "You are set *up!* That poof wanker wunt be no more trouble. Fact."

"I wish I felt that confident."

"Lissen, bub. You got Shorty…"

"Lofty."

"On yur side. You got *her*…"

"Laura."

"Yeh. On yur side, and you got *Mick* on yur side! Fuckinattrick!"

"What? Oh. Hat trick."

"Swot I said, yeh?"

I scratched my chin. No, really, I did. That bloody latex glue was playing havoc with my skin.

"I wish I could believe that," I said. "But you don't know what we're dealing with here. Dougy's not going to take this lying down. I just know it."

"Nah," he replied. "Tellyur what, though."

"What?"

"Might not take it layin' dahn. But I bet he'd take it bendin' over. Eh? Bendin' over? Gettit?"

Later, we did quite a bit of laying down and bending over ourselves. Something strange had happened to Paul. I think that somewhere within his deeply conventional view of the world, moving in with me had changed our relationship from man and mistress to man and wife. Or possibly wife and wife. Or wife, mistress and cat. Honestly, my grip on reality was getting looser than a suicide bomber's bowels.

Dave picked me up next morning. Call me psychic if you must, but somehow I knew that Dave would be picking me up and taking me home *for ever*.

Generally, I like the way the working classes are so shamelessly nosey. You could go to a middle-class dinner party with two black eyes and the word SLUT written on your forehead in cigarette burns, and nobody would be so vulgar as to enquire why. Get on a bus, however, and you could guarantee that within two minutes you'd feel like you were starring in your very own episode of *Trisha*. But sometimes, I admit, such ravenous curiosity can be tiring.

Dave was being tiring.

"So, tell us again, my brother," he said (for some reason I'd been promoted from mere "bro"). "First off Mick nearly catches you plating the missus…"

"Yep," I replied, a bit sharply. This was the third time he'd insisted on me telling the tale. Clearly I hadn't sounded sharp enough,. because he carried on regardless.

"And *then* Ducky – sorry, *Dougy* – nearly catches you plating *her* old man! Ah-ha! Ah-ha-ha-ha! Love it. LOVE it!"

"I was *concussed*," I said, sounding a bit queeny this time.

"Nah, I know, my brother. S'just so fuckin' funny! Oh, I wish I'd seen it! Where's Jeremy Beadle when you need 'im, eh?"

"In a cemetery, I imagine."

"Oh, yeah, right. Poor bastard. Kicked the bucket, didn't he? Here, d'ya reckon he had a little foot to match his little hand?"

"I don't know."

"Would've been a small bucket, eh? Like the ones you get at the seaside."

"Anyway," I laughed, despite my bad mood, "you haven't told me what happened after I left."

"Right, this is how it all went off," he said, settling himself back in his seat and putting the handbrake on. We were stuck at Deptford.

The night before I'd dashed out the door as fast as I could. Mick had tried to make me stay and get a cab but I was dazed, and somehow I'd known that things would be much better for me if I left.

"I get out of the motor with Laura," Dave began. "And I see you walking away – but Laura never. I go to give you a shout but I twig right off you wasn't right. Military training, see? Once a Para, always a Para."

"Thanks," I said, still not believing that this bumper bag of pork scratchings had ever served anywhere more dangerous than a Little Chef. "Good call."

"Pleasure. Anyway, we go indoors and the first thing we hear is someone crying, and going *No, please, I'm sorry...* Laura looks right panicked and she starts rushing towards the study. But me, see, I go straight into combat mode. I grab hold of Laura and put me hand over her mouth, and give her the signal to keep schtumm..."

He made a zipping motion across his lips, the way they do in the movies, presumably just in case I wasn't familiar with the word 'schtumm'. I nodded. I think I might have yawned, too. I'd had a restless night, one way and another.

"So then, right, I'm in full Falklands mode, ain't I? Port Stanley, crossfire, it's all coming back to me...."

Gawd, I thought, and not for the first time. Straight men. They're such bloody drama queens.

"So I press me body against the wall and make me way, inch by inch, towards the study, where the crying's coming from... And me brain, right, I'm like on autopilot, and – swear to God – I reach down for me weapon – and I ain't got one! And I'm thinking all of a sudden, you could be in trouble here, Dave my son."

"Why? What did you think was going on?"

"What?" he said, looking a bit irritated that I'd interrupted his flow.

"Well, sorry, but Dougy had only been in the flat for a minute."

"So?"

"So what did you think was going on?"

"Jeremy," he replied, easing the limousine forward a few feet and adjusting the controls on the air conditioning at the same time. "This world, O brother of mine, is a jungle. It can *wipe you out*. Just like – that!"

"Agh!" I shouted, as Dave illustrated his point by twisting the wheels of the Merc into the path of a cyclist.

"Yeah, you an' all!" he yelled at the poor woman, who actually looked quite nice, for a London cyclist.

"Right," I said. "I get you."

"Dougy could've gone in the flat and found two nasty pieces of shit, with sawn-off shotguns and poor old Lofty tied up in the corner with duct tape. Or worse."

"Of course," I said, wondering what it must be like to think that life really was like *The Sun*. Was it fun? Or was it horribly stressful?

"Anyway," he went on. "I creep along the wall, don't I? I can still hear the sobbing and I know by now it's Dougy. So I take a chance with me own life and I poke me head round the door…"

"And?" I asked, breathlessly. I know it was ridiculous – I knew perfectly well that there were no armed intruders – but Dave had managed to draw me in to his own personal version of *Die Hard*, whatever that would be called. *Fried Lard*, probably.

"And there's bleeding Dougy, on his knees, crying like a little girl, begging Mick not to hit him again!"

"*Again?*"

"Ohhhhh, yes," smiled Dave. "Again."

In fact, apart from Dave re-living his adventures in the Falklands, not a lot *had* happened. Mick had been in a thoroughly bad mood because Dougy had insulted his masculinity, and given him a slap. Dougy had become hysterical. Then Laura and Dave had appeared, and everything was patched up. I imagine there was also an argument between the newly-newlyweds, followed by as hot an evening of passionate make-up sex. Or as passionate as you could manage in a room full of pink ruched curtains and Beanie Babies.

If you thought Laura had been apologetic the day before, you should have seen her when Dave and I got to Coriander Wharf. I won't say she crawled across the kitchen on her belly, but she did hobble towards me with her knees bent, like a hunchbacked geisha.

"Jeremy, I am *so* sorry. I didn't think things could get any worse than yesterday.…"

Something told me to keep quiet, for once.

"And then they did," she said.

"Oh," I laughed good-naturedly. "I think it's just one of those weeks."

"Isn't it though?" she said, bringing me a cup of tea.

"I'll get me own," said Dave, grumpily. We ignored him.

"I really don't know what's up with Dougy at the moment," she went on.

"Time of the mumf?" offered Dave, pouring his tea.

"I've told him straight. Either he gets over this problem he has with you or it's goodbye."

"Did you?" I said. "But then who'd take his...."

"Oh, don't worry. I'm only trying to scare him. I couldn't function without him. But I've ordered him to take a few days off," she went on. "And hopefully, by next week, this will all have calmed down."

"I hope so, too," I lied.

"Anyway, look. I've really got a bitch of a day, now, especially without him to help me. R and J have got all the bloody Children of Courage coming into the studio today. Six wheelchairs, three guide-dogs and two mobile dialysis units are *not* my idea of fun. But I wanted to say thanks."

"To them?"

"No. To you."

"Oh. For what?"

"Well, everything. But mostly for those reports you wrote."

"Oh," I said, using every muscle in my body to keep composed. "The books?"

"Yes. Jeremy, they were absolutely *genius*. Honestly, you should think about taking it up professionally."

"What, writing?"

"Well, no, not *writing*. Report writing."

"Oh. Sorry. Yes, thanks. I'll think about it."

"Don't think about it too long. I need you!"

"For what?"

"To read the rest, of course. Look. I wasn't entirely honest with you yesterday. I really need to find a last book for the new list, and I want something… literary. A bit *challenging*."

"Ah," I said. "I understand."

"So, if you can just work your magic again… That would be fantastic."

Giggles are just like sneezes. When you feel one coming you just can't stop it. I thrust my mouth into the steaming mug of tea, until the pain wiped the smile off my face.

"OK," I said, hoping I hadn't actually burned myself. "Leave it with me."

For the first time since the whole idiotic adventure had started I felt ever-so-slightly confident. I won't say I could taste victory but I could certainly smell the raw ingredients. With Dougy out of the picture for a few days and my rep with Laura at an all-time high I couldn't really go wrong. I knew that he'd be absolutely driven to distraction by the fact that Laura had put a book on the list from my recommendation, but he was far too canny to kick up a stink. He'd just have to put on that eerie grin of his, and bear it.

Lofty went out to "see" his lady-friend at ten-thirty, and I set to work. Before I knew it, I heard his key in the door.

"You ain't never still sitting there?" he said, looking more than a little tousled.

"Yes," I replied. "What time is – gosh! Six o'clock!"

"Yep. I'll make us a brew."

"Thanks."

"Don't mention it," he said, leaving.

"Oh, Lofty?"

"Yuss?"

"You've got lipstick on your collar."

" Ta, Jeremy."

He chuckled and went off humming *Lipstick on Your Collar*, which he continued to hum and sing for the next hour. Hearing a man singing round the house always makes me feel that things are right with the world. I don't know why.

Laura came home just after seven, with Dave in tow, carrying some very shiny shopping bags. The sort that cost more than my actual shopping.

"Hello!" she smiled, at her sunniest. "How was your day? How was dad?"

"Both fine, thanks. We had a nice late breakfast, then he spent most of the day in bed, as usual."

"Oh, dad," she said, suddenly sad. "He's not old enough to be in bed all day."

"No," I replied, trying not to laugh. "But he does love bed. How was *your* day? How were the Children of Courage?"

"God, don't go there. You'd think cerebral palsy would keep them quiet, wouldn't you? Honestly, it should have been called Television Producers of Courage. Nightmare. But the switchboard was jammed with adoring viewers afterwards, so there you go. Job done."

"Good," I said, feeling a little disappointed that Laura was showing this cynical side to her nature. I suddenly realised: it would never have worked out between us.

"Now, Jeremy. I need your opinion."

"They're all here," I beamed, pushing my pile of book-reports across the kitchen table.

"No, not that opinion – we'll get to those. No, this is more important."

More important? What the bloody hell was she talking about?

"Dave," she went on, beckoning at him. Dave put the bags down on the table and grinned at me.

"Right," said Laura, opening a bag that, now I looked, said *Paul Smith*. "Tell me what you think of this. Honestly."

She pulled out an absolutely gorgeous men's suit. It must have cost more money than I got for my last advance.

"Wow. Well, it's fantastic," I said, honestly.

"You really think so?"

"Yes, really. It's manly, and elegant. And obviously expensive, without being spivvy."

"So, if your wife or girlfriend gave it to you you'd be pleased?"

"Pleased? I'd probably have to take her to the bedroom and say thank you immediately."

Dave chuckled fruitily.

"Oh," I went on, feeling myself redden. "I'm so slow sometimes. Yes, I think Mick will be very happy with it."

Dave laughed again.

"Well, I'm glad you think he would," smiled Laura. "But actually, it's for you."

"For *me?*"

"Yes, for you. Or have you changed your opinion?"

"No! But – for me? Why?"

"Oh, for God's sake! After all that's happened this week? I nearly bought you *two*."

"I… don't know what to say."

And for once, I didn't.

"Don't say anything," she said. "In fact, think of it as hush-money. Now, show me those reports."

- 23 -

Don't Forget Your Toothbrush

Needless to say, I hadn't been given a chance to wear the Paul Smith suit myself, because the second I'd shown it to *my* Paul, he'd snatched it and put it on. Well, almost put it on. There was the small matter of him being three inches shorter than me, and three stone heavier.

"Gotta lose some fuckin' weight!" he grizzled, sashaying from the kitchen to the far wall of the living-room and back again. Oh, the honour. I felt like I'd blagged a front-row seat at Sittingbourne Fashion Week.

"Yes, well, it is *my* bloody suit!"

"Yebbut I make it look good, innit?"

"No, Paul. You make it look like the glass slipper, and you're *not* Cinders."

"Sayin' I'm ugly?"

"No. I'm saying you're five-foot seven and fourteen stone, but the suit is meant for someone who's five-ten and eleven stone. Me, in other words."

"Gur," was all he said, suddenly tearing it off as though it were made of nettles, and leaving it in a heap on the floor.

"May I?"

"S'your suit."

"Thank you," I said, slipping it on.

"Yur, bub," he grunted resentfully. "Looks nice."

"Is that all?"

"Pwoppa nice."

"Honestly, you are such a big baby. Look, I promise – once this book gets on the list and the money starts rolling in, I'll buy you a Paul Smith suit of your own. One that fits. OK?"

"Ainchor fuckin' toy boy," he said, getting dressed again in his own togs.

"I never said you were."

"Paul Smiff *bollocks*," he added, as he went in to the bathroom.

God knows how many hours I've spent, ever since I first met Paul at that hole in the road, fantasising about having a proper life with him. But fantasies, at the risk of sounding obvious, aren't real. There we were, after just two nights as a couple, and I was going crazy. Now that we were "together", Paul suddenly seemed to be invading my space. In the past he'd been outside my life and I'd wanted him in; but now he *was* well and truly in, I wanted out. Did I ever tell you? I'm a bit gay.

However, I wasn't the only one feeling pressured by the new set-up. After we'd eaten (yes, I was back in the kitchen. Paul couldn't stretch to two signature dishes), and I'd told him about the latest developments, he'd announced he was going out on the lash with some of his mates. I felt quite guilty at how glad I was to get rid of him for the evening.

When I raised Robyn on the webcam I was shocked. She was wearing a dress. A really crafty little evening number that managed not to put a foot wrong in the sartorial minefield between sexy, smart and sluttish. She looked stunning, like a trophy wife with a degree in astrophysics.

"Blimey," I said. "Where are *you* off to?"

"Dinner, darling."

"In Swindon?"

"People do *eat* in Swindon."

"Yes," I said. "But only when they can walk at the same time."

"Actually, we have a Michelin starred restaurant. And I'm working my way through the menu. The puddings are divine."

"Hmm. So I can see. And they say black is forgiving…"

"Darling, are you just going to be bitchy? Because I'm expecting a car."

"A car? Ooh, get you!"

"Yes, darling. And *mine* doesn't belong to my boss."

"Sorry, Robby. You look fab. So it's going well with Mr Giraffe then?"

"He's asked me to move in with him and I'm probably going to say yes. What does that say?"

"It says I think you've been abducted by aliens and replaced with a lookalike."

"I suppose I have, in a way. I'm in love."

"I do hope you feel the same way when they bring out the anal probes."

"Oh, they won't be any problem for me, darling. I'll send those aliens home feeling *very* confused. Anyway, what's new at your end?"

"Well, in that strange way our lives have, Paul's moved in with *me*."

"Has he?"

"Yes."

I heard a car horn in the background.

"Darling, listen, there's my car. I'll have to process that news later. But quick – tell me about the book! Did you slip it under the radar?"

So I told her, as briefly as I could. All the advice she could manage, in between a final go with her lippy and spritzing herself with perfume was:

"I'm proud of you, darling. But please. *Don't* underestimate Dougy? Mwah!"

I once found myself playing proper roulette in a proper casino. I didn't have any more money then than I have now, but I was pissed and excited and I was in Cannes (I'd managed to blag a film festival freebie from a friend in magazines) and I'd found out that you can get gambling chips on Visa. Anyway, when you're playing proper roulette in a proper casino and you're totally broke to start off with, there's this funny thing that happens between placing your bet and waiting for the ball to stop bouncing around. You'd think you'd be frantically anxious, wouldn't you? But you're not. For those few seconds you feel free. You *totally* stop giving a toss. It's only when the ball settles down that you want to die. Or not. Though, usually, to be honest, you do. At least, I did – and that was before I got my Visa bill.

Anyway, that was how my evening went: like I was hypnotised by the roulette ball. I was going to think about the future, but I didn't. I watched the DVD of *Brief Encounter*, got pissed, and stroked Dolly who, for some reason best known to cats, was in the mood for love. I didn't even notice that Paul hadn't come home.

However, when I awoke next morning to an empty bed, I *did* notice that Paul hadn't come home. My first instinct was to phone him, but then I realised I wasn't quite ready to become a proper wife and start nagging. Not after two days. So I texted.

Dave and I were arriving at Cinnamon Wharf when Paul finally replied.

"Got 2 pissed. L8rs."

Ah, I thought, the poetry of love. Was that Sonnet 17? Or 21?

Laura actually kissed me when I walked into the flat. That was a bit disconcerting, because both Lofty *and* Mick were in the kitchen.

"I can't believe you found this!" she said.

"Found what?" I replied, silently praying to God, Loki, Vishnu, Allah and, just in case, L. Ron Hubbard.

"*The Thames Barrier,*" she said, waving my book in the air. "I've never even *heard* of Jeremy Canty!"

"No… Me neither."

"Well," she went on. "I stayed up half the night reading it. And it's *perfect* for my gap."

"Your gap?"

Dave guffawed dirtily.

"Shut up, Dave. Yes, you know. My gap in the *list*. Something a bit literary. A bit…"

"Challenging?"

"Exactly! God, I'm so relieved! You must be psychic!"

She actually sighed.

"Good," I said, trying not to faint. "Glad I could help."

"Honestly, Jeremy, you've been so much more than a help. Would you like another suit, or something else?"

"Oh. Hahah! One's enough."

"Get some new strides out of her, son," said Lofty.

"Look," said Laura, gathering her things together. "I'm in a hurry, as usual. But listen."

"Fire away."

"Are you free tomorrow afternoon?"

"Um…" I said, remembering to stay in character and look at Lofty for approval.

"Don't you worry about me, son," he answered, winking at me lewdly. "I'll find a bit of entertainment."

"Yes," I replied. "If he says so."

"Oh… *Jeremy*," she sighed. "Look, it's our summer staff party tomorrow. We're having a do. On a boat. Will you come? I want R 'n' J to meet you."

"Me?"

"Yes," she laughed. "You!"

"But why?"

"Let's just say you're part of my evil master-plan," she smirked.

I looked nervously at Mick.

"Don't look at me!" he laughed, raising his hands.

"So, will you come?" Laura went on.

"Yes, yes. Of course I will. Thank you."

"Fantastic. It's at lunchtime. R 'n' J have got to do the National TV Awards in the evening."

"Oh, yes. I think I saw that somewhere."

"I'll get Dave to collect you."

"Where's the boat setting off from?"

"There's a sort of jetty thing next to Hungerford Bridge."

"Don't bother Dave, then. I can walk from here."

"Ta, my bro," said Fat Dave. "Nice to know someone cares. Right, milady. Where to this morning?"

"Actually, Dave" said Laura. "Mick's driving me in."

"Oh," he replied, looking worried. "Right."

"Don't worry, mate," said Mick. "It'll only be today. Won't take me long to remember what she's like when you get her in the passenger seat."

"Hur-hur-hur," went Dave.

"*Dave!* " scolded Laura. "Please! We're not in a bloody Carry On film!"

"Oop, sorry," he replied, exchanging a wink with Mick. I realised yet again that, even if I'd somehow managed to give Laura a better ride than a bobsleigh on cobbles with dildos for seats, I could never have passed for straight. The only way I could safely get away with winking at a straight bloke is if he was in a wheelchair with flat tyres.

"All set then, son," said Lofty when everybody had gone. "Looks like it'll all work out."

"I wish I felt that confident."

"What? What can go wrong now?"

"Well," I said. "To put it in racing terms, this is the Grand National, not the Derby. I might be ahead of the field for now, but I've still got Beecher's Brook. And we all know what that can be like."

"Beecher's Brook? You're well past that. You're in the final furlong!"

"No, I'm not. There's Dougy for starters."

"Nah. He won't be no trouble. Wouldn't dare bite the hand that feeds him. Don't you worry about that poof. No offence, like."

"None taken. But – OK – say it all goes according to plan? The second my book gets on the list – *if* it does – I'll be exposed as a fraud!"

"So?"

"What do you mean, *so?* It'll be a disaster!"

"Fuckin 'ell. You read too many books, you do. Why will it be a disaster? What've you done wrong?"

"Errrrr… Assumed a false identity? Used unfair methods to get my book on the list? Shall I go on?"

"Garrr, button it. You need to spend a bit more time with proper villains, son. Far as I can see you ain't broken no laws."

"It's not the law I'm worried about. In case you haven't noticed, the newspapers don't only write stories about people who've broken the bloody law!"

"Alright, alright. Keep your hair on. You're forgetting summink."

"What?"

"*I'm* in on it, ain't I? So if it all kicks off, I'll tell her the lot. She won't wanna drag her dear old dad into it, will she? I tell ya, Jeremy, you're home free. 'Sides. Even if it all went belly-up, you know what they say."

"Not really. But I'm sure you're about to tell me."

"All publicity is *good* publicity."

If I'd been in the market for an old and slightly decrepit slave, Lofty would have fitted the bill perfectly that day. He was so thrilled that I'd played my part in getting Laura back together with Mick that I really think he would have cleaned my boots if I'd asked. It was terribly touching, and it made me realise how families can *work*. Lofty loved Mick like the son he'd never had. I wasn't sure who'd missed him more: Lofty or his daughter. Whatever, it had all worked out fine for them. For them.

As I sat on the bus to Woolwich all I could do was hope that my plans worked out as well. Dave had called at five, apologetic but very happy, because Laura and Mick had, indeed, already argued, and he was back in work.

Paul still wasn't there when I got home. I know I said I was glad for the break, but that was earlier. Now I was feeling a bit neglected. To distract myself I called Prue.

"Oh," she said. "*There* you are."

"Yes. Here I am."

"You know we haven't actually spoken since I took you to lunch?"

"Yes," I said, biting my lip to stop myself saying sorry. "Sorry."

"OK," she sighed, in that bloody voice she does, like she's my wife, forgiving me for going with a hooker. "So what's happened?"

"A *lot*," I replied, knowing that would get her interest.

Prue, it turned out, had also been invited to the boat-party next day.

"Jeremy, this is so exciting!" she squealed. "My plan is working out! It feels like… Like I'm having a baby!"

"Well, let's make sure it doesn't run before it can walk, eh?"

"Yes, yes, you're right We need a new plan. What do we do if it all goes tits-up?"

"What do we do? I don't know about you, Prue, but I'll *run*. And I'll keep running till I reach Kazakhstan."

"OK, right, OK. But, um, OK. What will *I* do?"

"You?"

"Yes, Jeremy. Me. It's not *all* about you."

I took the phone away from my mouth and sighed lividly.

"Jeremy? Are you there?" she whined, so I counted to ten. Then I realised: she had a good point. She was one of London's top PRs, and *she* had made this whole deception possible. This could ruin her.

"Fuck, Prue. You're right. I really hadn't thought…"

"That's OK. I *have*. If it all goes horribly wrong, we re-boot."

"Re-boot? Re-boot what?"

"The story. You'll have to say that it was all *your* doing. That you were fooling *me* before you were fooling Laura. Do you see what I mean?"

"Yes, yes, I do. "

"I do love you, Jeremy, but I couldn't let this ruin both of us, could I?"

"No," I replied, feeling a bit detached and floaty. "Of course not."

I was still trying to find the right answer when I heard Paul's key in the door. Yes, of course I'd already given him a key.

"OK, Prue," I said hurriedly. "You're absolutely right. We'll play it that way. Look, I've got to go. See you tomorrow."

I put the phone down as Paul slunk into the room. He held his chin to his chest and his electric blue eyes darted back and forth beneath his brows, like a fox that wasn't quite sure if it was out of danger.

"Hello, love," I said, knowing that something bad was coming, but feeling strangely calm about it. "You look like you've been caught out."

"Urr. Wanna lager."

Of course, I knew the truth. He had been caught out. What I

wouldn't learn until the next day, was quite how badly. But we'll come to that.

There was no point trying to play happy families. I was angry.

"Shall we get this out of the way?" I asked him, as he guzzled his third lager in as many minutes.

"What? Get what?"

"Come on, Paul. You said you were going out in Woolwich last night."

"Yerrawas."

"But you couldn't come home?"

"Tollja bub. Too pissed."

"Too pissed to walk a mile?"

"Ad me lorry, innit?" he said, pretending to concentrate on rolling himself a joint, but giving it all away by frantically bouncing his foot up and down on the spot.

"Paul," I said. "I know you don't like to think so, but you're a bloody useless liar. Why don't you tell me what you did last night?"

"Wennout."

"Yes, I know. But you didn't go out with your mates in Woolwich. Did you?"

"Shuttup, Jeremy! Always gotta know evryfink! Shuttup!"

"No, Paul. Just for once, I don't think I will shut up. Tell me what you did last night. I already know, but I want you to tell me."

When he did actually look at me there were tears in his eyes.

"Met a bloke, awight?"

"For sex."

"Yeah, for sex!"

"OK…"

"Dunt fuckin' OK me, cunt? Fuckin' gay now, yeah?"

"You're *gay* now? What does *that* mean?"

"You know what it means, Jeremy. S'all different."

"What is wrong with you, Paul? When you're with your wife, you want to be with me. Now you're with me, you want to be somewhere else. Most of the time you're stoned out of your box, or drunk, or whatever. Why? Why can't you make up your fucking mind? Why can't you just be *inside* your life?"

I looked at him for a minute, or maybe more. I really wasn't angry. I was disappointed. I know that makes me sound like a parent, but there's a good reason. Because I suddenly realised the truth about why I loved him. I wasn't his mistress. I was his mum.

He stood up, and started gathering his things. They didn't amount to much. Just a pack of Rizlas, a bag of grass and two last lagers. He hadn't even brought a toothbrush.

"Fick fuckin' cunt," he said, trying his best to cover the fact that he had tears rolling down his cheeks. "I'm all fucked up, innit? Fuckin' fucked *up*…"

- 24 -

Happy Now?

I cried myself to sleep that night, but not really because he'd gone. I'd never expected it to last beyond that first afternoon, when I'd driven my car into that hole in the road. I cried because love is the most fucked-up thing in this whole fucked-up life. Why are we born with this need to love unconditionally, only to have it disappoint us again and again? It's not just romantic love, either. How many parents love their babies to the point of madness, only to end up with a selfish little shit-bag who breaks their hearts? Plenty. Love is a trick played on us by Mother Nature, to make us propagate the species. And when she's finished with us, she couldn't care less. We've done her work and she's on to the next poor sucker.

Anyway, I dried my eyes and got myself ready for the big day. Ooh, and I did look *fab* in my new suit!

Lofty obviously held the same opinion, because he couldn't stop dusting me down with his clothes-brush as I prepared to leave for the party.

"Lofty, if you brush me one more time I'll catch fire."

"Just want you to look nice for the do, son," he said, flicking at my collar for the fourteenth time. "Big day."

"Yes," I said. "Big day."

"You'll be alright, Jeremy. Keep your nerve. It's all about keepin' your nerve. That's it. That's the secret."

"Lofty?"

"Yes, boy?"

"I've been meaning to ask. What *was* that about? That day in the betting shop?"

"Oh, that. Just sussing you out, weren't I?"

"So you never knew that guy? The one you spoke to?"

"That old bastard? Course I never! Wanted you to think I was a bit senile, didn't I?"

"But why?"

"Why?" he laughed. "Cos it suited me purposes."

"But why?" I asked again, stupidly.

He gave one of his chuckles and put his hands on my shoulders.

"Jeremy," he said. "I know you reckon you're a criminal mastermind. But you ain't. Now, go on. Piss off out of it. I've got a date, and so have you. Be lucky."

"Thanks, Lofty."

"Don't mention it."

And then, as The Crystals once sang, He Kissed Me. On one cheek. Just like I'd always wanted my own dad to do.

Never having had one myself, I've always wondered what the female orgasm is like. We all know that boys and girls are different when it comes to this simple human moment, but it would be so nice to walk in someone else's shoes for a night. Well, knickers.

Anyway, when a boy comes it's a bit like the last bit of Beethoven's Ninth. It's dee-dum, dee-dum, dee-dum, dee dum, dum dum. Didi dum-dum-dum. Dum…. DUMMMMMM!!!!

Actually that could have been the end of any number of symphonies, which probably explains why they've mostly been written by men. When a girl comes, on the other hand, I've always imagined it to be more like riding on a roller-coaster. It's "up, up, up – tummy over, SQUEAL!" and "up, up, up, tummy over, SQUEAL!" Or as Tinky-Winky used to say: "Again, again!"

Well, that's how I imagine it. There's a thread about it on the forum section of my website, if you want to tell me otherwise.

Anyway. As I walked down the gangplank to the party boat, I felt like I might be having a girly moment. My insides were churning around like a machine-load of dirty smalls (no, not the well-known gangsta rapper), and it wasn't all that pleasant. But every time the washing hit the top of the drum, I positively gasped with pleasure. I was about to *meet* Richard and Judy!

I had to laugh when I reached the end of the gangplank. The big goon on the door was the same one who'd been on duty that day when I'd gone to Saint Bernadette and dragged Gloomy Prue out from the Woman of the Year lunch. He hadn't grown any less gorgeous.

"Hello, sir. Can I have your name, please?"

"Robson," I said, *just* managing to stop myself saying 'Canty'. "Jeremy Robson."

As he scanned his clipboard, his lips moved. Honestly, is there *anything* sexier than a meathead trying to read?

"This way, please, Mister Robson," he smiled, lifting the rope. And I was in.

To be honest I thought it was a bit naff, having a do on one of those Thames party boats. I mean, be honest, they're no more than stretch limos with life belts. At least they'd spent a bit of money tricking it out with flowers and a few acres of tulle. And, outside of a dream, I'd never *seen* so much champagne.

It was a very hot day and I stood there for a few moments, anxiously pressing at my beard, making sure it wasn't about to peel off. The bloody thing itched so much I felt like I'd caught crabs off Captain Birds Eye.

I scanned the crowd and realised I didn't know a soul. I didn't even *recognise* a soul, which was a bit disappointing. I'd expected Joan Collins, at the very least; but I couldn't even see Richard. Or Judy.

One of my skills, apart from writing novels that don't sell, is grabbing a lot of free drink, very quickly. I'd barely gone ten yards and already I was on my third glass of sparkling wine. (Yes, I was wrong about the champagne.) A muscley-faced boy with dirty eyes smiled at me and I smiled back. He smiled again, and I was about to try chatting him up, when an arm snaked around my waist, and someone planted a kiss on my cheek.

"Hello, you little star!" winked Prue, kissing me again, which made the dirty-eyed boy turn away in disgust. "You made it, then?"

"Hi, Prue! Yes, I made it. You look…."

Ermm… How *did* she look? Oh, I don't know. Prue's dress sense drains my imagination.

"You look fab," I said. It was the best I could manage, considering she looked like a Christmas cracker with its own credit card.

"And look at *you*, in your posh suit!"

"Paul Smith."

"Laura really *does* like you," she smiled.

"Hmm. That can still change. I'm bloody terrified."

"Well, *don't* be terrified," she said, suddenly adopting a PR smile. "Because they're coming our way."

I followed her eyes and saw why she'd adopted the fake smile. The crowd was parting, like corn beneath a helicopter, and the Great Ones themselves were heading straight for us. Well, not really "us". Me.

I'm not proud of this, but it's not like I've held back so far, so I'll tell you. Guess what I did when Judy held out her hand to me? Go on, guess. What was that you said? No, I didn't wee myself. Go to the back of the class. What? No, I didn't throw up on her shoes, either. Eh? What did you say? Oh, well done! Ten out of ten! Yes, that's right! I curtsied. I CURTSIED, like a dopey debutante.

It wouldn't have been too bad (well…) apart from two things: (a) as I curtsied I somehow lost all my energy and collapsed like a failed soufflé at her feet; and (b) Dougy and Adam were standing right behind her, sniggering. To be fair, only Dougy was sniggering. Adam gave me a sympathetic look with his dreamy brown eyes.

As it happens, it was a brilliant stroke. If anyone did piss themselves it was Judy, who became semi-hysterical with giggles, for which I instantly forgave her because she tried so very hard to stop herself.

Richard gallantly reached out his hand to help me up.

"Excuse the missus," he said with a twinkle, shooting one of his mock-angry looks at Judy. "She's always like this."

"Specially when men *curtsy* to her," chipped in Dougy. It could have been funny, but he spat it with such venom that nobody laughed. In fact, it made Judy stop. Oh, it was a lovely moment. One for the album.

"Anyway," said Laura, whom I hadn't noticed until then. "As I was saying, this is the wonderful Jeremy. The man who's turned my life around!"

"Lovely to meet you," said Judy, holding out her hand – then snatching it back jokily. "You're not going to do it again, are you?"

"I promise. Sorry. I feel such a fool. I think I thought I was meeting the Queen Mother."

"Oh," said Judy. "Not sure if that's a good thing."

"God!" I started burbling. "No, I didn't mean…"

"Actually, love," Richard said to her smoothly. "If you could see yourself, you'd think it was a compliment."

"What? What?"

"Well, your slap's run a bit," he went on, turning up the twinkles so much he looked like the Christmas window of a Pound Shop.

"Oh, dear," she said. "Is it bad?"

"Like two crows on a windscreen, my love."

Now, I don't know if you've ever met any celebrities, but I have. I've met friendly ones and unfriendly ones. The friendly ones, strangely enough, are the problem. It's a bit like teachers at school. The unfriendly ones let you know from day one that they hate you. They are there to teach, you are there to learn, and they have no interest whatever in being your mate. The friendly ones, on the other hand, come on like they love you. Like they're just one of the kids. But the *second* you cross them they pull rank, and suddenly you're standing outside the headmaster's office, knees knocking, and still not sure what went wrong. All you did was take the piss out of a *mate*. Isn't that what mates do? No, apparently not. And it's just the same with friendly celebs. One minute you're snorting gak together in the ladies' loos, and it's giggle, giggle, I *love you!* Then, thinking she's your new best friend, you make a joke about her ex-husband the film star and what he did with the nanny… and you're in Siberia without an overcoat, never mind another line of charlie.

Where was I? Oh, yes. Crows on a windscreen. So Richard made the joke. It was a good joke. But then there was this frozen moment, like a scene in *The Matrix,* only camper. Nobody quite dared to laugh. Until… Judy laughed!

"You are a bastard," she went, slapping Richard (quite hard, I couldn't help noticing). "Isn't he, Jeremy?"

"Oh, well," I stuttered, thinking don't drag *me* into your domestics, love. "He's always been a perfect gentleman to me!"

Everybody laughed at that, thank God. Even Dougy. Adam, standing just behind him, actually gave me a thumbs-up.

"No wonder Laura wants you to come and work for us," she went on.

"Does she?" I replied, genuinely amazed, and looking at Laura. I hadn't realised this was what she meant when she said I was part of her evil master-plan.

"If you would," Laura smiled. "I think you're wasted where you are."

"Wasted?" I said. "I wouldn't say that looking after your… Ow!"

I wheeled round to see who'd just dug me in the ribs. It was Prue.

"I've been telling him that for years, Laura," she butted in, so smoothly that I finally understood: she really *was* good at her job. "But he never listens."

"Well," said Laura, looking me straight in the eye. "I hope he listens this time. Because television needs more Jeremy Robsons. Bright, passionate and most of all, *honest*."

"Here, here," said Richard, passing his glass to an anonymous assistant. I wondered why. Then I realised: he needed both hands free to applaud.

A moment later, everybody was clapping. I'm not really sure if they were clapping me, or the general idea of honesty, or simply copying Richard. But I tell you what: getting applauded feels *great*.

"Right, then. I'd better go and scrape these dead crows off my face," said Judy, poking Richard in his enviably flat tummy. Ooh, it was just like the telly! "Lovely to meet you, Jeremy. Can't wait to see you at work."

"Yes," I said, as she headed for the nearest powder room. "Me neither!"

"And remember" she grinned, giving me a professional little wave before she disappeared into the crowd, "it's a *bow*, not a curtsy!" You know, apart from the fact that Judy's teeth were perfect, it really *was* like meeting the Queen Mum.

"*That* went well," said Prue, when the whole entourage had moved off as a single entity, like a showbiz Portuguese Man-o'-War.

"Did it?"

"Errr, hello? You charm Judy; you charm Richard, and then their producer offers you a job. In front of ten people! Apart from a contract written in blood, what more could you want?"

"I don't want more, Prue. I want *less*. I just want *The Thames Barrier* on the list."

"But you've already done that! This, as we say in the trade, is gravy."

"I don't want gravy. I'll settle for the plain grilled steak. Can't you understand? How could I possibly have my novel on the list *and* work for Richard and Judy? Can you imagine? Trying to keep both identities going? This is real life, Prue – not Mrs bloody Doubtfire!"

"You know your problem, Jeremy?" she said, swiping a glass of bubbles from a passing Slovakian. "You're earthbound. Half the people on this planet are nine parts bullshit and one part Superglue. Would Jeffrey Archer worry about this sort of crap? No. Would any politician, come to that? Or..."

"Prue," I interrupted, before I lost my temper. "Can we leave it? I need to find a loo."

"All right, Mister Grumpy. And while you're there?"

"*What*?"

"Stick your beard back down. It's peeling off."

Another thing I hate about those party boats: the tiny loos. It's like having a poo in a wardrobe. When you're sitting down your knees bang on the door. When you lean forward to wipe, your head bangs on the door. And when you try to pull your knickers up, *everything* bangs on the bloody door. You sound like someone break-dancing in a coffin.

Anyway, I hadn't reached the standing-up stage. I think the drama of the last half hour had got to me, and I sat there for ages, not trusting my bum. The ladies' was the other side of the paper-thin plywood (*another* thing I hate about the loos on party boats – they're about as private as Jodie Marsh's lady-garden), so I got to listen to a procession of drunken women rabbitting on about men, work, cellulite, the usual. Then, just as I was deciding that I had to be the master of my botty, despite its skittish mood, two girls crashed into the cubicle behind mine, and immediately started cutting up lines of gak. Except it wasn't two girls. It was one girl and a bitch. Dougy.

"Hurry up with that," I heard him say. "I'm gagging."

"You could always bring your own," the girl said, dryly, chopping away frantically.

"Yes, well, sorry. I used all mine last night, and funnily enough I've not had a chance to call my dealer today."

"You are in such an arsey mood lately," she said, as she finished chopping. "There you go. You first."

"Sorry," said Dougy, nosing down what sounded like half a gram of gear. "It's that little fucker Jeremy. I want him to *die*."

"Aww, he seems sweet. Pass me that straw."

"Can't you roll a note? I don't like to share my straw. Germs."

"Dougy, we're snorting it off a bloody toilet! Stop being a wanker."

"Please don't tell me Jeremy's got *you* fooled as well," he said, bitterly. "I thought you were smarter than that. You know he's selected the last book on the new list?"

"No he hasn't. Laura selects all the books."

"Yes, um, OK. She does. But he helped her out."

"So? You help her out, don't you?"

"Yes," he said, getting a bit edgy on the coke. "But I'm not the fucking home *help*."

"I never know *what* you are, exactly. Shall we go back?"

"Not yet," said Dougy greedily. "Do us another one, hen."

"Christ, I only brought one wrap!"

"Go on, hen. chop us another and I'll tell you all about last night."

"Oh, yeah, last night. When you necked all the gear you were saving for today?"

"Precisely."

"OK. It'd better be good."

"Ooh, it *was*."

"You talk," she said, starting to chop again. "I'll do the work."

"Well! Adam dropped me off at Laura's the other day…"

"He's such a dreamboat. You're so lucky."

"Yes, aren't I, anyway, he dropped me off and there was this lorry outside Coriander Wharf. And there was this lorry driver. Well, honey, he was like a sort of chav version of Elvis…"

"Is that good?"

"Better than that, love. He had Paul Newman's eyes."

"Right now I'm getting sort of a freaky Celebrity Picasso."

"Will you shut up? He was fucking *gorgeous*."

You know I said I wasn't sure if I was going to poo or not? Well, I did. Right then.

"Carry on," said the girl. "Me *first*, this time."

"So I gave him the eye, and guess what he did?"

"Don't know," she said, in between snorts.

"Gave me the finger!"

"You're *such* a natural, Douglas. You radiate love."

"No, but listen to this. Two nights ago I was leaving Laura's – and there was his lorry, right outside the door."

"He didn't…"

"Oh, yes he *did*!" sniggered Dougy. "And then he did *again*! Last night! Only this time we had a threesome!"

"A threesome. You are such a greedy queen! Give me that bloody straw!"

"Too late!" he cackled, with one huge sniff. "All gone! Aha-hahah!"

He was right. It was too late. It was too late for everything.

As I stumbled out of the bog, Richard was waiting there at the front of the queue.

"You OK, mate?" he asked, in that man-of-the-people voice of his.

"Yes thanks. Fine. Sorry if you've been waiting. Nervous tummy."

He squeezed my shoulder and stepped into the coffin-bog. "See you next week."

"Yes," I mumbled. "Lovely."

As I staggered away my hearing was muffled by shock. Every sound seemed to be coming from inside a tin tunnel, lined with a duvet. But I still managed to hear Richard from the loo, clear as a bell.

"Jesus *Christ!*" he said, trying not to gag. "Thanks for the *warning!*"

Perfect. My humiliation was complete. I'd gassed Richard Madeley.

Not only deaf, but almost blind with grief and humiliation, I made my way to the exit; but the gorgeous goon blocked my path.

"Can't go that way, sir."

"But I want to get off!"

"Might be a problem for the next few minutes," he said, stepping to one side.

I looked through the window, or porthole, or whatever they're bloody called. I hadn't taken account of the fact that we were in the middle of the river. What with one excitement and another I hadn't noticed that we'd actually set sail, or whatever it is that horrible party-boats do. Chugged off?

"Oh," I sighed. "Right. How long?"

"Five minutes."

"OK, thanks. I'll, um. I'll…"

"*Jeremy!*" said the very last voice on earth I wanted to hear. "*There* you are!"

And there *he* was. Dougy. All coked up and ready to go. And you know what I did? I smiled. You probably think I'm a spineless excuse for a man because I didn't pick up the nearest fire extinguisher and mash his handsome face into baby-food, but let me ask you this: have you ever really been – really, properly been – in a state of shock? It had only happened to me once before, when I got mugged at knifepoint by a gang of youths. Believe me, when it happens, you don't think that clearly.

"I've not had a *minute* to congratulate you!" he went on. Cocaine and booze had made him sound even more like a bitter Morningside spinster than usual. "Welcome! Welcome to our happy little family."

"Er, thanks. Thank you."

"Oh, don't mention it. Come and talk to me. Come on. I don't bite. Unless you ask! Ahahahah!"

And, like a rabbit hypnotised by a snake, I followed the evil shitbag.

Somehow or other he'd managed to find a private space, behind the wheelhouse, or the bridge, or whatever it was. It was a little room about six by eight. I suppose it had a purpose other than letting evil coked-up shitbags have conversations in private, but I don't know what it might have been.

"Ssssoooo," he hissed, chopping up two fat lines of gak (the gak he'd lied about not possessing) on a tiny Formica table. "Things seem to be working out *just* as planned…"

"Planned?"

"Oh, come on, honey. No need to be coy any more. Have some of this and tell Auntie Dougy *everything*."

"Actually, I don't take drugs," I said.

"Suit yourself," he said, twisting his torso over the coke. He came up, throwing his head back theatrically. "But it really doesn't matter any more. I know another pro when I meet one, hen. *Respec*, as the niggers say."

"Dougy," I said. "I'm sorry, but I really don't know what you're talking about. And if you don't mind, I'd like to get some air. I don't feel very well."

"Aww, no. Poor baby. I can see that. You're sweating. Is that *fear*?"

"Yes. I've never liked boats."

"Hmm. If you're not going to…"

"Be my guest."

"Yes," he said, hoovering up the other line. "In fact. You're *very* sweaty…"

He stared at me intently. He'd spotted something. A weakness. His eyes narrowed, and suddenly I realised. I felt my hand going to my chin, but it was far too late. He'd already pounced.

"Ahhahahahaha!!" he went, in a new, extra-horrible version of his cackle. It sounded like a Scottish Kenneth Williams being buggered by the Devil. My fake beard fluttered in his claw, like the pathetic wing of a baby bird. I was utterly, utterly frozen.

His eyes glittered: beautiful yet dead as glass, as he looked at me for a second. Then he cocked his head. I could almost see his drug-enhanced brain making a million pitiless calculations a second. Meanwhile, the best I could manage was to keep breathing and await the inevitable.

"I knew it. I fucking KNEW it! I knew I'd seen you some-where! Jeremy Canty. You're Jeremy cunting *Canty*...."

It could have been worse. At least I'd already been to the loo.

"Yes," I whispered. "I am. Happy now?"

"Ohhhh, no," he hissed. "I'm not happy at *all*. But honey, let me tell you. I'm a lot happier than *you'll* ever be. Ever, ever, *ever* again."

- 25 -

Man of the Weld

Along with every other drama queen on this planet, I've had lots of moments in my life when I've contemplated suicide, but that afternoon was the first time I'd ever *really* wished I was dead. Heartbreak, humiliation, ruin and booze are a lot to take all at the same time. Oh, yes, I knew it was all my own fault; but knowing that something's all your own fault never quite cheers you up, does it?

Paul's betrayal was the hardest thing. Yes, OK, I know I said he was getting on my tits, but I never said I didn't *love* him, did I? I lay on my bed, swigging straight from the bottle, and crying into the Ben Sherman he'd left in the washing basket. It stank of dirt, diesel and most of all, *him*; and I knew I would never, ever wash it.

The next thing I remember, Paul was sitting on the bed, tugging at the shirt.

"Urr," he said, guiltily. "Ditn't wanna wake you up. Come for me Ben."

"*Who?*" I said, too pissed and strung-out to focus.

"Me shirt. Gotta have me shirt, innit?"

"Fuck off. I'm keeping this shirt. It's all I've got left."

"Come on, bub, gissit. She'll only give me grief."

"Who's 'she'? Dougy?"

I wasn't so pissed that I didn't see him turn crimson.

"The missus," he said.

"Oh, so we're *straight* today, are we?"

He looked at me, and I realised he was sober, for the first time since I'd known him.

"Always was, Jeremy."

"Then what the fuck have the last three months been about, Paul?",

He put his hand on my shoulder. Yet again I couldn't help noticing how beautiful it was, just like every last bit of him.

"I was curious," he said. "Sorry."

"*Curious?* Is that the best you can manage? I'm not some rat in a laboratory! I'm a *person*!"

"Chill pill, Jeremy. It was *you* what chatted me up. 'Member?"

He was right. Again, and for the very last time.

"Take your bloody shirt and piss off," I said, bitterly. "It needs a good wash, but I'm sure the missus will be happy to oblige."

He took the shirt and said nothing. Then he turned away and went to the door.

"Paul?" I said, feeling a bit more clear-headed. "Tell me something."

"What?"

"Why did you do that with Dougy?"

The door was half open, and for a second, I thought he'd run.

"Tell me," I said. "You owe me that."

"Wanted to test meself, innit?"

"In what way?"

"Cummun, Jeremy. You're a man of the weld."

"I'm not, Paul. I'm really, really not. Please. Tell me."

He looked at me, puzzled that I didn't understand.

"Cos he's double 'ansome, innit? Wanted to know."

And, at bloody last, I got it.

"You mean you wanted to have sex with another perfect-looking man? And that would tell you if you were gay or not?"

He looked at the floor, and suddenly I felt calm.

"Ah, Paul. There I was, thinking you'd understood from the start. Being gay isn't about your cock. It's about your heart."

He shifted from foot to foot, still not able to meet my eye.

"I know it's over, love," I went on. "But answer me one last thing. Why did you go back for the threesome with Dougy and Adam?"

"Oo?"

"Adam? Dougy's other half? About six foot? Jet black hair, built like a tank, looks like a better-looking version of Alec Baldwin?"

Paul looked utterly bemused.

"Nope."

"Come on, Paul. Don't lie to me now. There's no point."

"Ain't lyin'. There *was* annuvver geezer, yur. Ugly ginger cunt. Fuckin' munter. That Dougy aksed me if I'd do it a favour. And it wun't called Adam."

"Really?" I said, sitting up. "What *was* he called?"

"Andrew," said Paul. "S'all I know. Gunna fuck off now."

"No, no, wait!" I said, leaping off the bed, feeling more sober than I had in years. "Wait! One second!"

I belted into the living room, grabbed the book from my coffee table, and rushed back to Paul as he stood in the jamb of my front door.

"Was this him?" I asked, barely able to breathe. I held out the book. He snatched the copy of *In Tooth and Claw* from my hand and looked at the photo on the back.

"Thassim. Andrew Goodman. Nuvver fuckin' writer, izzit? You *all* queer, or what?"

Anybody in the midst of losing a battle would wish for reinforcements; but Paul had handed me a nuclear weapon, and it was so terrifyingly powerful I couldn't think what to do with it. I just sat there on the bed, frozen. My thoughts weren't the ones I should have been thinking. All I could say to myself, over and over again, was "Of course, of course, of COURSE! It all makes sense!" And "Andrew Goodman! That bastard! And he's *married!*" And "Wait till I tell Robyn about this!"

Just when I'd thought it was all over, the battle was still to be won.

If there's one character in this story who's always been utterly reliable, I think you know who it would be. Yep: Dolly. As I sat staring into space like a rabbit on Valium, Dolly showed the spirit of the woman she was named after. For reasons I don't understand to this day (apart from the fact that cats really *are* spooky) she sprang across the room and sank every last one of her claws in my thighs. I screamed and tried to push her off, but she wasn't having it. Her claws were deep in my flesh; her fur was all on end, and she hissed at me like I was trying to kill her kittens. I was genuinely frightened by her fury; and (to my permanent shame) I really did hit her. Hard. She flew across the room, smacked against the wall, landed perfectly and immediately raised her hackles for a fresh attempt.

I looked at her, stunned.

"Christ, Dolly! What is *wrong* with you? I don't need this!"

I looked down and saw blood seeping into the cloth of my expensive new trousers. Suddenly, everything stopped feeling like a dream. I stood up and went towards the bathroom.

"Just for the record," I said to her. "Don't think this means I'm going to turn into one of those queens who think their cats are human. OK?"

She didn't look all that bothered about my opinion; but as I closed the door, she purred, then settled down to lick the blood from her paws.

I must admit, I was starting to believe that Fat Dave did have *some* sort of military training. He may have looked more like Jabba the Hutt than Rambo, but his driving skills were straight out of *Bullit*.

"I am fuckin' *loving* this, my brother! LOVING IT!!!" he shouted, as he gunned the Merc the wrong way (I swear to God) round Trafalgar Square.

"Yes, yes! I believe you!!" I shouted back, closing my eyes as he drove straight across a pedestrian crossing.

"Calm yourself! Who dares wins!"

And with that we were driving the wrong way up the contra-flow bus lane in Piccadilly. With a bus coming straight towards us.

"Woo-hoo!" he yelled. "Deaf or Glory! Deaf or fuckin' GLORY!!!"

And then I closed my eyes once more, as he swerved to the left and did the pedestrian crossing trick again. I simply couldn't believe the police weren't on our tail. So much for the Surveillance Society.

OK. Rewind.

After Dolly had brought me back to reality I hadn't known what to do. All I knew was that I had to do *something*. Maybe. Ish. Hmm. But I didn't have the first idea *what*.

Then my phone rang.

"Alright," Dave had said cheerfully. "Where's you?"

"At home."

"Fought you might be. Laura said you was meant to be coming to this do tonight. Only you went AWOL from the party. Wossup?"

"Er, nothing. I'm fine. Got a bit drunk. Came home."

"So you goin to the do or not?"

"Um, I'd like to, but it's a bit late."

"Course it ain't! I'm right outside your gaff."

The first thing Fat Dave had said when I'd opened my front door was: "Shaved yer beard off, bro?"

"Not exactly. I'll tell you in the car."

"I'm all ears."

Obviously, I was wrong when I said that all straight men have limited powers of observation. Dave carried on asking probing questions from the second we'd set off. I told fibs for about half a mile but suddenly I didn't care. There was nothing to lose. So I told him everything. And that was how I found myself in a Merc, travelling at sixty miles an hour the wrong way up Piccadilly. Not only did Dave love the story, he loved *me* for telling the truth; he loved the chance to re-live his glory days; and, most of all, he loved the idea of seeing Dougy Dearest get his comeuppance.

"Right," said Dave, as the Merc screamed to a halt outside BAFTA. "Off ya go. And take this…"

"What is it?" I asked as he handed me a piece of laminated card.

"Me backstage pass, bro."

"Thanks, Dave," I said, not moving.

"Go on! Shift yer arse!"

"But what do I do, Dave?" I sighed. "This isn't me at all."

"You 'avin' a larf?"

"I wish I were."

"Listen, bro. Jeremy. I've seen a few brave geezers in me time, but you take the fuckin' biscuit. You're *nutty* brave. You get a job in some bird's house, wearing a disguise. You fool everyone you're one fing when all the time you're another. You're like fuckin' James Bond! Only mad. And bent! You're a *top* fuckin' *bloke*! Get out there!"

"And do what, though?" I whined.

"Oh, for…" he said, literally shoving me out of the Merc. "*Kill* the wanker!"

In the backstage gloom were dozens of beady-eyed media rat-children, scurrying back and forth with clipboards and earpieces, none of them paying the slightest attention to me. That was good. It gave me plenty of opportunity to find a dark corner where I could hide and collect my thoughts. Out on stage I heard Richard and Judy announce the winner for Most Popular Reality Programme. Can you believe that? I mean, really? *Most Popular Reality Programme.* What dead-eyed freak would want *that* award on the mantelpiece? It made me think of something I'd read on the web, about the Adult Video Awards in America. *Best Moaning in an Anal.* Classy.

One moment I was thinking about arseholes; the next I actually saw one. I spotted Dougy was heading towards me, with Laura hanging on his arm. I pressed deeper into the shadows as they approached, and then stopped, inches away from my hiding place.

It was weird, standing right behind Dougy and Laura, without them knowing it. I felt like I was there and not there at the same time, like a phantom limb. Richard and Judy were announcing the next award. I think it was *X Factor*. It could have been *Dancing On Ice*. Or was it *Chimpanzees Fucking*? I didn't notice. What I noticed was that Dougy clapped wildly, but Laura did not. In fact she looked miserable.

"How fab is *that?*" he squealed at her, still clapping away like a big queer seal. "Anthony and Tom *really* deserve it!"

Anthony and Tom, I assumed, were the clowns behind whatever had just won the award for Most Popular Talent Show.

"Yeah," Laura said, in a flat voice. "About time, eh? They really should've won it last year, for *Catwalk Pets*."

"Awww, *honey,*" said Dougy. "Why so sad? Be happy! It's been a good day!"

"Has it?"

"Oh, please. It's *me* you're talking to! "

"So?" she said. I couldn't see her face clearly, but I could see enough to know she was angry. And I could see enough of Dougy's to know that eight hours of coke and booze had made him forget his place in the world.

"Pardon me for breathing," he said, puffing up with that deadliest of all gases: pride. "If it wasn't for *me* you'd be looking at the shreds of your career."

"What?" she said, taking a sudden step back. "*What?*"

"Come *on*, honey. Don't give me that. Have you even thought about what I've done for you today? I mean, really. Have you?"

Laura turned away from him, and looked straight at me - except I was so deep in shadow that she still had no idea I was there "You can run," Dougy whispered in her ear, "but you can't *hide*. Oh, yes. That's right. Things have changed, haven't they? I'm not the scullery maid any more. You *owe* me…"

It wasn't so much that I hated Dougy; it was more that I liked Laura; that I knew she was a decent human being, and that she not only needed help but deserved it. Besides, the whole thing was a fuck-up. The least I could do was be a man.

"What are you doing, Dougy?" I asked, icily, stepping out of the darkness.

I've got to give it to the calculating twunt: he pulled himself together in an instant.

"Hello girlllllfriend," he sneered. "I had a *feeling* you'd crawl out of the woodwork, but I didn't think it'd be *this* soon."

"Oh, well," I said. "Here I am. And I'm waiting for an answer. What are you playing at?"

"Och, that's fucking rich, coming from *you*."

"I don't deny it. But I'd still like to know why you think you can blackmail Laura."

"Let me think," he replied. "Oh, yes. Because I *can*?"

Despite everything, Laura's mouth literally fell open in shock.

"Don't come the fucking innocent with me," he said to her, brazenly. "First of all you let a cuckoo in your nest, then you ignore my warnings a thousand times, and then I save your lazy arse – and now you don't expect to *pay* me? Stupid *bitch*."

Then Laura did the strangest, sweetest thing.

"Hiya, Jeremy," she said, giving me a little wave. "Weird day."

I looked in her eyes, and I knew, I just *knew* that she was all right. That she wasn't One of Them. And so I pressed the Big Red Button.

"You know what, Dougy?" I said. "You're right. She *is* stupid. But she's stupid in a nice way, unlike you and me."

"You *and* me? Ahahahaaha! Sorry, honey, could you clear that one up for me? I mean, it's fab to hear you admit it – but why am *I* stupid?"

"Come on now, *honey*. We're both fans of literature. Surely you're not going to make me count the ways?"

"What 'ways?' " he said, making those annoying little speech-marks in the air. "I mean, I know your *novels* make no sense, but maybe you could make an effort when you're actually *speaking*?"

"Sorry. Thought I was being clear. I'm talking about the ways that you're even more fucking stupid than I am. Starting with the way you had sex with my boyfriend."

"Is that right?" he sneered. "And what boyfriend would that be? The imaginary one?"

"No. Paul. The one who drives the Conway lorry?"

Dougy drew breath, ready to deny me; but something stopped him in his tracks. I glanced over my shoulder and saw that Adam was standing there. I could barely believe that anybody could live with a shitbag like Dougy and somehow think he was a trustworthy, decent human being; but from the way Adam's lip trembled, he very clearly did. Or had.

"Sorry, Adam," I said. "Didn't know you were there."

"Not your fault," he replied, covering his chin with his hand.

"There's more," I said to him. "I really am sorry."

He nodded, and looked past me hatefully, at the man he thought he'd known.

"Oh, for Christ's sake, Adam!" spat Dougy. "You don't believe *her*, do you? She wouldn't know the truth if it fucked her in the arse! Ask her to prove it! Go on!"

Adam looked at his boyfriend, or whatever Dougy now was.

"I don't need him to prove it," he said, quietly. I silently thanked my lucky stars. After all, there was no way *I* could have proved it.

"Anyway," I pressed on, while I had the advantage. "I didn't come here to have a cat-fight with you over a bit of trade. Did I?"

"Shut your lying pie-hole, bitch," growled Dougy. Ironically, he sounded truly butch for the first time since I'd met him. "Or I'll shut it for you."

He took a step towards me, and as the huge muscles in his back flared out, wrapped in his skin-tight black T-shirt, I felt like I was about to be engulfed by the cloak of some evil queen from a fairy-tale. Ooh, silly me. I was.

"Pick on someone your own size," said Adam, coming between us and pressing his meaty forearm against Dougy's seething chest. I know it wasn't exactly the moment, but all that pumped-up muscle did look rather lovely.

"You were saying?" asked Adam.

Suddenly it all felt so cheap and nasty that the fight went out of me.

"Oh, it doesn't matter," I said to him. "I don't even know why I came here. I'm no better than him. We're both conniving pieces of shit. You two should kiss and make up, and I'll go home."

The funny thing was, I really did mean it. All my reasons for being there were bad ones. Well, I'm saying "reasons". What I mean is "reason". Revenge. Oh, I know, we've all heard that line a million times. "Revenge is a dish best served cold". It sounds great in a Mafia movie, but you know what? Movies aren't real. And the truth is that revenge is a dish best not eaten at all. It's apt to give you indigestion.

But sometimes…

"That's it," crowed Dougy, as I walked away. "Piss off back to your smelly little hovel in Loserville! Go on! And leave that suit at the door on your way out! It's just not *right* on you, honey!"

…revenge is *just* the food you need.

"You know what, Dougy?" I said, walking right back again. "You're amazing. If you could have held on to all that poison for ten more seconds you would have won. As it is…"

"No!" he screeched, struggling with Adam, who now had him in some sort of neck-lock. "Noooo!"

"Laura," I said. "You'll never know how sorry I am for deceiving you the way I did. But at least I really liked your dad, and I'm genuinely pleased I played a part in getting you and Mick back together. Dougy here, on the other hand, can't say *any* of that. And the thing he hasn't told you, I'm sorry to say, is that him and Andrew Goodman… are *fucking*."

Poor Laura. No wonder she was so fond of fiction. Real life was obviously too much for her to bear. She looked so completely shocked I didn't know if she was going to burst into tears, or flames. Not that I got the chance to find out.

* * *

Here's another of my tips: if eighteen stone of prime beef is about to land on you, be ready with your mustard. When Dougy threw himself on me I was totally unprepared. Not that it would have made much difference: pound for pound, he could have worn me as a brooch. He reared up over me, and I realised – properly realised – that he was totally insane. He wasn't shouting, or swearing. He just closed his hands around my windpipe. Then he seemed to levitate away from me, very fast, and I saw that Adam had grabbed hold of him.

I took my chance and ran towards the exit; but Dougy had other ideas. I heard a loud thud and when I glanced over my shoulder Adam was lying flat out. Under any other circumstances I would have rushed over and given him mouth-to-mouth, whether he needed it or not; but these weren't any other circumstances: a poof the size of a heifer was heading for me at what looked like forty miles an hour and it wasn't because she wanted milking.

Apart from that thing the New Zealand rugby players do, I'd never heard a man roaring until then. Quite frankly I was surprised that Dougy could make such a noise. I mean, I knew he'd had plenty of men in him, but I had no idea he actually had *a man* in him. It was such a terrifying sound that it almost rooted me to the spot. Almost. I carried on running, and I really believed it was for my life.

Unfortunately, I soon got the chance to find out, because as I threw myself bodily through what I thought was the exit, I found myself in total darkness, tangled up in a curtain. There was no time to think, only react – to the approaching sound of Hurricane Douglas.

"Aaaaaaaaaaaargh!" he roared.

"Ooooooooooooooo!" I, replied. It sounded butcher in the flesh, honest it did.

There are times when a man's hot breath on your neck is *no* fun, and this was one of them. Just as I felt that hot breath I managed to disentangle myself from the curtain, and it was Dougy's turn to get caught up in it. I grabbed my chance and ran, as fast as I could,… straight onto the stage.

Oh, that Judy Finnigan. What a pro.

"Oh," she went, as though it were the most natural thing in the world to be confronted on stage by a panting, bug-eyed lunatic. "Did you get lost coming back from the loo?"

The audience roared. I think they thought it was a stunt. They didn't a moment later, when Dougy charged on, with smoke pouring from his nostrils and bloody murder in his eyes. I'll tell you this for nothing: it was a lot more entertaining than any of the shitty telly programmes that picked up the awards that night.

I will be forever grateful to Richard Madeley for what he did next. Judy Finnigan, on the other hand, probably won't. I fled across the stage, wondering what the hell to do next, when Richard, bless him, neatly stuck his leg out in Dougy's path, thus solving the problem for me. And creating one for Judy.

It's hard to describe accurately the sight of a very large, very angry homosexual, travelling at speed through the air, with nothing to grab onto except the evening gown of a rather small lady television presenter. On the other hand, it's easy to tell you what happened next. The poor cow was standing there in nothing but her high heels and knickers, while her frock and bra were wrapped round Dougy, who now lay unconscious at her feet. Richard, always the gent, whipped his jacket off and threw it over her in the blink of an eye. I'll tell you what. You can see an awful lot in the blink of an eye…

If you do *one* thing before you die, my top recommendation is this: make friends with a multimillionaire. They're fab! They're extra-specially fab if you have half the tabloid journalists in London camped out on your doorstep, offering your neighbours free crack if they'll dish some dirt. You see, if you find yourself in that situation, all you do is stay behind the tinted windows of the multimillionaire's limo, while your best friend (who also happens to be his fiancée) slips past the journos, pretending to be a Ukrainian cleaning-lady, and collects your cat. Then, off you pop to Biggin Hill, where you, your best friend, her fiancée *and* your cat board his private jet. Next thing you know, you're all lying by the pool of his villa on Ibiza. Except the cat, who's decided the accommodation's not up to scratch, and moved to the villa next door.

Cats, eh? They're such bloody queens.

Epilogue

I t's 5.15, and I'm enjoying four of my favourite things in the whole wide world: lying on the sofa with a triple G&T, a packet of Bensons, and Richard and Judy on the telly.

You know, I'm really not sure about these fifty-inch high definition plasma tellies. They certainly don't do Miss Finnigan any favours, and I can personally attest that she's much younger in real life. Still, I got the big telly to keep the other half happy. He does love his rugby, does my boyfriend. Funnily enough, seeing it on that big telly, I'm developing a bit of an interest as well.

Besides, you couldn't very well have a little telly in this room. It would look silly. In fact I sometimes wish we'd bought a bigger one. Maybe we will when the new house is ready. *If* the architects ever stop arguing with Camden bloody Council. Honestly, you'd think it was the first house in Primrose Hill to have an indoor pool.

Still, this flat suits us for the time being. At least it's on the top floor, so we don't have any neighbours clumping around upstairs; and on a clear day, from the south balcony, I can see all the way to Woolwich. I can almost see my old flat. Studio. Bed-sit. Whatever.

And it's nice having a gym and spa in the building. Nice for the other half, anyway, the bull-necked dreamboat. I can't say I'm a big fan of the gym but I'm a keen supporter of the results. Have you ever run your hands over eighteen stone of solid muscle? Think horse's arse, but without the hair.

It's lover boy's birthday today. He thinks I've bought him a new pair of trainers, but I haven't. I've bought him a new car. Little BMW 1-series coupé. I would have bought him something bigger, but I know he wouldn't want it. That's one of the many, many things I love about Adam. He's not the tiniest bit flash. He even wears baggy clothes most of the time because he doesn't want people gawping at his bod. And that suits me just fine.

Anyway, I can't lie here all afternoon boozing. I'm on the last chapter of the last book of *The Thames Barrier* trilogy. Fingers crossed it sells as well as the last two. It bloody better had, or my architect won't be having any more arguments with Camden Council.

I get up to turn the telly off. I'd use the remote to put it on standby, but his nibs will only nag me about global warming. Before I press the button I do what I always do when Richard and Judy are on. I kiss them both.

You know that old saying about all publicity being good publicity? It's true.

Burka, Schmurka, Mazurka!

O h, come on. Get a grip. You're not seriously telling me you thought that's how it ended? My insane best friend married a giraffe-fetish millionaire; I became a best-selling author with a perfect boyfriend, and we all lived happily ever after? Yeah. Just like life.

This is how it ended. Of course you don't *have* to read it…

Next morning, there really was a scum, sorry, *scrum* of reporters outside my building, and Robyn really did pretend to be a Ukrainian cleaner, so that she could slip past them and into the building.

I was buried under my duvet with a bottle of gin and Dolly when Robyn hammered on the door.

"Jeremy! Open the fucking door! It's me!"

I was terrified, paranoid and pissed. The only way my front door was going to open was with a battering ram. But then Dolly miaowed and slipped out from under the duvet; and I trusted her instincts. She recognised Robyn's voice, even if I didn't.

"Jesus Christ," said Robyn. "Shame they don't give BAFTAs for looking like shit."

"Thanks," I said, as she came in. "Why are you wearing a hanky on your head?"

"It's a Ukrainian thing," she replied. "Where's your suitcase?"

"I haven't got a suitcase."

"Don't be ridiculous. Everyone's got a suitcase. *Tramps* have suitcases."

"Good for them. I don't. Suitcases are for people who can afford to go on holiday."

"Well, you must have something! How about a holdall?"

"Nope. I've got a big plastic bag. For the launderette. In a rather fetching blue and red tartan."

"It'll have to do. But hurry. We need to get out of here. Now."

"Why?"

"Oh, you know why. Look out the bloody window if you need reminding."

I didn't need reminding. Even buried under the duvet I'd been aware that my doorbell had been going since six o'clock that morning. But I still couldn't help looking out of the window.

"Fuck."

"Yes, love. Fuck."

"That's quite a crowd."

"Hmm."

"Quite a hostile-looking crowd."

"Yes. I've met them. And right now, you're Marie Antoinette."

"Oooh…"

"Shut up, Jeremy, and find that bag."

I've got to be honest. Even though I knew that the people gathered outside on the street weren't exactly well-wishers I couldn't help feeling a bit Britney. You know: persecuted, and yet… wanted. I found my laundry bag and Robyn started running round my flat, tossing things in it frenziedly.

"Christ, love, calm down. It's not Supermarket Sweep! You're making me even more jumpy than I already am."

"Good," she replied. "I want you to be. I've booked us two tickets and our plane leaves in five hours. You *have* got a passport, haven't you?"

"What? Where are we going?"

"New York," she said, throwing my laptop in the bag.

"Are you out of your mind?" I squeaked. "I'm not wanted for manslaughter!"

"Try telling that to them," she said, pointing at the window. "Your life is going to be a total nightmare."

"Well, maybe. But not for long. I thought I could go to my cousin Diane's holiday cottage in Skegness."

"And have you actually asked your cousin Diane?"

"No."

"More to the point, have you ever been to Skegness?"

"No."

"Well, believe me, New York suits you better."

"Robyn, look. I appreciate you being so protective, but honestly, this is all too much."

"Oh really?"

"Yes. You're doing your usual."

"Which is?"

I really didn't want an argument, but not as much as I didn't want to go to New York.

"Over-dramatising."

"God, Jeremy, I never thought I'd hear myself say this. But you're *under*-dramatising. Go and look in my bag. Go on. Then tell me what you think."

* * *

I've got to give it to those boys and girls at *The Sun*. They know how to write a headline. Above a half-page picture of poor Judy with her tits out was the headline "PUT 'EM INNAGEN, FINNI-GAN!!" And then it got really bad. Unlike me, who'd spent the night hidden under the duvet with a large quantity of booze and a cat, Dougy had clearly been on the phone to all his media contacts, spinning away like the Black Widow. The result was that I'd been painted as "embittered gay author Jeremy Canty" who'd "sleazed his way into the life of lonely book wizard, Laura Morris", in a "desperate attempt to get his long-winded book on the famous Richard and Judy list."

It got worse.

"Canty's agent, Christine de la Silvestre, announced today that she wants no more to do with him. *'It's not just that Jeremy has ruined his reputation, and damaged mine,'* said the glamorous 52-year-old from the doorstep of her Holland Park home. *'It's that he's damaged the reputation of literature and of the Richard and Judy book list. That's unforgivable.'*"

"Cunt," I said, as Robyn waved my electric toothbrush under my nose.

"Don't be like that. I only wanted to ask if this'll work on American voltage."

"No, not you. Christine. More concerned about not pissing off Richard and Judy than she is in protecting me."

"Erm, she is an agent, hun. That's what they do. She's not your friend, is she?"

"Actually, I thought she was," I said. And burst into tears.

Funnily enough, it was the first time I'd had a good snivel.

"God, what have I done? What have I *done?*" I bawled. "At least James Frey made a few million before it all went tits up!"

"James who?"

"Frey. You must know about him."

"Yes. I'm only asking so you can feel superior."

"OK – he wrote a book called *A Million Little Pieces*. It was about his terrible struggle with booze and drugs, and how he reached rock-bottom, selling his arse for a rock, blah-blah. Then it got picked by Oprah and spent fifteen straight weeks at the top of the best-sellers. He made a fucking *fortune*."

"So?"

"So it was all made up, wasn't it? And he got found out."

"Oh. I see."

"Except, as I said, by then it was too late. He'd already made the money – and nobody made him give it back. Bastard even went back on Oprah to apologise, and the bloody book went *back* into the best-seller list!"

I started sobbing again. Robyn, to her credit, came over to cuddle me, which was good of her considering it must have been tempting to slap me behind the knees.

"Listen, hun. You don't know what'll happen with *The Thames Barrier*. If your publisher and your agent have got any sense they'll be working on it right now. But meanwhile you need to get away. Wait for the dust to settle. I hate to say it but your enemies are made of stronger stuff than you, darling."

"You mean Dougy."

"Yes. You were only *playing* mean. Dougy really is mean. And he's holding all the cards."

"He's not! He's the one who shoved Andrew Goodman's shitty book on the Richard and Judy list! That's worse than me!"

Robyn squeezed my hand.

"Well, actually hun, it isn't. Is it? And besides, you know as well as me that by now he's done a good job of convincing the world that you made it all up."

"Of course he hasn't! How could he?"

She looked at me – generously, considering – and pulled *The Daily Mail* from her bag. There was a picture of me from the night before, as I fled the scene. I looked like Countess Dracula making a dash for her coffin. Next to it was a picture of Dougy and Adam, looking like they just stepped off the set of a porn movie where they'd both played priests. And above it was the headline "WALTER MITTY LIFE OF FAILED AUTHOR."

That did it. I wasn't much of a contender to start with, and then I knew I was beaten.

I cried all the way to Heathrow. Actually that's not true. I didn't start crying again until we'd dropped Dolly off at Gloomy Prue's place in Battersea. Prue, true to form, was seeing things from her point of view.

"I've been dodging the paps *all day*," she said, jutting her chin out weirdly and tossing her hair like Marianne Faithfull just after Mick got busted for dope.

"Really?" said Robyn. "Why aren't there any outside?"

"I haven't worked in PR for twenty years for nothing," Prue answered sharply.

"No," said Robyn, taking in a few of the expensive things

in the room, and managing, somehow, to imply it was all a bit ostentatious. "I can see that."

Gawd, I thought. I really don't need Oestrogen Wars.

"I lured them out earlier," said Prue, trying to sound like Mata Hari but actually sounding like someone from *The Famous Five*. "And palmed them off in Waitrose."

"Ooh," said Robyn. "You classy bitch. I palmed someone off in Tesco's, once. But *Waitrose…*"

I've not told you before that Prue and Robyn aren't exactly a match made in a match-factory. But I didn't need to, did I?

"We'd better get going," I cut in. "Thanks for taking care of Dolly, love. If we're not back soon and she's too much for you, my mum'll have her."

"No, she won't be too much trouble," said Prue, eyeing Dolly nervously, as she crept around her perfectly tidy living room, looking for somewhere messy enough to call home. "She's not a scratcher. Is she?"

"No," I lied.

"And anyway," added Robyn helpfully, "surely *your* furniture's cat-proof?"

Anyway, as I was saying, it was after we left Prue's for Heathrow that I did start to cry. The taxi driver, a sweet, fat Pakistani, was very understanding. He even handed tissues to us.

"She's had some terribly, terribly awful news," Robyn explained to him, passing me the tissues. "Yes. Her sister and brother-in-law died in a suicide bombing in Baghdad. She's going over to look after the children. It's terrible."

"Poor lady, poor lady," said the taxi driver. "Good Muslim lady."

"Thank you," said Robyn, choked with emotion. "She's a saint. A *saint*."

Sorry. I didn't mention. Robyn had dressed me in a burka to escape from Woolwich. I won't say I felt happy in a burka (they're so hot!), but it cheered me up no end when our lovely taxi driver refused to accept any payment. Robyn did try to give him a tip, but he insisted that kissing my hands was tip enough.

Needless to say there was a price to pay for our free taxi. Women in burkas attract more attention at Heathrow than Brangelina. From the police, at least. No sooner had we entered the terminal than a scary man in a bullet-proof vest brandished a semi-automatic at us. Of course, as a good and innocent Muslim woman I had just as much right to be there as any other human being; but somehow, it didn't feel that way.

"We've got to get you out of the drag," hissed Robyn as the policeman looked at us beadily and spoke into his radio. "Let's find the nearest loo."

Finding the nearest loo was easy. Evading the Stasi wasn't. Have you ever had that horrid experience on the motorway, when you're speeding, and you suddenly see a police car, perched above you on a bridge? And you realise that, even if you slow down, it's too late, because they've clocked you, and half a mile ahead another police car will pull you over? Well, that's what it was like, trying to get to the loo. Policeman number one alerted policeman number two, who alerted policeman number three…. and so on.

"They're watching us," I said to Robyn.

"Yes, darling, I know that. We're only going to the loo, for Christ's sake."

"Yes, but what if they follow us? I can hardly go into a cubicle as a woman and emerge as a man, can I? Not without getting arrested."

"You've managed it before, hun…"

Thank God for sexism. I don't know how many female police officers in London are licensed to carry firearms but there certainly wasn't one available to follow us into the ladies'. The biggest problem was how to get out again, since the coppers were still watching the door. A problem for me but not for Robyn. She was in the next cubicle, dispensing with her Ukrainian cleaner gear. Then my phone rang.

"Have you got rid of the burka?" she asked.

"Why are you phoning me? I'm in the next cubicle."

"Shut up. Have you got rid of the burka?"

"Well, sort of. I've stuffed it down the loo. It looks like ten dead blackbirds."

"Don't worry about that. Strange things happen at airports. Now. You're going to start crying. No, you're going to start *sobbing*. And we're going to emerge together. You keep your face buried in my hair and I'll stroke you and make comforting noises. OK?"

"OK."

"And if one of the Nazis says anything, you just sob louder and leave the talking to me."

So we emerged from the ladies' together, with me sobbing like Sylvia Plath into Robyn's luxuriant hair. Wig. I'm never sure. I couldn't see where we were going and I didn't dare look. Then we stopped, suddenly, and I heard the unmistakeable tones of a policeman. Why *do* they always sound like the Monty Python voice of Neasden?

"Excuse me, madam," he said. "But are you sure that's your trolley?"

There was a pause. A very long pause. I carried on sniffling into Robyn's hair/wig/whatever.

"Is your friend all right?" asked the policeman.

"No," Robyn answered. "She's just lost a baby."

I heard the hiss and crackle of the copper's radio.

"Err, yes. We have a missing child? Repeat. A missing child. Copy?"

"NO, you…" said Robyn, with a slap in her voice. "She's had a *miscarriage*. God…"

The copper sounded horrified. "What, in the ladies?"

I realised this was a moment for me to sob louder.

"Jesus, what is *wrong* with you?" Robyn hissed. "Of course she hasn't had a miscarriage in the ladies! She lost her baby yesterday! Look, can we just *go*?"

"Umm…"

"Before you cause any more *pain*? Please?"

The copper was clearly too embarrassed at his own stupidity to utter an apology, and I risked opening my eyes for a moment. Through Robyn's hair/wig/whatever I saw him gesture with his big gun, and we were free. As was our luggage trolley. And we were on our way to New York.

Losing the burka had a *big* downside: I looked exactly like me. And looking exactly like yourself is not what you want when your face is on the front page of three quarters of the national press. In fact, it was more than three quarters. Only the *FT* and the *Independent* had relegated the story to the inner pages. All the others had decided that nothing adds to the gaiety of nations more than a pic of a pair of gays fighting, while Judy Finnigan flashes her tits. I can't say I blamed them.

Robyn tried to reassure me that nobody would make the connection but she would have had an easier job convincing Michael Jackson that he was black. So I went and hid in the loo until she phoned me to say our flight had been called.

You know, maybe there *is* no such thing as bad publicity. Because, as we boarded the plane, the purser winked at me, and gestured to the right. You know what a gesture to the right means, right? It means you turn left, because you've been upgraded to first. Hang on, I just want to say that again, since it's the only time it's ever happened, or ever will happen again. We were UPGRADED to FIRST.

Honestly, I don't know why the lucky bastards who can afford to fly first class ever bother getting off the plane. There can't be a hotel in the world that's nicer than a first-class cabin. You half expect a dwarf to come round with a tray of cocaine on his head. And the most amazing thing about it is the people. I'm sure this varies according to destination but on the London-New York flight there were none of your suited businessmen. Oh, no. They were all back in Business. In first there were two types: ludicrously over-groomed Park Avenue dames of indeterminate age, and ludicrously scruffy young people, who could have been pop stars, Internet millionaires or simply stinking rich. Oh. And us.

"Will you please *stop* opening and closing your mouth like that?" hissed Robyn, once we were in the air. "You look like a goldfish who just won the lottery."

"But I am," I replied, taking a hot towel from one of our designated cabin-crew and a glass of champagne from another. "How am I supposed to look?"

"Like you're *used to it*," she said, taking the rest of the bottle of champagne from the waiter, as though to the manner born. Two minutes later she was getting a head and neck massage, while I was quite happy to sit there with a daft grin on my face, knocking back the champagne.

I wish I could say that my joy continued unabated throughout the trip but that wouldn't be my life, would it? We were somewhere about an hour past Ireland. The lights in the cabin had been dimmed after dinner. Ooh, I must tell you about dinner in First Class. It really is dinner! You get a proper menu! And if you choose Chateaubriand (oh, of course I bloody did) they carve it at your table! And I just don't care if I'm using too many exclamation marks! It was exciting!!

Anyway. Sorry. I'd just finished my dinner, the lights had been dimmed, and I'd stretched out in my seat (oh, poor you, I can't bring myself to spare your feelings. It was a bed, OK?). I turned to Robyn, and I realised for the first time that day what an incredible thing she was doing.

"Hun," I said, mistily. "What did I do to deserve a friend like you?"

"Shut up," she smiled. "You're pissed."

"No, I'm not. I'm… grateful. You could've just let me go to Skegness. But you didn't. You did *this*."

The trouble with knowing someone too well is that, well, you know them too well. It's like playing poker with a child. Robyn's eyes flicked to the left – for a tiny second – and I knew, I *knew*, that something was up.

"You'd do the same for me," she said. "Now, go to sleep

and we'll be in New York before you know it."

"'Kay," I smiled dreamily, letting my lids close. "Love you."

In truth, beneath my eyelids, I was as wide awake as a Wurlitzer. There was something Robyn hadn't told me. I lay there and did a bit of fake snoring, my brain clattering away like an abacus. Then it occurred to me: she hadn't mentioned her millionaire fiancée all day. Not once. What was *his* opinion about his girlfriend suddenly swanning off to New York to look after her little gay friend? And where, for that matter, was his private jet? Why were we slumming it in First Class when the boyfriend had a private jet?

I lay there for ages, pretending to be asleep, desperately hoping that Robyn would go to the loo. That woman's got a bladder like the Hindenburg. Finally, she did, and I was pulling down the zip of her bag faster than a ten-quid hooker at closing time.

It didn't take long. At the bottom of the bag, under a ton of lady-rubbish, was a big, soft, grey leather purse, stuffed as full as a sturgeon. I didn't need to open it to confirm its contents but I did. Fifty pound notes. Hundreds and hundreds of them. Something told me we wouldn't be flying in a private jet anytime soon.

I saw Robyn coming back from the loo and quickly stuffed the purse where I'd found it. I took a deep breath in preparation for the Big Scene that was inevitable. And then, suddenly, it was all too much for one day. I fell fast asleep and didn't wake up until they were letting us off the 'plane.

Getting upgraded to first class does not, unfortunately, continue when you disembark. You have to go and collect your luggage along with the plebs. That was the first blow: remembering I was still a pleb. The second came when my foggy brain cleared and I remembered the purse.

Post-9/11, going through immigration at JFK is about as unpleasant as it could possibly be, without actually getting de-loused. I'd say the only thing the officers lack is cattle prods, but most of them have scowls just as effective.

Robyn and I were in different queues. It's something we always do at airports. The first one through goes and sorts out the taxi, which is good, because it's always Robyn. Always. Then again, the only time I get a plane is when she pays, so fair's fair.

That day was no exception. My queue got held up by an old lady in a burka. Actually I don't know if she *was* an old lady (those burkas, eh? You can't see a *thing*) but she did have a walking stick and she was bent over like a hairclip, so I assumed. And it wasn't her who held us up, it was the idiot in uniform, who thought she might be dangerous. A decent but misguided Englishman ahead of me in the queue decided to intervene on her behalf, which made matters much worse. So we all had to wait while both of them were carted off to JFK's outpost of Guantanamo Bay. Honestly, if I hadn't stuffed my own burka down the bog at Heathrow I would have put it on, just to be awkward.

When I finally emerged Robyn was standing outside, leaning against a yellow taxi, and chatting away to the cabby, an Indian so short his eyes were exactly level with her boobs. He looked happy; she didn't.

"Glad you could make it," she said. "He's only had his meter running for half a bloody hour."

"No he hasn't, Robyn. He's been far too happy having his little face buried in your bosoms."

"All right. But I haven't."

"Tough titty," I said, chucking my case in the boot. "And besides, you can afford it, can't you?"

"What did *that* mean?" she asked as we joined yet another queue to get out of the airport.

"What did what mean?"

"'You can afford it'?"

"I don't want to talk about it now. Let's just get wherever we're going. Where *are* we going, by the way?"

"A hotel, of course, darling. All paid for by Alan."

"Oh, your *fiancée*. I take it he knows he's paying?"

"Of course he knows! I've told you how generous he is."

"Mm. So he wouldn't be paying out of that twenty-odd grand I found in your bag?"

There was a loooong pause.

"You had no right to go down my bag," she said.

"Yes, dear," I replied. "And you had no fucking right to drag me to New fucking York to cover *your* fucking tracks. In fact, if you bought return tickets I'd like mine *now*."

The lovelorn cabbie looked at me in his mirror, as if to say "Don't you treat my woman bad, or I'll call my brothers."

"Let's just get to the bloody hotel," I said, turning my face away from Robyn and looking out at the neglected streets as we entered the tunnel into Manhattan.

-27-

The Absolutely End

I carried on sulking as we drove through Manhattan. I carried on sulking until I noticed we hadn't stopped in a shitty area. And I was still sulking (but only by making an effort) when we turned into East 57th Street, and pulled up outside The Four Seasons. Now, in case you were wondering, I'd never actually been to New York, except in my imagination. One of the characters in *The Thames Barrier* spends a lot of time in New York. And she always stays at The Four Seasons. So, when our cab pulled up outside the *real* Four Seasons, in Real Life… The only time I'd been inside a hotel that posh was when I once dreamed that I'd married Donald Trump (and that sort of took the shine off things) . When you go inside for real, well, you just have to stop sulking.

But not for long.

"Feeling a bit less sour?" asked Robyn, after the porter had left our room.

"I'll let you know after I've tested the bath."

"Tested the bath?" she said, following me into the bathroom, which was so huge and marbled I was surprised not to see a few Roman senators lying around in togas. "What about the bath?"

"Oh, just something I've read. You're s'posed to be able to fill the tub in sixty seconds."

"And what if you can't?"

"Then I'll definitely want that return ticket, cow."

Coming from a land, as I do, where your typical shower is like being pissed on by a tomcat with prostate problems, a bath (a huuuuge bath) that fills in sixty seconds isn't just amazing, it's terrifying. You stand and watch like you're witnessing the Bible. You half expect not to survive. At the very least you expect Shelley Winters to swim past, Poseidon Adventure stylee.

Anyway, I did (survive, not see Shelley Winters). And When I'd stepped into the small swimming pool that called itself a bath, and sank up to my chin, I let Robyn come in.

She'd poured us champagne.

"You're not getting round me that easily," I said.

"Darling, just take the glass and stop doing your serious face."

"I am serious."

"Not sitting in a giant bubble-bath you're not. You look like Jayne Mansfield."

"Fuck off."

"You fuck off. Who's paying for that bath?"

"Not *you*. Which is why I'm looking serious," I said, taking the champagne. "Your ex-boyfriend is paying. And I'm guessing he doesn't know that."

"He probably does by now. Look, let me explain."

"At last..."

Robyn sat on the bidet. As good a place as any to make a confession.

"It's not very complicated," she said. "He turned out to be a wanker. What a surprise."

"You'll have to do better than that, hun. Multi-millionaire wankers get more chances than poor wankers."

"Do they?"

"They do in my book."

"And when have you ever had one?"

"All right. Give us a bit more of that champagne."

"He flew us to Paris," she said, pouring another drink. "Three nights ago."

"In his private jet."

"In his private jet. It was lovely, it really was. Show me a woman who hasn't dreamed of being flown to Paris by a man with a private jet and I'll show you a big old lesbian."

I tried to give her a world-weary look, but it wasn't easy with bubbles in my hair.

"And we ate at Le Grand Véfour, which is like ten Michelin stars. Then we walked down to the Seine. Hand in hand. Don't laugh, but I felt like a lady."

I looked at her, squatting on the bidet with her knees together and thought *You are a lady. But I'm not bloody telling you.*

"Carry on."

"And then he asked me to marry him."

"This is sounding pretty good, so far."

"OK, fast-forward. So I said yes. He apologised because he'd left the engagement ring at the hotel. We laughed. Then we walked back to the hotel."

"Hand in hand."

"Shut up. I'm near the end."

"Sorry. Is there any more of that champagne?"

She stood up and poured some of hers into mine.

"So. We went up to the suite. He gave me the ring. It must've cost fifty grand."

"Ooh. Where is it?"

"My bag, in cash."

"Ah. OK. You're getting to the bad part, aren't you?"

"Yes, Jeremy. I'm getting to the bad part."

"Should I be listening to the bad part in a bubble bath?"

"Probably not," she said. "You get dried and I'll get more champagne."

When I emerged from the bathroom she was crying.

"OK," I said. "Tell me the last bit. Sorry I've been a twat all day."

"You've been a twat ever since I met you," she snivelled.

"Fair enough. So what happened?"

"So, went to bed. Well, I went to bed. He disappeared into the sitting room. He was gone for absolutely ages. I mean *ages.*"

"Erm, I think I'm ahead of you here. He came back wearing a giraffe outfit, didn't he?"

"I wish he had. No, he came back dressed as a nun."

"Oh. Is that *so* bad?"

"With a whip."

"Ah. Hmm. But still…"

"And an eight-year-old girl."

"Oh. Right. I'll shut up, now."

"Would you?" she said. "But I wouldn't mind a cuddle."

Didn't I say you should never trust an Alan?

"You know what?" I said, when her sobbing subsided a little.

"What?"

"You could've taken a bit more money off the perv…"

Later, over a third (OK, possibly fourth) bottle, we did sit and count the money.

"Ooh," I said. "Forty-five thousand. I wish I had a beret."

"But then you'd look like Frank Spencer."

"I was thinking Faye Dunaway in *Bonnie and Clyde*".

"Thanks. That makes me Warren Beatty."

"No change there, then," I replied, as Robyn swept her arms across all the neat piles of fifties and threw them in the air.

"Agh! Don't do that! We'll have to start again!"

"So? Who's in a hurry? I wanted to celebrate."

"Celebrate what?"

"Us! Friendship! And not being *too* fucked up!"

"*Not* fucked up?" I said. "Have you had a look at us?"

"Ohhh, yes," she replied, picking up a heap of money and rubbing it on her boobs. "But have *you* had a look at the rest of them?"

I must have drifted off. OK, I did drift off. I don't know what time it was when Robyn woke me , but it was daylight. She was holding a glass, full of something fizzy. With a slice of lemon.

"Please tell me that's not what I think it is," I moaned.

"Sorry, hun. I think it is," she replied, handing me the G&T.

"Oh, for fuck's… even *I* don't have gin for breakfast."

"I know. You don't have these, either," she said, waving a packet of Bensons. "I bought them at the airport. Just for you.

Come on, I want you to see something."

She went through to the sitting room. I couldn't believe I wanted a G&T and a Benson at that time of day, but then I thought well, you're jet-lagged. This must be five in the afternoon for you. So I followed her.

"What time is it?" I asked, flopping down on one of the sofas. Bloody hell, it really was a nice hotel.

Robyn looked naughty. "The broadband's *fantastic* here," she grinned, wriggling down next to me and plonking her laptop in between us.

"*Please* don't tell me you've been looking for punters," I said. "I can handle gin and fags for breakfast, but not men in nipple-clamps."

"Ssh. This is *much* better than men in nipple-clamps. Watch…"

She clicked the mouse.

"Oh, no! No, no, no! Don't do this to me!"

"Sssh. You know you want to."

"No, I don't, I don't, I don – ooh! Oooh! What *is* she wearing? She looks like a geography teacher!"

"Never mind what Judy's wearing," said Robyn, lighting me a Benson. "Just wait till you see *Dougy…*"

So. It wasn't five o'clock. But I *was* lying on a sofa, doing four of my favourite things in the whole wide world. Smoking a Benson, drinking a large G&T; watching Richard and Judy. And cuddling my best mate.

Judy had a glazed look about her, and I mean glazed like a fruit tartlet. Sort of shiny and fixed. It was weird. Well, it wasn't all that weird. It was Botox.

The camera zoomed in on Richard. Unlike his wife he looked animated – even more animated than usual, which is going some. He didn't just have ants in his pants. They'd crawled up his bum and thrown a party on his prostate.

"Oh dear," he said, looking out from under his fringe and trying – sort of – not to smirk. "We've only gone and done it again…"

He threw a naughty grin at the missus. She literally did not react. Not a T. W.L. in sight. Then Richard surprised me. Or perhaps he didn't.

"Well," he said, doing his own trademark poke-my-finger-in-my-hair-without-disturbing-it thing, and letting rip with a proper grin. "Maybe I don't mean 'we'. *She's* gone and done it again. Eh, love?"

He held up the *Sun*, with the Innegan, Finnigan headline and looked naughty.

I honestly could not breathe. Taking a glug of gin and a drag on my Benson, almost at the same time, I waited….

And suddenly, in one professional movement, Judy shrugged off her Botox shroud; twinkled to camera; turned to her hubby and smiled, "Yes, love, well. If you'd been a bit more interested in *me* and a bit less interested in the *men*…"

Then she turned back to camera and cracked what I can only describe as a record-breaking T.W.L. All it lacked was the late Roy Castle and his bloody trumpet.

"God," I squealed, rolling off the sofa, wiggling my legs in the air and clapping, all at the same time. "If only they knew how *much* I love them!"